Is Gretchen pregnant?

"Why are you taking prenatal vitamins?" Matt asked.

Gretchen's face fell as she saw Matt looking at the prescription from their mutual friend and obstetrician. He rounded on her, fury and disbelief streaming through him.

"I, uh—"

Matt picked up the book lying open on the counter. "And why are you reading up on pregnancy?"

Gretchen swept her hands through her hair.

And suddenly, Matt knew why Gretchen had been so desperate not to see him. "The baby is mine, isn't he?"

He stepped closer to her, the possessiveness he felt toward her and her unborn child growing by leaps and bounds.

"Isn't he, Gretchen?"

Dear Reader,

Texas wildcatter Matt Hale is looking forward to an empty nest now that his kids are grown up. And Gretchen O'Malley seems like just the woman to start his new life with. But he's in for a surprise because Matt is about to become an "Accidental Dad"!

From the author who brought you the "Too Many Dads" miniseries, Cathy Gillen Thacker takes you on a fun-loving ride all the way into the delivery room.

Don't miss the companion novel to this—
Linda Randall Wisdom's *Mommy Heiress*,
available right now!

Happy reading!

Debra Matteucci
Senior Editor & Editorial Coordinator
Harlequin Books
300 E. 42nd Street
New York, NY 10017

Cathy Gillen Thacker

DADDY CHRISTMAS

Harlequin Books

TORONTO • NEW YORK • LONDON
AMSTERDAM • PARIS • SYDNEY • HAMBURG
STOCKHOLM • ATHENS • TOKYO • MILAN
MADRID • WARSAW • BUDAPEST • AUCKLAND

ISBN 0-373-16607-9

DADDY CHRISTMAS

This edition published by arrangement with Harlequin Books S.A.

Printed in U.S.A

Chapter One

Gretchen O'Malley knew she was in trouble the minute it started snowing. Sure enough, twenty miles and a patch of ice later, she began an out-of-control slide into the oncoming lane of the steep and winding Colorado road.

Gripping the steering wheel with leather-gloved hands, she took her booted foot off the accelerator, ignored the brake and steered ever so gently in the direction of the skid. The defensive maneuver was supposed to steady her car. It didn't. Her rented sedan kept right on going. Sliding first to the left and along the berm of the deserted rural highway. Then veering right as snow covered the ice and her tires regained some traction. Sideways as she hit yet another patch of solid ice.

Gretchen gasped as her car spun into a wicked 360-degree turn. She felt as though she were inside a snow globe that had been given a hard shake. Trees flew by in a dizzying kaleidoscope. Snow pelted her windshield at a blinding rate. The next thing Gretchen knew the spin ended—with a jarring thud. Her sedan landed nose down in the ditch on the opposite side of the road. The back wheels spun. "Jingle Bells" played merrily on the car radio. Gretchen was shaken up, but unhurt.

Breathing a sigh of relief, she pulled herself together and turned off the motor. It didn't take her long to figure out there was no hope of getting the sedan out on her own, not when the car was sitting at a forty-five-degree angle. She would just have to go for help, she decided as she peered up at the sky. Damn, and in this weather....

Drawing a deep breath, she made sure she turned off the car lights, too. Her course of action set, she slung her purse over her shoulder, released the catch on her safety belt and reached for the door handle. It wouldn't budge. Gretchen knew a moment's panic, then realized she hadn't unlocked the door. Laughing at her foolishness, she released the lock and tried again.

It still wouldn't budge. Neither would the door behind her. *I can do this. I just need to stay calm.* Sliding across the front seat, she reached for the door on the passenger side. And the one behind it. Both were jammed, too.

Heart pounding, Gretchen tried to roll down one of the windows. Then the next and the next and the next. All were manual and *none* was operational. And still the snow was coming down furiously, coating the hood of the car with white. Praying someone was close enough to hear, Gretchen hit the horn. Once, then again and again...

MATT HALE heard the sound as he rounded the bend. Someone was honking a horn. Not rudely, but in the short-long-short pattern of an SOS. He slowed the four-wheel-drive Rocking S Ranch Jeep to a snail's crawl, just as he hit the ice. He skimmed over the surface, swaying dangerously, before his wheels once again found traction on the asphalt beneath the snow. The car in the ditch hadn't been as lucky. Hoping the occupants were all right, Matt sounded his horn in return to let them know they were not alone, then steered his Jeep safely to the berm up ahead.

He parked, then got out and started back, aware the panicky horn blowing had stopped. Whether it was because the car's occupants had realized they were about to be rescued or they had passed out from injuries, he didn't know.

His pulse racing, he stamped to the car and brushed snow off the passenger-side window to peer inside. There was only one occupant, an incredibly beautiful woman.

Matt rapped on the window. "Roll this down," he shouted, aware that snow was already dusting his shoulders and the brim of his Stetson. It wouldn't be much longer before the road was completely unmaneuverable, even for vehicles with tire chains and four-wheel drive.

"I can't!" the dark-haired woman shouted back, color flooding her cheeks. She grabbed the door handle with both hands and tugged ineffectually, then scowled and pounded on the door in fury. "Everything is jammed."

Matt brushed snow off the side of the car with one gloved hand and promptly understood why. The frame of the sedan was bent. "Hang on," he reassured in a low voice. "I'll get you out."

Face tucked into the collar of his shearling coat, he tugged the brim of his Stetson down over his brow and headed back to the Jeep. He returned with a crowbar. Short minutes later, he had done as promised and opened the stranded angel's car door. She vaulted into his arms, shaking from head to foot.

"Thank God," she said again and again, clinging to him as if her life depended on him. "I th-th-thought I was going to have to spend the night out h-h-here."

Matt checked her over for injuries and saw no bruises or bleeding. Nor were there any signs of shock or hypothermia. "How long were you stuck?" he asked, wrapping an arm tightly around her slender shoulders and holding her close.

The woman tilted back her head and looked up into his face. Her shoulder-length mahogany hair spilled across her shoulders in silky disarray.

"I don't know. At least half an hour. There wasn't another car."

Tears welled in her deep blue eyes and clung to the thick fringe of lashes. Her hand curled around the edges of his coat as her lower lip trembled.

"I d-d-don't know what I would have done if you hadn't stopped."

"I'm glad I found you, too. There's not much traffic on the highway, even when the weather is great. It's mostly ranches out this way."

Matt glanced up at the opaque pearl gray sky. Snow was still coming down in sheets. "Where are you headed?" He wasn't altogether sure he could get her there in this weather, but figured he might as well ask.

"The Stewarts' Rocking S Ranch. You know the place?"

Matt grinned. Maybe this Christmas wasn't going to be as bad as he'd thought. In answer to her question, he pointed toward the battered yellow Jeep with the Rocking S Ranch insignia on the side. "Sure do. I was headed there myself with a load of groceries for the Stewarts."

She looked at his truck in relief. Anxious to get a move on, he slid his arm down and firmly encircled her waist. "What do you say we gather up your gear and drive to the ranch? We can call the auto club and the highway patrol from there—although from the looks of things, it's doubtful we'll get anyone out here to pull the car out of the ditch until the weather clears."

"Sounds good."

The woman took another look at the wrecked car, then released a strangled moan and buried her face in her hands.

"You feeling okay?" Frowning in concern, Matt pressed a hand to her cheek and found her skin silky and warm, not burning up with fever, not clammy from shock.

She buried her face in his shoulder, and he was surprised at how natural and right her impulsive action felt.

"Actually, now that I've seen the car, no," she lamented with another heartfelt groan. "When my insurance company learns of this my premiums are going to go sky-high."

Matt chuckled as even more healthy color flowed into her sculpted cheeks. If insurance premiums were all that concerned her, she was more all right than she knew. "You a bad driver?" he teased with a grin, wondering when she was going to get around to giving him her name instead of just her life story in that lilting Texas drawl of hers.

She shook her head as she reached into the car to remove the keys from the ignition. "Actually, I'm an excellent driver. Just unlucky," she informed him, her eyes lasering in on his.

"So how come you headed out in a storm?" And was she who he thought she might be?

She offered a shrug as she unlocked the truck and began handing out a stack of ribbon-wrapped packages. "It wasn't snowing when I left the Denver airport. There was only a twenty percent chance we would even see flurries, according to the weather report."

Matt carted the gifts over to his truck, then returned swiftly to her side. "Snows come in fast in the mountains. Weather can turn on a dime." Seeing that her trunk was empty, he reached past her and shut it.

"I'm sure there are some who would say my being in a wreck was probably my penance," she muttered, reaching back into the car to grab a Pullman case and a small leather carryon.

Matt tore his eyes from the graceful lines of her long legs. He had never realized loose wool slacks could drape like that. Struggling to keep his mind on their conversation and not on the slim, supple body beneath her navy blue parka, he said, "Penance for what?"

She straightened to her full five feet six inches and squared off with him amicably. "For telling a little white lie."

He laid a hand across his chest. "I'm shocked," he announced.

"Yes, well..." She rolled her eyes at the sky. Snow coated the tip of her nose and her cheeks. "I didn't want to hurt Marissa's or Cal's feelings. I know they mean well, even when they do the wrong thing."

Marissa and Cal... Matt tensed as he realized she had to be talking about lying to the Stewarts. Maybe he'd better find out more. Just because this woman looked angelic didn't mean she was. "What kind of fib did you tell?" he asked casually, following her back around to the Jeep.

"We were supposed to all fly out together from Texas. But I pretended there was a glitch in my reservation that bumped me onto an earlier flight, and I switched my flight from Austin so I'd arrive in Denver much earlier. Then I told them that instead of killing time at the Denver airport all day, waiting around for them, or checking into a hotel for a few hours, I'd just rent a car on my own and come on out to the ranch. Maybe even get a head start on making some pies for Christmas dinner. I mean, I knew their hired man—you—was going to be here. So it wasn't like I was putting anyone out. Just the opposite. Still—" she sighed, regaining her composure at a rapid rate "—it was a lousy thing to do."

Yes, Matt thought, it was, more than she knew. And that in turn made him wonder if he should correct her misimpression or just let her continue chatting away, to find out everything he could. *Then* he would decide how to deal with the situation. And her, too.

"Especially since I think they went to a great deal of trouble to try to fix me up with someone for the Christmas holiday," she added.

"And this fix-up doesn't interest you?" he said carefully, wondering why in hell it wouldn't. He watched as she thrust out a pouty lower lip that looked every bit as soft as it did kissable, before she answered.

"No way."

Matt rankled at her tone. She was presuming a lot on very little information. Deliberately he tamped down his reaction to her attitude. What she did or did not feel toward the guy Marissa and Cal were fixing her up with was nothing to him. "Nevertheless you feel guilty about what you did," he stated, trying to figure out how often she pulled stunts like this.

"To a point. I don't like being dishonest. Then again..." Her lips curved wryly as she folded her arms in front of her and admitted, "Neither do I like being backed into a corner and forced into a situation against my will."

She tilted her chin up, and Matt realized she was waiting for his reaction to her confession. Determined to play his cards close to his chest, he shrugged offhandedly as he hauled her luggage to the Jeep and tossed the bags in beside her presents and his holiday groceries. "A person's got to do what he or she's got to do," he said. He already had an idea what *he* was going to do next.

He snapped the rear cargo door shut. "Though I don't understand why you didn't want to drive out from Denver with the Stewarts," Matt continued conversationally as they stamped through the snow toward the front of the Jeep. Unless..."

"It's a long story." She watched as he opened the passenger door, then accepted the hand up he offered her and climbed into the Jeep. "Hadn't we better get a move on?"

"Of course, Miss—" Matt prompted, realizing he still didn't know her name.

She smiled at him winningly. "O'Malley. Gretchen O'Malley."

GRETCHEN WASN'T SURE what she'd said. But he looked as if she'd just sucker-punched him in the gut, instead of stated her own name. "And you must be... Mr. Roper, isn't it?" she guessed lightly, having already concluded as much for herself right from the start. The Stewarts had only one hired man at their Colorado ranch-vacation home these days.

He shook his head, then said, "My friends call me 'Matt.'"

"But you are the man who takes care of the ranch in the Stewarts' absence?" Gretchen asked, just to be sure, as he circled swiftly around the front of the Jeep and climbed in behind the steering wheel.

"I'm doing the chores around the Rocking S for the time being," he said flatly, looking slightly irritated as he fitted his key in the ignition. "But I'm not an employee per se," he replied as he glanced out the windshield. "More a friend of the family," he added as he started the Jeep and turned on the heater full blast.

"Oh, I know," Gretchen said quickly, wanting to save him further embarrassment before he could continue explaining. "I heard about the accident that forced you to retire from the rodeo." The Stewarts had generously offered him a place to recover. "Your leg seems to be okay now, though." At least, he wasn't limping.

Matt followed her gaze and glanced down at his worn Levi's. He rubbed his thigh contemplatively. "Most days it doesn't trouble me a bit," he agreed sagely.

Gretchen paused. Matt was wearing a thick shearling coat and a bone-colored Stetson. Button-fly Levi's clung to his long, muscular legs. His feet were clad in sturdy leather winter hiking boots and thick Ragg socks.

But it wasn't just his clothing that made him look like a Marlboro Man extraordinaire. It was everything about him, from the thick, unruly, jet black hair escaping from beneath the brim of his hat to lie against his brown corduroy shirt collar, to his deeply suntanned skin, ruggedly handsome profile and intent silver gray eyes.

"Then you knew I was coming?" she asked, not sure why her heart was pounding, only knowing that it was.

Matt nodded. "Marissa mentioned the family had invited some guests when I talked to her long distance this morning, which was why I was rushing to get groceries in before the storm hit."

"So no one else is at the Rocking S Ranch right now?" Gretchen wasn't sure how she felt about that. She didn't want to be alone with Matt. The temptation was too great.

"Except me, no. But don't worry." He reached back into the middle seat of the Jeep and picked up the folded wool blanket he kept there for emergencies. He wrapped it around her shoulders, then tucked it in at her waist and down over her legs. "We're all ready for company. I spent the morning doing all the usual precompany stuff—putting sheets on all the beds and getting towels out and so on."

Somehow she couldn't quite see Matt dusting, sweeping and changing sheets. He was a man's man in every sense. "In addition to taking care of the horses?" she asked in astonishment as Matt adjusted the controls on the heater and waited for the windshield to clear of the fog their breaths had generated.

He shrugged his broad shoulders and tugged off his worn leather gloves, to reveal strong, square hands with thick, capable fingers and clean, neatly trimmed nails.

"Someone's got to do it. Even a small ranch like the Rocking S, which is kept mainly for pleasure, doesn't run itself. What about you?"

He paused to search her eyes, as if her reply were of utmost importance.

"Do you mind routine chores?"

"Only when they're expected just because a person happens to be wearing a wedding ring," Gretchen replied primly as she snuggled under the blanket.

Matt digested the answer. "Do you object to spending time with someone who doesn't mind getting his hands dirty to make a living?"

"Of course not!" Gretchen replied, incensed as he pulled a thermos out from under the seat and uncapped it. Steam rose from the lip of it as he poured her a cup of black coffee. "Why would you ask such a thing?"

He rummaged around in a restaurant sack and produced individual packets of sugar and powdered creamer. "Some women don't like men who labor physically for a living," he said, waiting while she removed her gloves before handing her the cup.

"Well, I'm not one of them," Gretchen responded staunchly, as she balanced the cup of fragrant coffee on her blanket-covered knees.

He looked skeptical as she tore open a packet of creamer and sprinkled it into her coffee.

"Sure about that?"

She resented being thought a snob, even as she stirred her drink with unnecessary vigor. "My father supported us by working in a peach orchard outside Fredericksburg. I have never been, nor will I ever be, ashamed of that,'' she stated calmly, lifting the cup to her lips.

He grinned approvingly. ''Good for you.''

Gretchen didn't know why, but she felt elated, as though she had just passed some major test as far as Matt was concerned.

''So, back to the story of how you happened to be driving out to the ranch alone...?'' he prodded. Having no cup for himself, he drank his coffee straight from the thermos.

''I was supposed to drive out from Denver with this friend of the Stewarts, not with them,'' Gretchen said, noting the windshield had almost cleared.

''That's a problem?'' Matt asked as he took another swig of coffee, then recapped the thermos with the silver top.

Gretchen savored the warmth of the cup between her hands. ''It is if I'm going to be stuck in a car for several hours with him.''

Matt grimaced as he set the thermos on the floor, between their two seats, then reached for his safety belt and pulled it across his chest. ''You've met this guy, I take it?''

''No.'' Gretchen watched as he fastened his belt. ''But I can imagine what he'd be like.''

Matt paused, his hands on the steering wheel. ''And that is...?''

''Someone about my age. Someone looking for a wife.''

Matt checked the rearview mirror, then carefully shifted the Jeep into drive. ''But you're not interested,'' he guessed, as he eased out onto the road.

''No way.'' Gretchen tensed and pulled the blanket up around her as Matt eased the Jeep into the center of the snow-covered highway. ''I've done my time in matrimonial prison.''

Matt grinned but didn't look at her. "That's an interesting way to put it," he remarked.

Gretchen thought she'd been tactful, under the circumstances. She took another deep draft of hot coffee. "You ever been married?"

"Once," he replied casually.

"But you're not still married," she continued, turning to look at him directly. At least, she hoped he wasn't.

Glancing at her, Matt grinned. "I broke out of jail, too," he said gently.

She smiled and took another sip of the steaming coffee. "Your choice or hers?" she asked, admiring the way he controlled the Jeep on the slippery pavement.

"Initially hers, although now that we're divorced I'm not sorry that we are," Matt said calmly as he slanted her another glance. "What about you?"

"I was dumped by my spouse, too," she said wryly.

"Sorry," he said sympathetically.

"Don't be," she replied breezily, meaning it. She set the thermos cap down in the built-in cup holder between the bucket seats. "It worked out for the best in the end."

"Yet you're reluctant to move forward, at least in your personal life," Matt noted.

"Look, just because I don't want to have anything to do with this mystery man the Stewarts have set me up with doesn't mean I'm afraid to have another relationship," she said hotly.

"How do you know the mystery man is all wrong for you?" he challenged with a grin.

Gretchen closed her eyes and leaned back against the headrest. "For starters, he's probably a physician."

"That's not surprising, since the Stewarts are both physicians," Matt remarked.

"I know, but I've got my reasons for staying away from doctors." Feeling restless again, Gretchen straightened and peered at the snow still coming down. She still felt as though she were trapped in a snow globe, only now the scene was pleasant and Christmasy.

Matt arched a brow at her remark, but kept his eyes on the road. "Physician phobia?"

She gave him a droll look. "Very funny."

"I thought so." He arrowed a thumb at his chest.

"Anyway," Gretchen added, sighing, "it just never would've worked with said mystery man and we are now both spared the agony of having to try to make it work one on one."

Matt braked as they approached a single black mailbox beside the road. A wrought-iron sign emblazoned with the words Rocking S hung above the snow-covered lane. Five acres or so behind that, a rambling two-story, log-cabin-style ranch house with a wraparound front porch sat majestically among the pines. A weathered gray barn and stable stood just behind that. All were blanketed in snow. Gretchen leaned forward and, stunned by the sheer beauty of what she saw, peered out the windshield. "So," she breathed at last, "this is the Stewarts' place."

Matt nodded as he turned slowly into the lane and drove beneath the arched entryway to the ranch. "You've never been out here, I gather?"

"No. We were never able to get our schedules to coincide and I didn't want to come up unless they were going to be here, too." Eager to explore the place, Gretchen was already inching on her gloves again. "But I've heard a lot about it over the years. I know Cal Stewart grew up here and inherited the place after his dad died. Now the Stewarts use it mainly as a retreat. What about you?" Gretchen asked as he parked next to the house. She climbed down from the

Jeep and met him at the cargo area. "When was your first visit out here?"

His gaze contemplative, Matt opened up the back of the vehicle. "It was probably about thirty years ago. I worked on the ranch as a hired hand the summer I turned fifteen, and have come back occasionally to help out or just visit with the Stewarts ever since."

Which meant he was forty-five, Gretchen thought, exactly ten years older than she. Yet she didn't feel the age difference between them at all.

He carried her suitcases in, and Gretchen ferried a load of groceries. With a quick call, Gretchen notified the highway patrol and auto club about the wreck. Several trips to the Jeep and some quick work later, they had all the groceries put away in the spacious ranch-house kitchen. While he went back for her presents, Gretchen took a moment and toured the downstairs, which consisted of three large wood-floored rooms that flowed effortlessly one into another. The kitchen was huge and open, with a long, rectangular center work space and state-of-the-art appliances meant to serve a crowd. The adjacent dining room featured an enormous pine table with trestle seats, beneath a rustic wagon-wheel chandelier.

One whole wall of the high-ceilinged living room was glass, with a panoramic vista of the mountains beyond. A huge fieldstone fireplace with a massive hearth encompassed the second wall. Overstuffed sofas and chairs in a striking Navaho print were grouped conversationally around the large room.

Gretchen was deciding where Marissa and Cal would put the tree, when Matt came in, a load of firewood in his arms. Kneeling before the fireplace, he spread out the dying embers of last night's fire.

"So what are you going to do when this mystery man arrives?"

Gretchen watched as Matt arranged two logs perpendicularly on the ashes. "I figure as long as I don't have to be alone with him that I can manage."

He paused to shrug off his shearling coat. Muscles flexing beneath his shirt, he tossed the coat on the floor beside him. "But it bothers you anyway—this business of being fixed up?"

Aware it was quite cold inside the house, she edged closer to the fireplace and sighed. "So much so that I almost canceled my vacation to avoid this umpteenth fix-up," she admitted. He was very good at building a fire, she noted. But then, so was she.

"Why *do* the Stewarts want to fix you up?" he asked, curious, laying a third log slant-wise across the other two.

Gretchen knelt beside him and rolled up newspaper from the stack in the bin. She stuffed it between the logs, then added another cylinder of paper and another. "That they didn't say precisely, but most likely they feel sorry for me, now that it's the holidays." And, Gretchen acknowledged, she had reason to feel down this Christmas.

"Sure you're not feeling sorry for yourself?" he asked.

It was almost as if he'd been there himself and knew the signs, she thought.

The challenge in his silver eyes had her lifting her chin a notch. "What have I got to feel sorry about?" she asked lightly, swiveling slightly to face him. Their knees bumped in the process, but she refused to move away. She had plenty to feel good about this Christmas, he might as well know that. "I'm a single woman, about to fulfill my lifelong dream of finishing college and becoming a teacher." And she had wanted this for so long! Only now did she have the courage and the wherewithal to go after it.

"So you're about to graduate, then?" Matt asked, his glance roving first to their touching knees and then her upturned face.

Gretchen flushed self-consciously and moved back a bit. "In three and a half years, give or take a semester or two," she explained, watching as he lit the end of a newspaper and stuffed it in among the others. "And in the meantime," she continued with determined cheerfulness as the fire crackled noisily and began to take hold, "I'm free as a bird." *With no one to account to or please except myself.*

"And all alone for the Christmas holidays," Matt added. Satisfied the fire was started, he stood.

"I'm not alone. After all, you're here," she stated, irritated he had seen through her so easily. Nevertheless, she accepted the hand he offered her and moved to her feet.

"True," Matt agreed, as their fingers meshed and held and then just as naturally drew apart.

"And the Stewarts, all fifteen of them, will be here in a few hours," Gretchen said over the pounding of her heart. "Soon we'll be tripping over people right and left and it will be gloriously fun and exciting."

Matt grinned at her prediction but didn't discount it. Which meant, Gretchen thought, as she slid her still-tingling hand into the pocket of her wool slacks, that he expected and looked forward to the same. She sighed. Sometimes it was easier to be with a crowd than to be alone, or worse, be with someone who wanted to know everything about you, past, present and future. She had the feeling much time spent with Matt would have her examining much about herself, and she wasn't sure she wanted to do that. Not this Christmas anyway.

Oblivious to her thoughts, and still smiling in anticipation of the coming holiday, he looked past her out the winlow. Gretchen followed his gaze. The sky had turned from a pearly gray to nearly white.

"It's really coming down," Gretchen said softly. The footprints they'd left as they'd approached the ranch house were already covered over.

"Yeah, it is." Matt grimaced at the worsening weather and grabbed his coat. He settled his Stetson on his head. "I better get down to the stable and see to the horses before it gets any worse."

Gretchen hastened to catch up, and fell into step beside him as he reached the back door. "Mind if I tag along?"

"Suit yourself." He tugged his collar up against the blowing wind and snow.

"So how come you're here for the holidays?" she asked, keeping her head bent and staying close to his side as they trudged a snowy path from the house to the stable. "Don't you have family to see, too?"

Matt brushed against her as he slid open the stable door, let her through, then slammed it shut. "My three kids are with my ex-wife, Vivian, and her new husband in Aspen."

"Oh. Sorry."

Matt shrugged as he went down the stalls, measuring out feed. "It's only fair. I had them with me last Christmas. Besides, I'll see them on the twenty-sixth. I'm driving down to ski with them a bit, before New Year's."

Finished with the horses, he led her back to the house. The phone was ringing when they entered.

Gretchen went to answer it, while Matt brought in more wood.

"Oh, good, you're there!" Marissa Stewart told Gretchen, in lieu of a greeting.

Gretchen shrugged out of her parka with one hand and cradled the phone with the other. "Where are you?"

"In Denver. We managed to land, but the roads are too bad to travel, so we've opted to stay in a hotel here overnight."

Gretchen was silent as the implications of that sank in. Deciding she would just have to make the best of it and ignore the simmering attraction she felt to the Stewarts' hired hand, she said, figuring she could tell them about the wreck tomorrow, "Not to worry, Marissa." She started to say "Matt," then worried it sounded too familiar. "Mr. Roper is here."

Marissa sputtered in amazement. "Mr. Roper is in Idaho."

But that couldn't be! "Then who was the man driving the ranch Jeep? The man who carried my luggage in?" Gretchen demanded, perplexed.

There was a pause on the other end, interrupted only by the static on the long-distance line. "I presume we're talking tall, dark and handsome in the Marlboro Man extreme?" Marissa drawled.

Heat started in Gretchen's chest and crept up into her neck as she thought about the way she had tingled at his touch and admired his broad shoulders and rock-hard thighs. "Yes."

"You must've met Matt Hale. He's our guest, Gretchen."

"But he was feeding the horses," Gretchen protested weakly, as heat flooded her face.

"Right. But he doesn't work for us. Surely he said as much."

Gretchen closed her eyes in abject misery. She could just die, thinking of all the things she had confessed to him in the past hour and a half.

"Gretchen?" Marissa pressed. "Are you still there?"

"He mentioned he wasn't an employee," she mumbled. *More like a friend of the family, he had said. But he sure let me go on thinking he was an employee,* she thought, furious.

"Listen, Gretchen, I've got to go—Cal needs to call the hospital to check on one of his patients. But I'll phone you as soon as there is any change in the roads to let you know our estimated arrival time."

"Thanks, Marissa." They said goodbye and hung up. Just as Gretchen put down the receiver, the front door blew open. She turned to see Matt Hale framed in the doorway. A load of firewood in his arms, snow dusting his broad shoulders and the brim of his hat, his cheeks red from the cold, he looked very strong and at ease.

Matt zeroed in on her expression. "Problem?" he asked mildly.

Gretchen glared at him, her temper flaring. "You bet there is."

THERE WAS GOING to be hell to pay, judging by the fire in Gretchen's blue eyes. But then, Matt thought as he set the load of firewood down in the bucket next to the grate, he had known that all along. "Who was on the phone just now?" he asked casually.

"Marissa Stewart."

Oh, hell.

Gretchen advanced on him like a gunslinger stepping into the street. "I want to know why you let me think you were Mr. Roper."

Matt shrugged and, not bothering to take off either his jacket or his hat, braced both hands on his waist. "I told you my name was Matt. You're the one who assumed the 'Roper.'"

"You could have corrected my mistaken impression just by giving me your full name, Matt Hale!"

Matt moved forward until they were standing toe to toe. "And missed the way you were pouring out your resentment about being scheduled to spend time with me, said mystery man? Not a chance."

"You're in on this matchmaking scheme, too, aren't you?" Gretchen accused, whirling away from him. "You changed your travel plans just so you could intercept me."

Matt watched the silk of her hair swirl about her face before settling on her shoulders once again. She walked toward him, her full breasts rising and falling rapidly beneath the soft knit of her ski sweater.

"I am here early for one reason only—because my flexible work schedule allowed me to help out the Stewarts," he explained as tranquilly as he could.

"As well as romance me," Gretchen added.

Matt recalled all the erroneous assumptions she'd made about him and grinned. "As delightfully troublesome as that experience might prove to be, no, you are not the reason I changed my travel plans." He arrowed a finger at her heart. "You are, however, the reason I didn't mind arriving early and missing the long, prearranged, fixed-up drive out with you."

"You're saying you wanted to avoid me, too?" Gretchen demanded, feeling unaccountably hurt as she drew herself up to her full five feet six inches.

"You're damn right I wanted to avoid you," Matt shot back, deciding it was high time they set the record straight about his participation in this fiasco. "What do you think? That I need or want to be fixed up with a potential love interest any more than you do? But I—unlike you, my spoiled Gretchen—was prepared to grit my teeth and do my duty and be polite to you in exchange for the Stewarts' kindness to me over the Christmas holidays."

She folded her arms in front of her and fumed. "So you came early to do just that."

"No, I came early because Mr. Roper's mother fell ill and had to be hospitalized. He went to Idaho to be with her yesterday morning. I flew in and got here by nightfall yesterday to take care of the horses in his absence."

"Oh."

"Yes, oh. Furthermore, I think if I could bring it upon myself to do my duty and drive out to the ranch with you, you could have done yours and followed the original travel plans the Stewarts set out for you."

She flushed with guilt. He was pleased to see she had a conscience.

"Why does it matter to you what I do?" she demanded in a chilly voice.

"Because it's winter in Colorado. And because your foolhardiness could have easily cost you your life had that wreck been any worse or had I not come along to get you out when I did."

"But that wreck wasn't any worse, and you did come along to save me," Gretchen retorted.

"And someone still needed to teach you a lesson," Matt responded equably, unable to tear his eyes from her face. "I figured it might as well be me."

Her eyes widened in astonishment and fury. "By making me eat my words where you're concerned?"

Matt shrugged. He knew he'd misbehaved—he hadn't been able to help it—there was something about her that pushed all his buttons, something about her that drew him in the way no other woman did. "I never would have done it if you hadn't started talking ill about me first," he replied casually. Because she still looked furious, he stepped closer and playfully wound a finger in the silky ends of her hair. "Admit it. You got your tail feathers trimmed." Satisfied he had her full attention and had made his point, he dropped his hand from her hair, offered another shrug and stepped back. "And now the lesson is over."

She pressed her lips together grimly. "Like hell it is."

He quirked a brow. "Meaning?"

"I am *not* staying here with you," she announced loftily, already going for her coat and gloves.

He clamped a hand on her shoulder and pulled her back to his side. "You have no choice. In case you haven't noticed—" Matt nodded at the darkening sky outside their window "—it's almost nightfall and there's a blizzard blowing out there."

"I don't care." Gretchen wrenched herself from his grip. "I want you to take me to a hotel."

"If you want to go in the morning, fine. Until then," he warned grimly, not about to let her have another car accident, "you and I are staying put."

Chapter Two

Snow piled outside Gretchen's window in two- and three-feet drifts, and it was still coming down, further closing them in at the Rocking S Ranch. The smell of frying steak teased Gretchen's senses. Her stomach growled, reminding her she hadn't eaten in hours. So, she could either wait it out here, or do the sensible thing and go down to the kitchen, where Matt was obviously cooking dinner, and get something to eat. Forsaking her pride for the good of her stomach, she headed downstairs.

Matt was standing at the sink, mashing potatoes with a mixer. He was wearing a navy corduroy shirt that, although comfortably loose, emphasized the broadness of his shoulders and the firm musculature of his chest and arms. Levi jeans gloved his trim waist and long legs. Unlike her, he hadn't given much thought to his appearance since they'd come in from the storm. His jet black hair hadn't been touched with a brush or comb; it curled down around his neck and over his ears in rumpled waves. His suntanned face, though closely shaved earlier in the day, showed a hint of evening beard. He was humming along with the Christmas carols playing on the stereo.

Becoming aware of her presence, he flashed her a blinding grin. "Decided to forgive me?"

Gretchen folded her arms in front of her and looked stubbornly up into Matt's silver gray eyes. She wasn't about to let him off the hook that easily, even if he had made dinner for two. "Not telling me who you were right off was a lousy thing to do." She'd been made a fool of by a man before; she wasn't about to let it happen again.

"So was ditching me before we even met," he drawled, sliding the pan of mashed potatoes into the oven to stay warm. "I'd say we were about even. Right?"

As he neared her, she caught a whiff of his after-shave. It was brisk and outdoorsy, just like Matt. Aware her heart was pounding, she held her ground determinedly, despite the dwindling distance between them. "Blunt, aren't you?" she remarked.

"To a fault, or so I'm told. So..." He looked her over, noting with approval that she'd changed clothes, brushed her hair and applied fresh makeup before coming downstairs.

Without warning, his look softened, she saw, and his eyes glowed with a disarming light as he extended a hand in friendship.

"Truce?"

What choice did they have? They were stranded there in the Rocking S Ranch; to continue to declare war on each other would serve neither. Besides, it was the Christmas season, and it was hard to stay angry with someone when "Silent Night" was playing on the stereo, reminding her that there should be peace on earth and goodwill toward men.

"Truce." Gretchen took his hand, reveling in the warmth and strength of his fingers as they closed over hers. She couldn't help but wonder what it would be like to kiss him. Would he exhibit the same capable tenderness with which he'd rescued her? Or would he be all fire and passion? Did she really want to know, now, when her life was finally becoming settled again?

Swallowing hard around the rising tightness in her throat, she disengaged their hands. She was fantasizing about Matt, just as Marissa and Cal wanted. And though she would have liked to think it was just the holiday and their isolation drawing her in, she knew it was Matt and the essence that was him. He gave her a good-natured look, then returned to his cooking.

Telling herself to concentrate on supper instead of him, she peered over his shoulder as he removed squares of the browned round steak from the skillet and added flour to the drippings like a pro. "Looks good."

"Thanks. Should be." Matt slid the steak in the oven to keep warm, too. "Chicken fried steak is one thing I know how to cook."

A traditional Texas dish, it was one of Gretchen's favorites. It had also been a while since she'd enjoyed the home-cooked and not the restaurant version. Her mouth watering, she watched as Matt added milk to the browned drippings, stirring the mixture into cream gravy with long, easy strokes. He added salt and pepper and stirred some more.

"I was thinking we should get a tree tomorrow, since Marissa was worried about it on the phone."

His concern for their hosts' happiness melted the ice around her heart a little more. Telling herself to watch it—she didn't want another broken heart for Christmas—Gretchen eased onto a stool at the counter. "You mean drive into town?"

"Cut one down," he said.

Gretchen blinked and nearly fell off her stool. "Ourselves?"

He shrugged unconcernedly. "Unless you know any Christmas elves willing to do it for us."

Very funny. "But—I've never done that before," she protested as warm color filled her cheeks.

"Nothing to it. I'll do the heavy work," Matt promised. "I just need you to help me pick one out and then decorate it once we get it back to the house. Marissa said the ornaments and lights are in the attic."

Visions of the two of them tromping merrily through the snow-covered property already filled her head. She figured the busier they were, the better. Because when she was this close to Matt, this comfortable with him, all she could think about was the snug, warm way his arms had felt around her when he'd rescued her from her wrecked car, how he had held her against him until she'd regained her bearings and how safe she felt when she was with him. And she hadn't felt that way with a man in a very long time, if ever. "I'd be glad to help," she said finally, telling herself it was not desire she saw in his eyes whenever he looked at her.

"Say, first thing tomorrow morning?" Matt asked casually as he set her plate in front of her.

Gretchen nodded, already anticipating the activity. She could not believe her instant and overwhelming attraction to Matt. "First thing."

"THIS ONE! No, maybe this one. No, that one over there." Gretchen bypassed a bristlecone pine and directed him toward a towering blue spruce.

Matt threw up his arms in exasperation. "You know, I never would've asked you to help me if I'd known you couldn't make up your mind," he drawled.

Gretchen planted her hands on her hips, aware she and Matt were both standing nearly knee-deep in snow and had been at the selection process for nearly thirty minutes. "You could be of some help here, you know."

Shading his eyes against the brilliance of the morning unlight reflecting off the snow, he squinted at her and said, 'I plan to be. I'm the one who's going to cut down the tree ınd drag it back to the house, remember?''

True, Gretchen thought, as she stopped in front of a par-icularly lovely Scotch pine with well-proportioned branches ınd abundant greenery. She knew at a glance it was just erfect for the Stewarts' living room. "This one here.''

"You're sure now,'' he commented drolly.

"Positive.''

Gretchen watched contentedly as Matt chopped down heir Christmas tree with powerful strokes of the ax. Long ninutes later, they were dragging it back toward the house. The morning was beautiful, cold and still. Alone with Matt out in the glistening, snow-covered field, she could easily believe they were the only two people in the world. Gretchen found herself wishing that were so, for just a little while. She had been pushing herself like a maniac the past four months, going to school all week, working all weekend and studying every spare second in between. It was a relief to do nothing for a while, but just be. And Matt was a delightful companion when he chose.

The tree thumped as Matt tugged it up the porch steps. He stood it upright. Snow coated its limbs. He was about to open the door, when she laid a hand on his arm.

"If we take it inside like that it's going to drip water all over the place.''

He grinned at her and leaned toward her just a little. "No joke, Sherlock.''

Aware of how solid his biceps was beneath her fingers, and how much she liked it, Gretchen wet her suddenly dry lips and stepped away from him. "So now what?''

Matt lounged against the side of the house and studied the tree. The outdoor thermometer beside him registered twenty-eight degrees Fahrenheit. "It won't thaw off out here on the porch."

"Maybe we should get a whisk broom and try to brush most of the snow off the branches," Gretchen suggested.

"I'm game if you are."

"Wait here. I'll be right back." Gretchen knocked the snow off her boots, wiped the soles of her boots on the mat and hurried inside.

When she got back, Matt was hanging the tree over the side of the porch, shaking off as much snow as he could. A fair amount still remained. Gretchen went to work with the whisk broom. Fifteen minutes later the tree was about as snow-free as it was liable to get. Matt sawed off the end so the tree would stand straight, and Gretchen knelt to help guide it into the stand. He held the tree in place while she tightened the screws around the base. As she worked, snow fell onto her collar and began to melt against her neck. Finished, she struggled to her feet and tried in vain to get the snow out of her collar, but all she succeeded in doing was pushing it farther down her back.

"Here, let me help you," Matt said. Hands on her shoulders, he turned her around so her back was to him. Working his hand beneath the collar of her parka, he scooped out the snow, then promptly smeared it across her face.

Gretchen screamed at the feel of the cold, wet snow on her lips and cheek. "Very funny."

His eyes gleamed with mischief. "I thought so."

She reached behind her and surreptitiously scooped up a handful of snow from the porch railing. "But enough fooling around," she continued with as much seriousness as she could muster. "Let's get this tree inside."

He studied her candidly. "Sure you don't want revenge?"

She shook her head matter-of-factly. "I'm not into childish games."

He paused, then nodded. "Hmm. Well, you want to hold the door for me?"

"Sure. Just let me get by."

As she sidestepped past, she smeared the snow in her hand across his mouth and chin. He let out a yelp of surprise. The next thing Gretchen knew, he had scooped up two handfuls and was chasing her down the steps.

"Now, Matt," Gretchen panted, as she raced across the front yard, "don't do anything you'll regret."

He transferred the snowball from hand to hand and grinned mercilessly. "Who says I'm going to regret this?"

"Then don't do anything I'll regret," she advised, scooping up another handful of snow herself as she ducked behind a pine tree laden with snow.

"Too late," Matt sassed back. He darted sideways and hurled a snowball at her shoulder. It connected with a painless *splat* that had her aching for revenge.

"Matt!" Gretchen reprimanded as she put one snowball in her pocket and, stealthily scooping snow off the branches of the pine, made another and another.

Again a snowball came whizzing at her leg, this one catching her just above the knee. Grabbing up two more handfuls of snow, he approached from the side, all big, taunting male.

"Give up?" he demanded, making it clear he would accept nothing less than her unconditional surrender.

"Never!" Gretchen darted around the tree and aimed a snowball at his head. She missed completely and he laughed uproariously, the mellow sound of his voice echoing in the snow-filled silence around them. He stopped laughing when she quickly pulled out her backup ammunition. Her second snowball caught him in the chest, her third in midcalf.

Matt took three great strides and caught up with her. "Now, that one," he drawled, scooping up a huge amount of gleaming white snow with both hands as they both broke into a run, "is going to cost you!"

Delighting in their cat-and-mouse play, Gretchen darted past the porch and around the side of the house. Unable to resist, she taunted breathlessly, "You have to catch me first!"

He clamped his arms around her waist, pulled her against him and backed her up against the wall. Feet planted on either side of her, he aligned his body with hers and stared down at her. "All right," he said softly, possessively. "I caught you."

"Now what?" she demanded, afraid she already knew.

Dropping his hold on her waist, he yanked off his gloves and took her face in his hands. "Now this."

His lips captured hers in a millisecond. Gretchen didn't think Matt thought about what he was doing any more than she did; she knew only that his lips were cold and his tongue was warm and the mixture of the two sent the most delicious heat spiraling through her. Her lips parted, not in surrender, but with an answering urgency that rocked them both and left them both shaking and gasping for air.

He drew back and looked down into her face. Gretchen saw herself mirrored in his eyes and inhaled sharply. And then she was in his arms once more, kissing him again, sweetly this time, unapologetically, experimentally. Driven by feelings she was loath to name, she let herself go, let herself feel and be, let herself drift mindlessly into pleasure—into passion.

When they drew apart, she was completely at a loss as to what to do or say or how to behave. Once again, Matt came to the rescue. He looked at her a long, telling moment, letting her know that he hadn't expected what had just happened between them, but that he didn't regret their reckless kiss any more than she did. Then he smiled and gently touched her face with the side of his hand. "I guess we better get that tree inside and up before the Stewarts arrive," he said.

"WHAT DO YOU THINK?" Matt asked a scant two hours later.

They stood back to admire their handiwork. The tree was beautiful, Gretchen thought. With garlands of red wooden beads, red velvet and red taffeta ribbons, assorted ornaments and sparkling white lights, it was as pretty as any department-store display she had ever seen.

The phone rang. Tearing her eyes from the tree, Gretchen went to answer it.

"Bad news," Marissa began without preamble as soon as Gretchen answered. "The interstate is still closed. It looks like it'll be tomorrow by the time we get out there. How are you and Matt doing?"

My lips still tingle from his kiss, Gretchen thought. *Worse, I'm wishing he would kiss me again and again and again.* She didn't know what had gotten into her. Maybe it was the season. Maybe it was just a fleeting, reckless whim or the long-buried playfulness that he brought out in her, but she wanted to enjoy their flirtation while it lasted, and so apparently did he, judging by the ardent looks he gave her whenever he thought she wasn't aware.

Gretchen glanced back at Matt and smiled. "Matt and I are fine," she told Marissa.

There was a short, disbelieving silence on the other end. "You sure, now?"

Gretchen laughed. She knew she and Matt had gotten off to a rocky start, exacerbated by her blatant attempts to avoid spending time alone with him. But that was all past them now. "Don't worry about a thing."

Matt was watching as she hung up the phone. "They're not coming," he guessed.

And looked not the least bit disappointed by the news, Gretchen thought. She glided back to his side, feeling giddy and alive with anticipation. She hadn't planned this, but she was more and more loath to turn away from it. "Tomorrow afternoon at the earliest, they think," she said solemnly. Which gave them nearly twenty-four more hours completely alone. A lot could happen in twenty-four hours, and Matt knew it, too.

He tried hard but couldn't completely suppress a smile. "I see." His eyes roved her upturned face.

At the raw, sexual energy in his gaze, her heart skipped a beat. Maybe she wasn't as ready for this as she thought she was. She turned away nervously, stepped past the glittering tree and headed for the kitchen determinedly. "It's my turn to cook tonight," she announced carelessly over her shoulder. "I'll go in and start dinner."

He nodded agreeably, already reaching for his coat. "I'll bring in more wood."

"Tex-Mex okay with you?" Gretchen asked, her hands a flurry of activity as he rejoined her short minutes later.

"Sounds great."

He was wearing a sophisticated pewter-and-navy flannel shirt that brought out the silver in his eyes. He looked masculine and inherently at ease with himself, Gretchen noted admiringly. Aware she was digressing again, she turned her attention back to her task.

He leaned against the counter, arms folded in front of him, then watched as she spread zesty refried beans onto tostado shells and liberally sprinkled on grated cheddar and Monterey Jack cheese before sliding the tray into the oven and setting the timer for fifteen minutes. "Those nachos look great."

"I thought they'd be a good appetizer. We can eat them while I fix the fajitas," Gretchen added, as the phone rang.

Matt reached for the receiver on the wall. "It's probably my kids. I gave them this number." He picked up the phone on the next ring. "Hi, Angela. Yes, I was hoping you'd call," he murmured affectionately. "I miss you, too, sweetheart." His face split into a concerned frown. "You want to what?" he said incredulously. "No," he continued gently but firmly, "I don't agree that's the thing to do. Not at this late date, but we'll talk about it when I see you next week. Yes. Put Luke on. Hi. Merry Christmas to you, too. What do you mean, where am I? You know where I am, Luke, at the Stewarts' ranch. No, I'm not going to do anything rash just because I have to spend the holiday alone. Oh. You heard the Stewarts got stranded in Denver. Yes, well, I made it here before the storm. Yes, there is another guest here—a very nice young woman—and that is all you need to know on the subject, Luke." Matt rolled his eyes, and struggled for patience. "I forgive you this time, but you've got to stop asking so many questions. Everything in life is not a mystery just waiting to be solved. Okay, bye. Hi, Sassy. How's the skiing? Good. I'm glad you all are enjoying yourselves. The day after Christmas. Yes, I'm driving down to Aspen that very morning. I'll leave as soon as I can. What time? I'm not sure. Yes, I understand your need for me to be precise, Sassy. How about I meet you at the ski lift at noon? Right. If anything at all happens to change things, I'll call you and leave a message with the hotel concierge. Yes, absolutely. You have a Merry Christmas, too, sweetheart. I'll see you in a couple of days." He hung up the phone.

"Everything okay?" Gretchen asked as she slid sliced onions and strips of marinated beef into the sizzling-hot cast-iron skillet on the stove.

He nodded, looking very much the devoted father. "My kids. They called to wish me a Merry Christmas."

"You have three children, I gather?" Gretchen said. Noting the nachos were done, she removed them from the oven, then cut them into fourths and slid the piping hot, pie-shaped wedges onto a serving dish that had lettuce, tomatoes, guacamole and sour cream artistically arranged in the center of it.

"Yes." As Matt brought out napkins and plates, he continued with unabashed pride, "Angela is twenty-three, a great kid and a student at the University of Texas. Her grades are wonderful. She's carrying close to a 4.0. The problem—if you can even call it that, given her sensitive artistic nature—is her inability to decide on a specific major. She's such a versatile and gifted kid. She wants to do absolutely everything and hence ends up changing her career plans every other term. As a consequence, she has plenty of credits but not enough to fulfill any particular degree requirements, even after six years of full-time enrollment."

Gretchen offered a commiserating smile. "I can see where that would be a problem."

He devoured a nacho and reached for another. "Unfortunately, you can't stay a student forever. To aid her in making the leap to adulthood, I've threatened to cut her off financially if she doesn't pick a major and stick with it soon, but I don't think she takes me seriously."

Gretchen paused, not sure she could see Matt behaving so harshly. "Are you serious?" she asked, curious.

Matt shrugged. "To be honest, I'd have a hard time throwing any child of mine out on the street. Besides, I want her to have an education. These nachos are great, by the way."

"Thanks." Gretchen smiled, then got up to give the fajitas a whirl with the spatula. Noting the sizzling beef had at least another ten minutes to go, she slid the foil-wrapped tortillas into the oven to warm. "What about Luke?" She sat down with Matt again, picked up a nacho and loaded it with extras.

"He's twenty-one and our middle child." Matt stepped outside onto the porch and brought in a six-pack of Colorado beer, which had been chilling out there. Gretchen watched as he opened two and handed her one. Gretchen brought down two glasses.

"Luke's at Texas A & M and although he's extremely bright and energetic, too, he's not doing as well academically as either of his sisters. He says it's because his classes in petrochemical engineering and business management are largely irrelevant. He wants to drop out of school altogether and become a private eye."

"But you object?" Gretchen sipped the icy beer.

Matt ignored the glass and tipped the bottle to his lips. "I admit I don't see much future in it. Although he is one of the nosiest, most suspicious people I've ever chanced to meet and he does love to check things and people out. So who knows? Maybe that is the place for him. Only he can decide."

"Still, you'd rather see him doing something else," Gretchen guessed.

His expression reflective, Matt nodded. Together, they finished off the last of the nachos. "I had hoped he would join me in the oil business someday—I'm a wildcatter and I've got my own firm."

Realizing there was one child they hadn't yet talked about, Gretchen got up to bring the skillet of sizzling fajitas to the table. "Sassy is your youngest?"

"Right." Matt watched as she got the tortillas from the oven and brought out another tray of salsa and grated cheese. "She's twenty and a prelaw major at Southern Methodist University. She's the most serious of my three children, very cautious and detail oriented."

"Which is why she wanted to know precisely what time you're going to arrive," Gretchen stated.

"Right. She can drive me nuts that way sometimes."

"But you love all three of them dearly, don't you?"

"Yes." Matt uttered a contented sigh and leaned back in his chair. "They are the best thing that's ever happened to me. I can't imagine my life without them."

Neither could Gretchen. Matt was very much a doting father. His kids were lucky to have him.

He looked down at the fajitas they'd built.

"Not exactly traditional Christmas Eve fare, is it?" Gretchen guessed at what he was thinking and wondered if he knew that she could have handled anything but a dose of sentimentality this evening. This Christmas Eve she didn't want to think about all she had lost. She wanted to think about all that lay ahead of her.

Matt grinned appreciatively. "Right now Tex-Mex is just what I need. What about you? Do you wish you were back in Texas?"

"Not so much...home is all relative to me.... But I do miss my dad." Gretchen found she trusted Matt enough to confide, "It's my first Christmas without him. He died last winter." And now that the holiday was upon them, Gretchen was finding the going a little rough.

"What about your mom?" Matt asked gently, reaching across the table to cover her hand with his.

"She died when I was ten."

"No other family?"

"None. Which is, of course, why the Stewarts invited me here. They took pity on me." Recovering, Gretchen shot him a flip glance. "What about you? What'd you do to earn the invitation?" she asked dryly, taking another sip of beer.

"It's my first Christmas without my kids. Last year I had them. This year it's my ex-wife's turn."

"So they're in Aspen," Gretchen said, recalling tidbits of his phone conversation with them.

Matt nodded. "Their new stepfather owns a hotel there." His mouth crooked up ruefully. "He owns a lot of hotels."

Gretchen noted there was no envy in Matt's voice; he'd simply stated a fact. "Do you and your ex-wife get along?" she asked, curious.

"As much as any two people who've been divorced for just under two years. Sometimes we do—sometimes we don't. Mostly she just thinks I am too hard on the kids, and hence have let them down that way."

He hadn't sounded like a bad father to Gretchen. "Hard in what way?" she inquired, taking a bite of her fajita.

"I'm the family disciplinarian and taskmaster. My wife doesn't have much of a work ethic."

"Not much of one or none?"

His eyes lasered in on hers. "You are shrewd, aren't you?" he said softly, admiringly.

Gretchen shrugged noncommittally. "From what I overheard just now, it sounded like you're doing okay as a dad, Matt."

Matt flexed his shoulders restlessly. "Even so, the teen years are rough. Thank God they're about over. I know everyone complains about an empty nest, but I for one am looking forward to being footloose and fancy-free again." He dug into a fajita with relish.

Gretchen studied him. "You really mean that, don't you?"

Matt nodded. "Having kids is a tremendous responsibility. I've devoted the past twenty-four years of my life—since I was twenty-one—to making sure they had everything they needed, from prenatal care on up. It'll be a relief to know they're grown up and okay, and just worry about me for a change."

He paused as their eyes locked once again. "You understand where I'm coming from on this, don't you?"

"Maybe because I feel the same way," Gretchen confided softly, then found she trusted Matt enough to be even more candid. "I put my dreams of becoming a teacher and having children on hold and spent the past ten years seeing my husband through medical school and residency, only to get dumped when he fell in love with another physician. Then my dad got sick and I took care of him. When he died, I knew I had a chance to start all over again and make a brand-new life for myself."

"Which is why you're back in school," Matt added.

They shared a smile. "Just call me 'studious.'"

"What about children?"

"That will come, in time, when I find my own Mr. Right, but now I'm more concerned with getting my education before I get any older." It was just too bad Matt was past that phase in his life, she thought, for he would've been the perfect father for her children, and perhaps even the perfect husband for her.

But that wasn't going to happen, she reminded herself sternly. The best she could hope to find with Matt was a fling. And even that might not happen. Aware they had both finished eating, she looked down at their plates. "And speaking of moving on, these fajita dishes need washing."

Matt pushed back his chair and stood. "I'll take out the trash and bring in more wood for the fire, then come back to lend you a hand."

"How'd you finish so fast?" Matt asked, when she joined him in the living room five minutes later.

"The Stewarts have a dishwasher, remember?" Gretchen replied.

A CD of Christmas carols performed by the London Symphony was playing on the stereo. He had turned down the lights and the tree sparkled in the darkened room, while a roaring fire crackled in the stone fireplace. Outside, snow piled up in deep white drifts beneath a black velvet sky sprinkled with stars. The night was peaceful, quietly romantic and very much Christmas Eve. Not in Texas, but in Colorado. Gretchen felt a deep, unexpected pang of loneliness as she realized once again this was the first year she would celebrate the holiday without any family of her own.

Deliberately, she pushed the melancholy thought away. There would be no feeling sorry for herself tonight, she scolded silently. Only enjoyment of life as it was. She still had much to be grateful for—her health, the limitless opportunities afforded her, her friends.

Blinking away unshed tears, she stepped closer to Matt and forced a smile as she watched him wrestle with a length of red ribbon and a sprig of evergreen leaves and berries. Was it her imagination, or did he suddenly look a little lonely, too? "What are you doing?"

"Hanging mistletoe—or trying to. What do you think? Should it go here by the staircase or over by the front door?"

Gretchen studied both places. "The staircase, I think."

He fastened the mistletoe securely on the chandelier next to the staircase, then peered up at it consideringly. "Think that will hold?"

Gretchen walked over to stand beside him. He had double-bowed the ribbon, albeit a little clumsily. "It's fine, Matt."

"Sure?"

Gretchen shrugged and gave him her best devil-may-care look. "I can live with it."

Hands braced on his hips, he grinned down at her wickedly. "Think we should we test it out?"

Chapter Three

Gretchen knew he expected her to say no and back away. But she'd spent a lifetime playing it safe. Maybe this once she should live dangerously, she thought. After all, it was Christmas Eve. They were both alone. Sure, they wanted different things out of life. She still had yet to experience having children and raising a family. He was all through with that part of his life.

But what did it really matter? she wondered passionately. After the holidays, they'd probably never even see each other again. So why not do something wild and wonderful just for herself? Why not prove, once and for all, that she could make love with a man and emerge with her heart and soul intact? Why not do something that would make them both feel less alone this Christmas Eve?

"Merry Christmas, Matt," Gretchen said, throwing caution to the wind.

Standing on tiptoe, she pressed her lips to his, drinking in the warm, smooth texture of his lips and the essence that was him. He opened his mouth to the explorations of her tongue and, groaning, pulled her all the way into his arms, anchoring her against him. She reveled in the tantalizing hardness of his chest and, lower, the rigid proof of his arousal.

Threading one hand through her hair, he tilted her head back, giving him fuller access to her mouth. And still the kiss continued, lush, hot and full of promise, until she could no longer deny the tenderness or the need in his touch.

Matt couldn't believe this was happening, that Gretchen was surrendering herself to him this way, but he didn't want it to stop. Even knowing she was too young, too cynical yet too idealistic, too feisty and independent for him, he still didn't want it to stop. Lowering his head, he pushed the rolled collar of her sweater aside and pressed his lips against the soft, vulnerable hollow of her throat. Her breath caught and she trembled at his touch, and he lightly traced the curve of her face, before once again possessing her lips and kissing her with white-hot desperation.

Basking in the quickened beat of her pulse, Gretchen shivered as he forced his knee gently between her legs, opening her to his touch. She hadn't planned for this to happen, but she wasn't sorry that it was, even as his palm swept from her thighs to her breast, testing the strength of her yearning through the curtain of her clothes.

She was filled with the warmth and steadiness of his presence, the way he'd made her forget how alone they both were this holiday. He'd made her aware moments like this were not lost to her forever after all. And she knew that if they went upstairs together he was going to make love to her, and she wanted it. For once in her life she wanted to luxuriate in the moment, and relish the magic that was them this Christmas Eve. Her heart pounded as he kissed her temple, her cheek, her ear, then he captured her mouth again, and this time there was no holding back, nothing but slow, inexorable passion and inevitable demand.

Finally, he lifted his mouth from hers. "Last chance to bail out," he murmured, his voice ragged with need.

This was reckless. But it was right. She splayed her hands across his chest, her fingers curling into the soft flannel of his shirt. "I understand what you're saying, Matt, and... I pass."

The next thing Gretchen knew, she was swept up into his arms, carried upstairs and lowered ever so gently on his bed. A moan escaped her as she thought about the lovemaking to come. Already her body was throbbing, aching to be filled, aching for the tenderness that was him.

If Matt had thought she looked like an angel before, it was nothing compared with the reality of her in his bed. Her dark hair spread out like a cloud of silk around her face. Her cheeks glowed with excitement. Anticipation danced in her blue eyes. Matt knew that Gretchen was thinking of nothing but the moment, and dammit, for once tossing aside his own innate gallantry, neither was he. Although rushing into a love affair was not at all his style, they were old enough and wise enough to handle this.

Shucking his shirt, boots, thermal undershirt and jeans, he joined her on the bed. With a sigh of surrender, she came eagerly back into his arms. Her lips were as soft and sensuous as her kiss, her caressing fingertips just as enticing. When her hands slid inside his briefs, tugging them off, demonstrating the passion she had yet to thoroughly unleash, he groaned. It was time she undressed, too.

He slipped her sweater over her head, unzipped her jeans and drew them down over her slender hips and sensational legs. She stretched out next to him, clad in pale pink silk long johns that were at once a considerable deterrent and terribly sexy in a pure, all-American-girl way.

"You have too many clothes," he murmured, dispensing with the long johns, too.

"So take them all off," she told him with dangerous abandon.

Matt caressed her face and grinned. Somehow he had known Gretchen would be uninhibited in bed...she was too strong willed and confident a woman not to be. He unclasped her bra and swept off her bikini panties. He had never seen a more beautiful sight—inches of flawless cream, interspersed with sexy touches of rose. Drinking in the fragrance of her skin, he bent his head to her breasts, enticing the nipples to dewy pink pearls with the masterful ministrations of his lips and tongue.

Her head thrown back in abandonment, she strained against him, relishing his skillful adoration. Then, with a murmur of desperation, she dragged his lips back to her, demanding he take more. And more, as she kissed him again and again and again.

"Don't make me wait," she pleaded, her voice soft and breathless, her legs shifting restlessly beneath him. Then her hands were everywhere. She couldn't seem to touch him fast enough. Couldn't seem to hold anything back.

And neither could he, as he slipped his hand between her thighs and discovered just how dewy and hot and hungry for him she was.

Gretchen shivered as Matt took her to new heights of arousal, her body tightening, until she couldn't suppress a moan. She had expected this to be the worst Christmas ever. It was turning out to be one of the best. For the first time in months, she felt incredibly alive and very much a feminine, desirable woman. That alone was a powerful Christmas gift, and one not to be denied.

"Oh, Matt. Matt, I want you," she whispered wistfully, as powerful convulsions were set off inside her. "I want you so much."

And it was true, she thought, as he flattened a hand beneath her and slid on top of her. The firm press of him as his body intimately draped hers felt so good, so right and natural. They were meant to be together. They were meant to have this one wonderful night. As he possessed her in one long, flowing stroke, she gave herself over to him completely, indulging the need that drove them, delighting in the joining of their bodies and the excitement-filled ascent, in the white-hot flash of fulfillment and the slow, floating feeling of release.

For long moments afterward they stayed just as they were, entwined, both of them silent, enjoying the aftershocks of passion that rocked them both. Finally, fearing he was too heavy for her, Matt kept both arms around her, but rolled onto his back. Gretchen collapsed on top of him, unwilling to admit she'd never been like that with a man before, not sure why it had happened with Matt—a man she barely knew—only aware that it had, and that as crazy as it was, their coupling felt right, at least for tonight. *My Christmas present to myself.* And oh, what a sweet, wild, wonderful Christmas present it had been.

"Tell me I didn't just dream that," Matt said, caressing her back with languid, circular strokes.

The demand in her already building again, Gretchen fought back a shudder of need and sighed. "You didn't."

He looked at her, searching for some explanation in her eyes. As always when backed into a corner, Gretchen resorted to being flip. She moved back and away from him, falling onto the pillows on the other side of the bed. Covering her eyes with her forearm, she drawled with a purely Texas wisdom that Matt Hale was sure to appreciate, "You know the old saying, Matt, a drought usually ends with a flood. And the longer the drought, the bigger the flood."

Matt grinned. "You're telling me that was a fluke? That we made love like that because we're both victims of abstinence—*yours and mine,*" he stressed softly, letting her know the drought hadn't been at all one-sided.

Gretchen tried not to feel too happy that it had been a long time since Matt had been with anyone, too.

"Or because it's Christmas and we don't want to be alone?" he continued.

Gretchen knew what a sentimental evening it had been and, in many ways, still was. She splayed her hands across his chest, still holding him at bay. "There's no denying we were both missing our families tonight."

"And also no denying that we might not have ended up in bed together tonight if we hadn't been snowbound—alone—here the past two days," Matt said, trailing his hands down her back.

But that didn't mean it hadn't happened, Gretchen thought. Because it had, and she was tingling all over from the aftereffects of his lovemaking.

Still trying to make sense of the winter storm she found herself caught up in, Gretchen regarded him solemnly. "When combined, all three elements are a lot to deal with at once. And as long as we're hunting for excuses, don't forget to factor in the wreck. Trauma makes people do crazy things. And sliding off the road into that ditch was definitely traumatic for me."

Though being rescued by Matt was anything but upsetting. Just as being made love to by Matt was anything but upsetting.

"But the lovemaking helped, didn't it?" Matt said.

Gretchen couldn't lie. He knew that it had, even before she flushed and stirred restlessly against him.

"It did for me, too," Matt confessed, kissing her neck, then her chin, then her lips. "So come here," he said.

With a wicked grin, he dragged her into the warm solace of his arms, securing her against him and taking her mouth with a consuming kiss that set her aflame anew. He tangled one hand in her hair, while the other stroked down her body, until she sighed her surrender and relaxed against him.

"And let's try that again...."

GRETCHEN AWOKE to sunshine streaming brightly into the room. Glinting off the snow, the light was almost white. She snuggled into the warm, love-scented flannel sheets and quickly became aware of two things. It was Christmas morning. And the shower was running.

Matt.

She had...they had... Gretchen buried her face in the pillow. The lovemaking that had seemed like a brilliant idea Christmas Eve now seemed glaringly inappropriate in the light of Christmas Day. What had she been thinking? She didn't have casual affairs with men. Before last night, she had never even entertained the notion. Yet she had slept with Matt. And they had made love, again and again and again.

And now she was going to have to face him. She was going to have to tell him that although it had been nice, it was not going to happen again. Not in this lifetime. She had school to finish. She couldn't afford to get sidetracked by a romance again, because if she did, she would never realize her dream of becoming a teacher.

As for her hope of having a family, children of her own, time was running out there, too, she thought with a frown. Matt might have already been there and done that, but she hadn't.

She stood, then headed for one of the other bathrooms at the end of the hall. She took her time in the shower, rehearsing over and over what she was going to say to him.

She had just finished drying her hair, when the sound of car doors sent her rushing to the window. The Stewarts, all fifteen of them, were piling out of an assortment of four-wheel-drive vehicles. Matt was walking out to greet them. As she looked down at him, Gretchen recalled their time together and was filled with warmth and tenderness.

Even so, she knew she was going to have to tell him that what they had shared the evening before was only a one-shot deal. She wanted to start a family. Matt was through with that. Their encounter could be nothing more than one night.

"LOOK, if you won't tell me who the father is, you at least have to tell him," Marissa Stewart told Gretchen several weeks later, after she had finished the physical exam and run the tests.

Gretchen shook her head as memories of that one fantastic night came flooding back to her. "I don't think he wants to know, Marissa." Although she had never had the chance or privacy to talk to Matt about the matter directly, in the twenty-four hours they'd had together before he left for Aspen to see his kids, she had let him know in dozens of ways—by the way she didn't touch him or look at him or talk to him one on one again—that their lovemaking was not going to happen again. Ever the gentleman, he had taken his cues from her and not pushed. At least not too much. There had been those phone calls later—calls she had not returned. And his being pleasant to her, but not pushing her, was exactly what she wanted. Wasn't it?

"You can't be sure of that," Marissa continued. "I can't think of any father who wouldn't want to know."

Gretchen thought back to what Matt had told her. *I've about had it with child rearing.... I'm looking forward to an empty nest.* She sighed. Like it or not, those words had come straight from Matt's heart. "Take my word on it, Marissa. He doesn't want to know this." Because Matt was inherently gallant, he would feel he had to do something if he knew. And Gretchen didn't want to trap him or force him into parenthood again. It wouldn't be right, for any of them, no matter what Matt said to smooth things over.

"Now, now, I know the timing is bad," Marissa soothed.

Gretchen grimly let out a breath as she tugged a hand through her hair, shoving the length of it off her face. "That's an understatement and a half." Even so, she wanted this child. Wanted it more than anything in the world. Of course it hurt that her baby wasn't going to have a father or the two-parent family she had dreamed about, but Gretchen also knew she could do it alone. She had enough love in her heart to rear a whole brood.

"But Cal and I will help you," Marissa went on practically. "I'll waive my obstetric fees and I'll get Cal to do the same with the pediatric."

Gretchen knew the husband-and-wife doctor team was among the best of the best in the Austin medical community, but her friend's offer felt like charity. Her Irish-immigrant father and hardworking German-American mother had raised her to be independent. She didn't want to be a burden to anyone, pregnant or not. "I can't let you do that," she said stubbornly.

"Of course you can." Marissa smiled and closed Gretchen's file folder decisively. "We'll call it professional courtesy for all those long years you worked in my office, running it like a well-oiled machine. I owe you, and you know it."

MATT HALE parked in front of the apartment complex where Gretchen O'Malley lived. He didn't know what was going on with her, or why she had done such an about-face on their love affair as soon as the Stewarts arrived at the Rocking S Ranch—could it be she was embarrassed by her relationship with him?—but now that his time with his kids was over, the latest crisis with his West Texas oil field averted and he was back in Austin again, he was going to find out.

She answered the door promptly. In jeans and a casual V-necked light pink cotton sweater that brought out the blue in her eyes, she looked even prettier than he remembered her. Glowing, almost. Until she saw him, that was. Then her expression fell and her face paled to an alarming chalky white.

"Matt." She whispered his name with remorse.

Trying not to be discouraged by her reluctance to deal with him, he cradled the bouquet of flowers in his hands. "Hello, Gretchen." Feeling a little foolish—it had been years since he'd come calling like a schoolkid, but that was how she made him feel—he thrust the flowers at her.

Their fingers brushed, and where her cheeks had been pale, they now turned a bright, self-conscious pink. He watched as she lowered her long-lashed eyes and wet her soft pale pink lips.

"Listen, I really. . . I, uh, I can't talk now."

Practically crushing the flowers, she held them so tightly, she looked behind her nervously in a way that made him wonder if she was hiding something—or someone—in her apartment. Jealousy rose within him, and that was something else he hadn't felt in years and years. Had he been edged out by another man?

"Then when?" Matt asked Gretchen patiently. He folded his arms and braced a shoulder against the doorframe. "You've been avoiding me for three weeks now, and don't try to deny it. You haven't returned any of my calls."

"There were only four of them."

Four, Matt thought, seemed like more than enough. Especially since he'd never had to chase a woman in his life. "I want to know why you're ducking me, why you won't even look me in the eye. Is it because of what happened between us?" He grasped her shoulders. Though he had been intent on keeping his own emotions under wrap, his voice dropped an anguished notch as he whispered, "Are you angry with me for making love to you that night—is that it?"

"No, of course not." Blushing all the hotter, Gretchen took his sleeve and drew him into the tiny efficiency apartment. She shut the door behind him. "I wanted what happened to happen as much as you did. We both know that."

"Then why won't you return my calls?"

Gretchen strode to the kitchen area at the far end of the room and got down a vase, adding water to it, before putting in the bouquet of flowers and baby's breath he'd brought her.

Returning to his side, she set the vase on the coffee table and sat down on the sofa, a sofa Matt was sure turned into a bed.

"Because it's not Christmas break anymore and I have to go back to class."

Matt sat down opposite her, leaving as much space as possible between them. As skittishly as she was behaving, he didn't want to crowd her. "Is that the only reason?" he asked gently.

Gretchen began to look a little panicked as she vaulted to her feet again and began to pace. She stopped next to a stack of textbooks on the folding table that served as a desk. She flipped through pages idly.

"What other reason could there be?"

"I don't know." Matt clasped his hands between his legs and stayed where he was only by supreme force of will. "That's what I'm here to find out. We never had a chance to talk in Colorado once the Stewarts arrived."

Gretchen lifted a shoulder. "There was a lot of confusion."

And she had played it to full advantage, making sure she and he never had an instant alone. Matt had understood her desire to keep their feelings for each other private; their brand-new friendship had been at a very delicate stage. It was the way she continued to cut him off, long after they were both out from under the watchful eyes of Cal and Marissa Stewart that had him confused.

"Are you angry because I had to leave the next day to go visit my kids?" he asked gently, aware that if that was the case it put a different spin on the situation.

She stiffened and whirled to face him, upset he would think that even for an instant. "No, of course not."

"Then what happened to make you stop speaking to me entirely?" Matt stood and crossed to her side. Had he done something, said something? Had he *not* done something, *not* said something?

She clamped her arms in front of her and pressed them against her waist. Her emotions under tight control, she tilted her head up at him stubbornly. "I just had a change of heart, okay?"

Matt wished he could believe that was all it was, but his gut told him there was a lot more to it. She had given herself unreservedly. They'd had a connection that was more than just physical. And now she was acting as if she were seeing a ghost just looking at him. She was acting as if she were, deep down, very upset.

She turned her face to the side and looked out the window at the parking lot below. "It was an emotional time for both of us, made worse—or maybe even brought on—by the holidays. We were both lonely and alone and feeling very sentimental."

Matt cupped her shoulders gently between his palms and recalled how soft and loving she had felt against him when he'd held her in his arms. "And we still never would have made love if we hadn't been very attracted to each other,'' Matt said.

Tears glistened in her eyes but did not fall. She continued looking out the window. ''It was the isolation of the ranch...cabin fever,'' she insisted stubbornly.

''It was chemistry, pure and simple, the kind that comes along once in every lifetime if you're lucky.''

''Even so, we were wrong to get involved so quickly.''

''I'm willing to start over,'' Matt said, dropping his hands and stepping back, ''slowly this time.''

Gretchen gaped at him. ''You want to date me?''

He grinned. ''That was the general idea, yes.''

''I can't.''

Maybe teasing her was the way to go. ''Why not? When I talked to Marissa yesterday, she said you were fine.''

Without warning, Matt had the feeling Gretchen was hanging on to her composure by a mere thread. The color drained from her face.

''Is that all she said?'' Gretchen asked.

Which was another thing. Marissa had been unusually closemouthed. Downright tongue-tied, as a matter of fact. And that wasn't like Marissa, who, Matt suddenly realized, had suddenly stopped trying to match him with Gretchen. After weeks of pushing him to pursue Gretchen, Marissa had said nothing at all yesterday on the subject. The question was, why hadn't she? Obviously Gretchen knew.

Matt replayed the brief but telling conversation in his head. ''Marissa wanted to know why I was asking about you,'' Matt replied cautiously.

Gretchen blushed bright red. ''What did you say?''

''Nothing incriminating.''

Gretchen looked relieved. Too relieved, for the circumstances, Matt thought.

"But I think she guessed anyway," Matt continued. "That I'm attracted to you." Which was putting it lightly. He hadn't felt this way about a woman since—hell, he'd never felt this way about a woman.

Gretchen returned to the sofa and collapsed onto it. "Oh, no."

"Relax. She doesn't know we made love," Matt reassured her quickly as he sank down beside her.

Gretchen stared at her shoes. "No, but she's smart and she can sure put two and two together," Gretchen said miserably.

Matt's glance narrowed. Since his conversation with Marissa had been by telephone, he hadn't had the advantage of seeing her expression. He wondered what he would have seen if he had talked to Marissa face-to-face. "Did you say something to her about us?" he inquired.

"No. Of course not." Gretchen nervously pleated the fabric of her jeans with the tips of her fingers.

"Then what else does she know that she can put together?" Matt asked, watching the smooth nimbleness of her fingers and recalling how those hands of hers had felt, feverishly caressing his skin.

Gretchen's chin set with customary stubbornness. "You're asking too many questions," she complained, deliberately averting her eyes.

Matt cocked his head. "It seems to me I'm not asking enough."

"How about some coffee?" Gretchen looked agitatedly around her. "Or maybe we should just go out for coffee. Yes, that's it." She had already snatched up her purse. "We'll go out."

Matt stared at her. Gretchen was not the kind of woman who got in a dither about much of anything, including being in a car wreck. Yet this afternoon, seeing him again, she was practically a basket case.

"I'd like that," Matt said gently, deciding that whatever was going on, Gretchen needed him more now than she had when he had pulled her out of her car. "But let's make it dinner." Matt figured he was going to need some time with her to have even a chance at jump-starting his blossoming relationship with her again.

"Fine." Purse in hand, Gretchen headed for the adjacent bathroom. "I just need to freshen up."

"Mind if I use your phone while you do that? I'd like to check in with my office."

"Go right ahead." Gretchen waved absentmindedly. "It's in the kitchen."

She disappeared. Matt stood and went toward the phone. As he moved, his glance fell on the large pharmacy bottle. At the same instant Gretchen came barreling back out of the bathroom.

Her face fell as she saw him looking at the prescription from their mutual friend, obstetrician Marissa Stewart. He rounded on her, fury and disbelief streaming through him. "Why are you taking prenatal vitamins?"

"I, uh—" Words failed her. But the telltale blush in her cheeks was back.

Looking around for further evidence, Matt picked up the book lying open on the counter. "And why are you reading up on pregnancy?"

Gretchen swept her hands through her newly brushed hair, dislodging the barrette she had just put in it. "I don't believe this," she whispered to no one in particular.

Matt recalled Gretchen saying that every drought ended with a flood after they made love. And suddenly, Matt knew why Gretchen had been so desperate not to see him. And why she especially hadn't wanted her physician, Marissa

Stewart, to know that he and Gretchen had been intimate. Because if Marissa had guessed Matt was the father, Marissa would have insisted Gretchen do the right thing. Namely, tell him. "The baby is mine, isn't he?"

Gretchen looked all the more miserable and didn't answer.

He stepped closer to her, the possessiveness he felt toward her and her unborn child growing by leaps and bounds.

"Isn't he, Gretchen?"

Chapter Four

"We have to get married," Matt said over dinner at Chili's restaurant.

Gretchen settled into her own corner of the brown leather booth. Even though she knew it was necessary, she fervently wished they were not having this conversation. She'd barely had time to get used to her own feelings on the matter, without dealing with his, too. Never mind the social implications! She angled her chin at him defiantly. "These are the nineties, Matt. No one *has* to get married anymore."

Matt rested his forearms on the ceramic-tiled tabletop. "I don't care what is or is not politically correct, Gretchen. Every baby still needs a mom *and* a dad, whenever possible. And for you and me, it is possible for us to get married and give our child that."

Hope rose within Gretchen, but her innate common sense gave birth to a whole new round of worries. "Every baby also needs two parents who love each other dearly," she said gently. Thinking about all she had dreamed of giving her child, and now would not be able to, she forced a smile. "We don't fit that description, Matt," she said, her voice laced with misery.

He was silent. "I know it takes more than physical passion to make a marriage."

Gretchen knew that, too, since physical passion had abounded in her previous marriage almost to the end.

"And I know this is all very sudden. But maybe with time...if we worked at it...we could...come to love each other."

Like brother and sister? Gretchen wondered, as she eyed him uneasily. That was not what she wanted, either. "Look, it's decent of you to offer, but I know how you feel about rearing any more children. You were very clear about that in Colorado. You've been there. Done that. And now you're actually looking forward to having an empty nest."

"So? That was before I fathered another child. This is now, when I have."

Gretchen knew what a chivalrous man Matt was at heart. That was one of the things she admired most about him. It didn't mean she had to take advantage. She toyed with her bowl of southwestern vegetable soup. "I'm not going to force you into anything, never mind twenty-one years of parental responsibility."

Ignoring his plate of steak and fries, Matt fixed her with a brooding stare. "You wouldn't be forcing me into anything. I'm volunteering, remember?"

Just as he'd effortlessly stepped in to make love to her when the time was right. Ignoring the thrill the memory evoked, Gretchen lowered her gaze to the grilled chicken sandwich she'd ordered with her soup. "Duty makes a very poor substitute for love, Matt."

To her disappointment, Matt didn't counter with an argument, but forked his salad purposefully. "At least let me give my child a name and be financially responsible," he persisted.

His proposal sounded simple on the surface, but Gretchen knew life had a way of becoming complicated, and quickly. What if the idea of having another child grew on Matt? What if Matt decided he did want a baby in his life again and didn't want Gretchen and decided to try to take their baby away from her? Was she up for that? she wondered shakily.

Gretchen forced herself to project some calm. "It's not that simple, Matt," she said cautiously, as the waiter returned to refill his iced tea and bring Gretchen a second glass of milk.

"It could be," Matt said as soon as their waiter had left again. "All you have to do is say yes."

Her pulse racing, Gretchen regarded Matt solemnly. She knew by the banked fires in his intense silver gray eyes that he wanted her. Perhaps more than just a lover now, but as the mother of his child. But was that enough? Could she ever be happy without commitment? Never mind being married to a man who was there only because he felt he had to be. "I want this baby, Matt. I didn't plan to get pregnant. And the timing couldn't be worse. But I also know this could very well be my only chance ever to have a baby. So for me it's still a dream come true."

His gaze softened. He reached across the table and covered her hand with his, instantly suffusing her with warmth.

"Despite the timing, despite the unexpectedness, I want this baby, too."

The feel of his hand on hers generated tingles of awareness and a melting sensation in her middle. Yearning to be in his arms again, making love, Gretchen frowned. "And yet, that fact aside, you act as if you feel every bit as ambivalent as I did at first," she stated, tamping down her own growing wonder and joy.

He flexed his shoulders, released her hand and returned to his dinner. "You have to admit it's quite a shock."

"Tell me about it," Gretchen commiserated. It seemed she had run the gamut of emotions since finding out. Elated one moment, terrified the next, while constantly wondering how she was going to manage the nine months ahead more or less alone. Wise or not, she realized she wanted to share this with Matt. And it was easy to understand why. They were going to have a baby. A baby who was part Matt, part her....

"Marry me," Matt insisted, his look gentle and persuasive. "Give it at least a year."

Gretchen sipped her milk, and found once again she was having trouble not succumbing to his wishes. Nevertheless, she had to be practical here. She met his eyes with trepidation. "And then what?" The last thing she needed was to fall in love with Matt and end up with a broken heart.

Matt shrugged, his broad shoulders looking impossibly strong and wide beneath the soft corduroy of his shirt.

"If it doesn't work out, we'll split amicably. You will retain full custody of our child. I'll visit and pay child support."

He made it sound so easy. She knew it was much more complicated. "We could do all that without getting married." Finished with her dinner, Gretchen pushed her plate away.

"Yes." His expression both restless and determined, Matt signaled for the check. "But this way, our baby will have the best start we can possibly give him or her."

"YOU HAVEN'T answered me," Matt said as he parked in front of her apartment building. Since they'd left the restaurant, she hadn't said much at all. Which in turn gave him the feeling he had mishandled the proposal, that he should have courted her more first. But it was too late now for backtracking. He had already laid the option on the table. They might as well deal with it, and expediently.

Gretchen unfastened her seat belt and turned toward him. Her face was clearly defined in the glow from the street lamps overhead. She seemed edgy and confused.

"Do I have to decide tonight?"

Matt blew out an exasperated breath. He rested an arm on the steering wheel. "What's the point of waiting? We have all the information needed to make the decision." Abruptly he had the feeling that if he let too much time elapse, she would lose her nerve, cut and run.

Gretchen laid a gloved hand on the console between them. "I disagree. There's a lot we still haven't discussed, Matt," Gretchen said, her lips forming a troubled moue.

Matt slid a hand beneath her chin and tipped her face up to meet his. He had never seen her look more vulnerable. He wanted to take her in his arms and comfort her. Sensing such a move would be interpreted as a pass, and an unwelcome one at that, he reined in his desire.

"The only way I would ever want to marry you is if you were marrying me because you wanted to marry me, because you loved me, not just because we were going to have a baby together." She shook her head in regret and released a tremulous sigh. "I don't want a loveless marriage, Matt. I've already had that."

Matt hadn't expected her to be so blunt, but now that she had laid her cards on the table he was glad she'd spoken her mind. The more honest they were with each other from the get-go, the easier this would be. "I don't want a loveless marriage, either," he said gently. "But there's no getting around the fact you're carrying my child. We have to do what is best for the child, and that means marriage. Fortunately we've got plenty of time to really get to know each other and work out some kind of feasible relationship before it is born. And once the baby is born...who knows...the love we feel for it may draw us together faster than we could ever imagine. And all of that can only benefit us all in the long run, whether you and I stay married or not," Matt finished firmly.

"Okay, I agree it's necessary for us to forge a sense of family—a foundation of mutual friendship and respect—for our child, and maybe our being married—at least in name only—and living under one roof is the way to do that. But what about the rest of it?"

"Such as?" Matt prodded.

"With a baby on the way, it's more important than ever that I complete my education. Which means I can't afford to miss a whole semester. I plan to enroll for the fall term, have the baby in mid-to-late September and go back to class as soon as possible after the baby is born."

"Wait a minute," Matt interrupted. "Although I agree you should complete your education, I don't think you should plan on going back fall semester. Taking care of a newborn baby is exhausting. It could be six months before the baby even sleeps through the night. And though I plan to do my share of nighttime feedings and diaperings, I won't always be there, which means sometimes you're going to have to get up."

Gretchen threw up her hands. "You see? We're arguing already and we haven't even applied for a marriage license. This is a bad idea, Matt. A very bad idea." She pushed from the car and hurried up the walk.

He caught up with her as she reached her door. The light above her door was on and he could see the tears shimmering in her eyes. He clasped her shoulders. "Gretchen—come on. We'll work everything out. I promise. It's a stretch for me sometimes, but I can be a very enlightened, nineties kind of guy."

She swallowed and her lower lip trembled, but she did not—would not—look him in the eye. "I know you mean well, Matt."

Mean well? He was fiercely possessive. That was his child she was carrying. "We'll work everything out," he soothed, stroking her hair. Somehow he would do what was best.

She shook her head. The tears she'd been holding back spilled through her lashes and tumbled down her cheeks.

Giving in to impulse, he wrapped his arms around her and folded her close. She was wearing the same perfume she'd had on the night they'd made love; the scent brought back a wealth of both erotic and tender memories. Matt knew he would not be able to let her go without at least trying to make this relationship of theirs work for the long haul.

"It's too complicated," she murmured, her voice breaking as she burst into new tears.

"No, it's not." Matt stroked her spine from nape to waist, welcoming the chance to hold her close, while she cried herself out. "It's easy. I'll do everything. Notify people and make all the arrangements for the ceremony. All you have to do is go with me to apply for a license and get a blood test."

Gretchen took a deep, shuddering breath and drew back to study his face. Tears still coursed silently down her cheeks. She regarded him with a woebegone expression. "What are we going to tell people?" she whispered.

Matt shrugged. As far as he was concerned, that was the least of their worries. "That we met over Christmas and we're going to get married," he said nonchalantly.

"Just like that?"

Matt inclined his head to the side. "If they need further illumination, we'll just tell them we've recently discovered we were meant to be together. And it's true. Right now, we are." Who knew what would happen in the long run, Matt thought wearily. So they would concentrate on the present and let the future take care of itself.

Gretchen leaned against her front door, her arms folded in front of her. She was no longer crying. "What about the baby?"

"We don't have to go into that until you start showing. Unless you want to tell people now?"

"No," Gretchen said swiftly, her already heightened color darkening across her cheeks. "This is going to be hard enough as it is."

"Agreed." Matt had the feeling news of their marriage was not going to be welcomed in all quarters, especially his own. "Then it's settled." Matt moved away from her and took a long, deep breath. "You'll marry me?"

Gretchen frowned. "It doesn't look like I have any other choice."

"GRETCHEN O'MALLEY?"

Gretchen lifted a sack of groceries from her car trunk and turned in the direction of the low, distinctly Texan, distinctly cultured voice. "Yes."

"I'm Sassy Hale, Matt's daughter."

The prelaw major at SMU. Gretchen smiled and extended a hand in greeting. "Matt's told me a lot about you."

Sassy watched as Gretchen shut and locked the trunk of her car. Matt's daughter was tall and athletic looking, with long, black hair. She was dressed in tailored gray slacks, a white cashmere sweater, suede jacket and tassled loafers. Preppy silver glasses rimmed her pretty and intelligent blue-gray eyes.

Sassy followed Gretchen up the walkway to her door. "Dad told me the two of you are getting married on Saturday."

"Yes. At Cal and Marissa Stewart's home here in Austin." Gretchen unlocked the door and led the way in to her apartment.

Sassy looked around. Gretchen thought she knew what Sassy was thinking. Her place was small and economically furnished.

"Dad also mentioned you'd be keeping your apartment here after the marriage," Sassy continued casually.

Gretchen nodded, grimly aware that Sassy was hanging on her every move. She had been expecting the third degree from Matt's nearly grown children. It would be a relief to get it over with. "It's convenient to UT. And I'll still need a place to study."

"I think it's wise." Sassy nodded solemnly as her voice dropped conspiratorially. "I mean, this was awfully sudden. Who knows if it will even work out?"

Sassy, it was clear, was hoping it wouldn't.

Gretchen busied herself putting away the milk and orange juice and tried not to feel discouraged. "Marriage is always a risk."

"Precisely my point." Sassy edged closer. "Which is why, Gretchen, I think you should definitely sign a prenup agreement with my dad. You know, stating you have no interest in the family money if or when the marriage dissolves."

Gretchen paused as a chill of foreboding ran down her spine. "Did your father send you here?"

"No, of course not." Sassy took offense. "You must know Dad is way too gallant to ever suggest such a thing."

Gretchen had hoped that was the case.

"But if you love him..." Sassy's expression gentled persuasively as she persisted. "If you really love him, then you'll want to protect him and give us all some peace of mind."

"All?" Gretchen prodded, wondering just whom Sassy was speaking for now.

"Luke, Angela and me. Fortunately, I've spent the past two summers working as a runner at a law firm here in Austin, and I know exactly who to contact about drawing up a simple prenuptial agreement for you and Dad. So what do you say, Gretchen?" Sassy edged nearer, her expression one of unbridled enthusiasm. "Shall we go and get this taken care of right away?"

"HEY, MATT. There's someone named Gretchen in the office to see you."

"Thanks, Pete." Matt wiped the grime off his face. Gretchen couldn't have come at a worse time. After a day spent repairing and replacing parts on malfunctioning oil rigs, he was filthy and sweaty. He'd be lucky if she didn't take one look at him and change her mind about marrying him.

As he strode into the office adjacent to his Austin headquarters warehouse, he considered her comment about not minding if a man worked with his hands for a living. Now was as good a time as any to put it to the test.

She was seated in a straight-backed vinyl chair, her posture as formal as the demure navy dress, stockings and heels she had on.

"I've come at a bad time, haven't I?"

Hell, yes, Matt thought, zeroing in on the official-looking manila folder in her lap. "Not at all," he lied. Aware of her eyes upon him, he walked over to the sink in the corner and turned on the spigot. Methodically he lathered soap to his elbows, then, aware of her eyes tracking his every move, scrubbed the skin-deep oil and grime off with a brush. "What's up?" he asked casually, as if he couldn't tell at a glance it was some kind of trouble.

"I brought by a prenup for you to sign."

Matt dropped the brush. It hit the bottom of the sink with a clatter. He jerked the towel off the drying rack and pivoted toward her. "A prenup that says what exactly?"

Gretchen averted her eyes from the towel he was rubbing over his forearms. "That we leave the marriage with the property we entered, that any children from the marriage will be shared jointly and without rancor. It also provides for a no-fault divorce if either of us becomes dissatisfied with the marriage."

His temper simmering at this unexpected—and unnecessary—development, Matt looped the towel over the rack and closed the distance between them in three long strides. He glared at the official-looking document in her hand. "May I?"

Her hand trembling, Gretchen handed the folder over.

Matt sat down at his desk and read the brief document in its entirety. Finished, he glanced back up at her face. "You really think this is necessary?"

Gretchen nodded brusquely. She seemed to be holding his gaze with difficulty.

"Your children are bound to feel less threatened if they know I have no designs on your money or your company."

"Uh-huh." Matt rocked back in his chair grimly. "Who's been talking to you?"

Gretchen was silent. Pink color filled her cheeks.

"It was Sassy, wasn't it? You don't have to answer. I recognize the name of the law firm she worked for last summer." Matt grimaced and reached for the telephone. "I'm going to talk to her."

"Matt, don't." Gretchen was out of her chair before he could dial. She put her hand over his, effectively staying him. "It doesn't matter who initiated this. I think it's a good idea."

Matt resisted the urge to touch the soft, silky nape of her neck as he studied her upturned face. "You're saying you want to sign it?"

Gretchen lifted her shoulders in an eloquent shrug. Her eyes darkened and she said softly, "Don't you?"

NO, Matt didn't want to sign a prenup. He didn't want to go into this marriage planning for it to fail. But he also knew in his heart that it was unrealistic of him to think he and Gretchen had even a slim chance of pulling this marriage off for a year, never mind making it work for all eternity.

The facts were clear. He had trapped Gretchen into marrying him because of the baby—their baby—and she had gone along with him, getting the marriage and the license only because she wanted to give their baby the best possible start in life under the circumstances. Still, he couldn't help but wish she were marrying him for more romantic reasons. He couldn't help but wish that she loved him, the way she might have been able to love him had the two of them met at some earlier, less-complicated time in their lives.

"Matt, I...I'm sorry if I've hurt you or handled this badly. It's just...I don't know what the protocol is in a situation like this."

"Not to worry. I'll be fine. We'll both be fine." He simply had to remind himself to keep his guard up, his heart closed against the possibility of getting too close to her; to not think that miracles might happen, that she might fall in love with him as time passed and decide to stay.

"The attorney said we could take this to their office and sign it in front of witnesses, or simply sign all three copies n front of a notary public for it to be legal. I noticed there's a bank not far from here—"

"Right. About a mile down the road," Matt said, already locking up his desk.

"You're sure this is okay? I mean, if you want another document or... or some other c-clause—" Gretchen stammered nervously.

Matt didn't want any clauses at all between them. But that wasn't about to happen. She was only marrying him because of the child—because they'd been foolish and reckless enough to have a one-night stand.

"This'll be fine," Matt said gruffly. "I just need to put on some clean clothes and then we'll go."

"ALL DONE," the notary public said as she finished affixing her seal. She handed the copies back to Gretchen.

As Gretchen and Matt left the bank, Matt grinned and shook his head.

"What's so amusing?" Gretchen asked.

Matt's lips crooked up ruefully. "I was just thinking that signing a prenup agreement is kind of like getting married with both feet out the door."

Gretchen leaned against her car, which was parked directly next to his Jeep. She folded her arms in front of her and turned to look at him. His eyes were brooding and intent. There was a new distance to his expression, as signing the papers had created even more constraint between them. "Is that what it feels like to you?"

He skimmed her face, lingering on her lips, before returning his gaze to her eyes. "What will you call it when those papers we just signed settle our divorce?" he asked, too lightly for comfort.

Gretchen drew a bolstering breath. "We can't pretend it's not coming."

"No," he replied shortly. "I guess we can't."

Gretchen straightened. *Sassy, if you were trying to drive us farther apart, you succeeded.* "Well, anyway, here's your copy," Gretchen said, handing it over.

Matt shoved both his hands in the pockets of his jeans. "Why don't you keep it?"

"You should have one."

But he didn't want one. "I trust you," he said diffidently.

She got out her keys and worked to keep the conversation casual. Lifting her eyes to his, she handed him the document, which he reluctantly accepted. "I guess I'll see you at the wedding then?"

He nodded, his expression contemplative, and continued to regard her in taut silence. "First thing tomorrow."

"I THINK it's great you're going to marry Dad," Angela Hale told Gretchen the moment she walked into the Stewarts' guest room.

Gretchen finished laying out her clothes and turned to Matt's eldest child, Angela. At twenty-three, she was petite and pretty, fashionably dressed and perpetually in motion. Her jet black hair was cut in a bob that made the most of her patrician features and silver blue eyes.

Gretchen gripped the belt of her pale pink robe, shocked by the warm acceptance flowing from Matt's daughter. "You don't mind?" She had not just expected all-out opposition from Matt's children on her wedding day, she had braced herself for it.

"No, not at all. I think it's great we'll be in college together." Mindful of Gretchen's wedding dress, which was laid out on the bed, Angela sat down and smoothed the skirt of her flowing pale blue dress. "I'm at UT, too, but then Dad probably told you that," she said.

Finished applying her makeup, Gretchen recapped her lipstick and slipped it back in her cosmetics bag. "Yes. He told me you're about to graduate soon."

"Well, that was the plan," Angela confided optimistically, "but it's not now. I just changed my major again and—"

"You just did what?" Matt thundered from the open doorway. He was dressed casually and had a garment bag over his shoulder.

Angela whirled toward Matt and put a gently admonishing fingertip to her lips. "Keep your voice down, Dad, or you'll upset the Stewarts."

Matt shut the bedroom door firmly behind him. "Forget that. I want to know what's going on." He released an exasperated breath. "Angela, I thought we had agreed you would finish your business degree and leave UT–Austin as soon as the spring semester is over."

Angela stood, her expression going from conciliatory to defiant in an instant. "No, Dad, we didn't agree on anything. You told me at Christmas that this was what I should do. You didn't listen to me when I tried to tell you that I made a mistake, that I should have a degree in psychology, instead."

Matt made a strangled sound of dismay. "How many more years is that going to take?" he demanded impatiently.

"About two and a half, my adviser said."

Matt looked like he was going to explode. Which, considering the fact his daughter had already been a full-time 4.0 student for six years and had yet to earn any undergraduate degree whatsoever, was not such an unexpected reaction, Gretchen thought. Sooner or later, Angela was going to have to make the transition from dependent student to responsible income-earning adult.

"You know, I think I hear Marissa calling me," Angel said, inching toward the door. "In fact, I'm sure I do." Sh slipped out before Matt could say anything else.

Gretchen laid a calming hand on Matt's shoulder. Lik her, he was not yet dressed for the ceremony, though he ha showered and shaved. Keeping her voice low in commiser ation, she edged closer, inhaling the tantalizing scent of hi after-shave. "It's not so bad. Psychology is a good field."

Matt shook his head, his expression unerringly grim, dis appointed. "She won't stick with it more than a year, if that She'll change her major again. I should just face it. Tha child is *never* going to graduate from college."

"Matt, what are you doing in here?" Marissa Stewar scolded from the doorway, hands on her hips. "You are no supposed to see Gretchen before the ceremony. It's bac luck." Marissa shooed him out. "Let Gretchen finish get- ting ready in peace."

When Matt had gone, Marissa turned back to Gretchen. "We've got fifteen minutes before the judge arrives and we start. You going to be able to make it?"

If I don't run out the back door in terror first, Gretchen thought wryly. "Sure."

As soon as Marissa left, Gretchen slipped out of her robe and into the demure, lacy white tea dress with the handker- chief hem. Aware her hands were shaking, she turned side- ways and checked her reflection in the mirror. Good. She wasn't showing. Yet, anyway. But then, she was only one month along. How was she going to get through eight more months of this? She sat down at the vanity. Realizing she had forgotten her hairbrush, she got back up. Marissa would probably have one she could borrow.

Gretchen started down the hall—then stopped again as she heard Matt's daughters talking in the bathroom.

"Stop being such an idealistic fool, Angela," Sassy said. "This marriage, if you can even call it that, is not going to last."

"How can you be sure?" Angela replied in a low, challenging tone.

"Because it's all happened too quickly," Sassy replied. "It isn't like Dad to be so impetuous."

You're right there, Gretchen thought.

"So how do you explain his marriage?" Angela scoffed anxiously, from just around the corner. "Don't tell me you think Gretchen is blackmailing him or something?"

"Don't be ridiculous," Sassy retorted hotly. "Dad would never allow anyone to jerk him around in that way. It's probably just a midlife crisis or something that's causing him to act this way."

A midlife crisis, Gretchen thought sickly, as some of the girls' anxiety was transmitted to her. *How aptly put....*

"And when that passes," Sassy continued irately, "he'll go back to normal and get out of this foolhardy marriage. Until then, we just have to humor him and pretend to accept her."

You're wrong, Matt. This is not going to be easy. Gretchen thought. *Nor is it going to be simple.* Why hadn't they talked more about his children? Just because none of them lived at home any longer did not mean they would not be affected.

"But you don't accept her, not really?" Angela asked Sassy.

"No, I don't. And I never will, either," Sassy said firmly.

Figuring she'd heard enough, Gretchen went back to the bedroom. A look in the mirror confirmed what she already knew. She was as white as a sheet. And with good reason. Matt's daughters were right. She and Matt were behaving crazily. And they had been since the first moment they'd met. It wasn't like him to have a one-night stand. Or her, either, Gretchen thought as the music floated up from downstairs, signaling the beginning of the wedding ceremony.

The song played through, ended, then began again. Gretchen knew she had missed her cue to sweep out of the bedroom and down the stairs, but she was so distressed she couldn't will herself to move. What if she was making a mistake—the worst mistake of her life?

Finally, a knock sounded at the door.

She went to answer it, expecting Marissa, and once again found herself staring up into Matt's face. Unlike her, he was ready—no, impatient—to get married and get on with their lives. But then, perhaps he didn't know what she did about his children's concern. Or perhaps he just didn't want to know.

His eyes roved her pale face and trembling lips. "Gretchen?" he said.

The concern he felt for her was evident, as he reached out to catch her in his arms and pull her close.

"Oh, Matt," she murmured on a weary breath, even as she struggled against the welcome warmth of him. What happiness was possible if it was at someone else's expense? She had not been brought up like this.

"What's wrong?"

"Everything," Gretchen whispered, as tears flooded her eyes. She shook her head in abject misery, laid her hands across his chest and stepped back.

"Matt, I can't go through with this."

Chapter Five

"What are you talking about?" Matt demanded.

His silver eyes gleamed as he closed resolutely in on her. Downstairs, the pianist switched to Brahms.

Gretchen took a deep hitching breath and moved away just as determinedly. "I can't marry you. I can't make a temporary mistake into a permanent or even a semipermanent one."

Her confession made him grin and edge closer yet. "Is that what we're doing?" he drawled.

"Darn it all, Matt, this isn't funny!" Gretchen reprimanded as the inches between them dwindled one by one. Suddenly she found it very hard to catch her breath.

"Actually, it is," he countered, eyeing her simple ivory tea-length wedding dress approvingly. Gently he touched the spray of flowers she'd pinned in her hair in lieu of a veil, let his fingertips glide to her lips and caressed them, too. "Who ever would have figured you'd have the prewedding jitters?" he teased.

Her lips tingling, Gretchen inhaled jerkily and stepped back a pace. She had to make him see reason. "Matt, it's more than that."

He thrust his hands in his pockets and lounged against the dresser as if they had all the time in the world, looking elegantly handsome and relaxed in a dove gray suit, pale gray shirt and tie, after-shave clinging to his jaw.

Lifting a dissenting brow, he countered resolutely, "Is it? You're not signing your life away or trapping us into anything."

"But your children—"

Matt crossed wordlessly to her side, sat down on the bed and, with unnerving tenderness, pulled her onto his lap. "My kids never approve or like or agree to anything I do anyway. They're at that age where they think I don't have any sense at all. They'll get over it, or so I'm told."

Gretchen splayed her hands across his hard chest. "But in this case, Matt, they may have a point. We are acting hastily."

He covered her hand with his, holding it over the slow, steady beat of his heart. "That's because we're in a situation where time counts." He twined his fingers intimately with hers. "Unless..." He hesitated, studying her flushed, upturned face. "You want to wait until the last possible second to marry, to further minimize our risk? 'Cause if you do," he continued with impeccable logic, "we could keep our license and blood tests current, put the justice of the peace downstairs on standby alert and then exchange vows and rings on our way into the delivery room."

"Hilarious," Gretchen decreed.

He tilted his head to the side. "It probably would be," he agreed.

His mock solemnness hitched her pulse up another notch.

Gretchen flushed. Fighting him on this was like fighting a brick wall. There was no way she could win. "Matt—" she protested softly. Only to have him reply in kind.

"Listen to me, Gretchen."

Matt turned her squarely in his lap and cupped her face with his hands. Warmth flowed through her in undulating waves, and she longed to bury herself in the haven of his arms and stay there forever.

"I don't give a hoot what anyone else thinks or says about us. We know we are doing the right thing, the only thing."

He took her hand in his, squeezed it in an almost familial way. "I know you're panicked by the commitment angle of it," he said.

With that soothing insight, he let her know in an instant that he, too, wanted to minimize their risk.

"But you needn't be," he soothed. "Our marriage is a temporary solution to a mutual problem. And that's all it is."

He was so sure of himself, of what they were doing. Gretchen only wished she felt the same. Oh, she knew it sounded uncomplicated. But things that looked easy or simple did not always turn out to be so.

Yet he was correct about one thing. When it came to doing right by their baby, what choice did they have? None, she knew. Slowly she extricated herself from his caressing hold and stood on legs that trembled.

Matt rose and laid a gentle hand on her shoulder. "I said I wouldn't hold you to the union much past the birth of our child, and I won't," he reassured softly. "All you have to do is trust me, and everything will turn out great. You'll see."

All you have to do is trust me.

Gretchen looked into Matt's eyes and knew that, crazy as it was, it was still within the realm of possibility: she could trust him not to hurt her or their unborn child.

Downstairs, the Brahms ended and the Pachelbel "Canon in D Major" began once again. Matt squared his shoulders. "I think that's our cue," he said, taking her hand.

"MARRIAGE IS a serious business," the judge, a well-dressed woman in her early fifties, began.

Don't I know it, Gretchen thought wryly, beginning to flush self-consciously.

"And to that end, Matt and Gretchen have written their own wedding vows," the judge continued.

On that Gretchen had insisted, and after getting over his initial resistance to the idea, Matt had agreed.

"Gretchen, do you promise to be generous and giving, steadfast in your loyalty, devoted to making your union with Matt work?" the judge asked.

Gretchen nodded, the nosegay in her left hand growing damp with perspiration. At least she wasn't promising more than she could reasonably deliver. "I do..."

"Matt, do you promise to be generous and giving, steadfast in your loyalty, devoted to making your union with Gretchen work?"

Looking even more sober than Gretchen felt, Matt took her right hand in his. His palm was warm and dry. Ignoring the skeptical, slightly horrified looks of his children, he gazed deep into Gretchen's eyes and said firmly, "I do," again behaving as if he didn't have a doubt in the world.

"Matt, Gretchen, you may exchange rings...."

Gretchen's hands trembled slightly as he slid the ring on her finger, and even more as she slid the wedding band on his.

The judge smiled. Matt squeezed Gretchen's hand.

"According to the power vested in me by the state of Texas, I now pronounce you husband and wife. Matt, you may kiss the bride. And Gretchen—" the judge grinned "—feel free to return the kiss."

Matt needed no further encouragement. He took her in his arms and there, in the circle of family and friends, he kissed her thoroughly, kissed her until her senses swam and her knees nearly buckled. And when he was finished,

Gretchen felt, to her ever-growing dismay, even *more* like a real bride.

Heaven forbid, what had she done?

"What happened to all that 'to have and to hold' stuff?" Luke asked casually, after the cake had been cut and the buffet supper drew to a close.

In a sport coat and tie, his cropped jet black hair tousled, blue-gray eyes intent, he looked like a younger version of his handsome father.

"Gretchen and I opted for a more modern ceremony," Matt said, as he forked up the last bite of cake on his plate and held it to Gretchen's lips.

Or in other words, Gretchen thought, *neither of us wanted to make any promises we knew we couldn't keep. It was more comfortable for us that way.*

Unfortunately, she still felt very married. But perhaps that would pass when they were no longer dressed in their wedding clothes, sitting in the Stewarts' festively decorated living room, surrounded by family and friends.

Matt's eldest daughter, Angela, shook her head at them disapprovingly. "I thought age was supposed to make one wiser, not less romantic, Dad," she chided.

Sensing another round of suspicion coming on, Gretchen jumped into the fray. "Matt is plenty romantic," she said, defending staunchly. And it was true. She only had to recall the way he'd made love to her Christmas Eve to know that.

"Oh, really? Then how come the two of you are passing on a honeymoon?" Sassy asked in blunt, lawyerly fashion.

"I've got class at UT on Monday morning," Gretchen explained.

"I wouldn't let that stop me," Luke murmured, with a typical twenty-one-year-old's enthusiasm for all things amorous.

Matt wrapped his arms around Gretchen's shoulders. "We didn't see the need to travel at this point. Perhaps later. On Gretchen's spring break—"

"Really, Dad. Why put off till tomorrow what you can do today?" Angela suggested brightly.

Sassy stated smugly, "You're always telling us not to procrastinate."

Gretchen was filled with dread. For once, Matt seemed just as wary as he admitted, "True, but—"

"No, buts," Angela said firmly, taking charge. "The three of us have arranged for you to have the honeymoon suite at an elegant hotel downtown." She smiled happily. "Now, where did that photographer go? I want him to take some photos of the five of us. Sassy, come help me find him."

Sassy glanced protectively at Matt. "We'll be right back, Dad," Sassy said.

"Some wedding present, huh, Dad?" Luke said, watching his sisters move off among the guests.

"Actually, I had a blender or a new coffeemaker in mind," Matt quipped.

So had Gretchen.

Luke regarded Gretchen with a smugly suspicious look. "Gretchen, are you feeling all right? You're a little pale."

No kidding, Gretchen thought. "Too much excitement, I guess." Gretchen forced herself to smile brightly.

"Yet I noticed you didn't drink any champagne," Luke continued. "Not even when you and Dad toasted each other. Instead you just pretended to take a sip."

"Luke," Matt reprimanded sternly. "I think that's enough."

Gretchen knew the questions would only resurface later if they didn't answer now. With a great deal more tranquillity than she felt, she laid a hand on Matt's arm. "It's all right, Matt. I don't mind." She turned back to his son. Knowing Luke was only trying to protect his dad made his curiosity easier to take. "You're very observant, Luke," she said kindly.

"Which is exactly why I'd make a crackerjack private detective," Luke said.

Matt tensed. "I thought we'd tabled that discussion until you were through college," he said.

"Not by choice," Luke replied.

"Table it anyway," Matt advised with a warning look. "At least for tonight."

"Fine. Back to your abstinence this evening," Luke continued. "Is there a particular reason you didn't drink, Gretchen?"

Yes. The baby. "Champagne makes me light-headed. Plus I'm not much of a drinker, although there are times—" like now, she amended silently "—when I think maybe I should be, at least in social situations. It might help me relax." And deal with all this. She was beginning to feel overwhelmed; Matt's college-age kids were a handful.

"I see." Luke mulled over her answer.

"Back to tonight," Matt said, changing the subject smoothly. "I don't have any luggage. So—"

"Not to worry. I packed an overnight bag for you," Luke replied.

"Thanks for making the arrangements," Matt said, affectionately lacing an arm about Gretchen's waist.

"No problem. It's not like I'm harboring the same theories my sisters have regarding your sudden marriage, anyway," Luke replied.

"Such as?" Matt prodded tensely.

Luke shrugged. "Sassy thinks that this isn't a real marriage...not in the traditional 'love, honor and obey' sense anyway."

Sassy was right, Gretchen thought.

"Whereas Angela absolutely refuses to believe you have blackmailed Dad into doing this. She said you are too nice a person to ever do anything so underhanded and manipulative."

"How reassuring to hear," Matt said dryly.

"And what do you think, Luke?" Gretchen asked, curious.

"That I've never known Dad to do anything without a damn good reason," Luke replied bluntly.

"Matt, maybe we should tell them why we got married," Gretchen said, beginning to feel a little panicky again.

"I've got a better idea. Let's just show them," Matt said. He took her into his arms and delivered a searing kiss.

Gretchen had thought that their kiss after they'd recited their vows was something. But it was nothing compared with this. She was dizzy from head to toe, aching all over in that peculiar sensual way. She leaned into the embrace, allowing his tongue entry into her mouth.

Suddenly the girls were back, the photographer in tow. Matt and she were breaking apart. Gretchen didn't need to look in a mirror to know she was as radiant as a new bride should be. Obviously Matt had made good on his purpose. Even Luke looked a little convinced.

"Did Luke tell you he's rented a limo?" Angela asked.

"And we're all three going to drive you and see you settled," Sassy added.

Recovering from his shock, Luke continued studying both Matt and Gretchen with thinly veiled suspiciousness. "Unless there's some reason the two of you would rather not stay in the bridal suite tonight?"

"None," Matt promised glibly, as the five of them lined up for the photographer.

Determined to hide her nervousness over the evening ahead, Gretchen smiled for the "family" photo, then added, "It sounds lovely, really. What a nice gift."

"THEY KNOW something's up," Gretchen said, as she and Matt went up to the guest room to gather their belongings.

It bothered Matt that Gretchen did not look thrilled at the idea of spending another night alone with him. Hadn't they managed just fine in Colorado? But he forced a smile anyway. "Those kids always could read me like a book."

Gretchen zipped up her garment bag containing the street clothes she'd had on earlier. "Face it, Matt. They don't believe our marriage is on the up-and-up. And they are out to use our slipups to prove it."

Gretchen was right, Matt thought. His kids were up to something. This honeymoon was some kind of test. But there was no reason for Gretchen to be upset about it. As a soon-to-be-parent herself, she needed to learn how to roll with the punches, because kids were full of surprises, almost from day one. He shrugged. "Then we'll just have to show them how serious we are about seeing this union of ours through, won't we?" Matt said softly.

"Ready to go, Dad?" Sassy asked.

Interrupted again, Matt thought, frowning.

Regaining her composure, Gretchen turned away in relief. "Just about," she answered Sassy lightly.

"I'll take the stuff out to the limo," Luke said.

"Gretchen?" Angela chimed in. "Marissa wants you to throw the bouquet before you leave."

"And Cal said something about a garter possibly needing to be removed," Luke added helpfully.

Matt was looking forward to that event himself. Gretchen had spectacular legs.

"I hope I catch the bouquet," Angela said dreamily.

"Oh, no, you don't," Matt told Angela. "No getting married until you finish college."

"Ha! And just what do you think you're doing, Dad?" Angela replied. "Marrying a college freshman, no less!"

"That's different," Matt said, unperturbed as all five of them headed down the hall. "We're older." He looked at Gretchen meaningfully, letting her know with a glance they had not made a mistake, despite his children's assertions to the contrary. "We know what we want." And what he wanted was Gretchen and their new baby, unexpected as both might be at this stage of his life. He could only hope that this slam dunk into stepparenting had not soured Gretchen on the idea of somehow blending his two families, past and present, into one someday soon. Because as time passed, Matt was seeing that it was the only way to go. The hardship would be in convincing Gretchen of the same. Thus far, because of their hurry to get married, she had only seen his kids at their collective worst. She hadn't seen how sweet and caring and supportive they could be under ordinary circumstances.

"So getting older makes it okay to rush into something?" Luke persisted.

His son's remark drew Matt's attention vigorously back to the present. *No, but having a baby on the way does,* he thought, which brought him to the next question. When exactly would be the right time for them to tell his kids about their new half-sibling? That was something he and Gretchen were going to have to decide, and soon. It went without saying the moment would require careful handling if he didn't want to completely upset everyone, especially Gretchen.

"Well?" Sassy demanded, when Matt didn't come up with some fatherly homily right away.

Matt was loath to confess he'd been so lost in his thoughts he'd already forgotten the question.

"I don't think I can bail you out of this one, Matt," Gretchen quipped, her eyes sparkling with amusement.

The reality of being married to Gretchen—of becoming a couple, even temporarily—was beginning to sink in. The truth was the baby on the way was a blessing in disguise, and so was their marriage.

"WELL, DAD, what do you think? Is this a bridal suite or what?" Luke asked.

"It's great, Luke. Thanks," Matt replied, as he and Gretchen took in the lavishly appointed living room. The bedroom beyond was equally luxurious, with a king-size bed. The adjoining bathroom had a bathtub big enough for two, and a separate glassed-in shower.

Sassy stayed close to Matt's side as the kids carried in their luggage. "You know we can hang out here for a while if you like," Sassy offered protectively.

"Thanks, but that won't be necessary," Matt said. He drew Gretchen close and wrapped his arms around her waist. "Gretchen and I can take it from here."

Maybe company would be a good idea, Gretchen thought. Anything to delay the inevitable discussion of who was going to sleep where and when. She didn't want Matt assuming this marriage of theirs came with any lord-of-the-manor rights. She turned to face him and lifted her eyes to his. "I don't mind if they want to stay, Matt."

He grinned. "I do."

Lowering his mouth to hers, he delivered a brief, breath-stealing kiss to her lips that had her senses swimming.

"You know, I think I'm finally beginning to understand what's going on here," Sassy mumbled as Matt and Gretchen slowly drew apart.

Angela elbowed her sister. "Cut it out, will you?" "Bye, Dad," she called cheerfully. "Gretchen. Have fun."

"And try acting your age," Luke ordered sternly as Angela pulled him and a still-stunned Sassy out the door.

"What's that supposed to mean?" Gretchen asked the moment the door had closed and they were alone. She thought the entire wedding day had been very dignified.

"If I were to guess, I'd say no sex," Matt remarked dryly.

"Oh," Gretchen said as he opened the door just long enough to put the Do Not Disturb sign on, then shut and locked it again. The casualness of his action, and the thought behind it, sent chills of anticipation coasting down Gretchen's spine. What was Matt expecting from her tonight, now that they were here in the honeymoon suite? She realized in retrospect that events had unfolded so rapidly she and Matt hadn't really come to any understanding about the evening ahead.

He studied her, his mouth crooked up in a wolfish smile. "You look disappointed," he commented softly, after a moment.

"Don't be ridiculous," Gretchen said, quickly drawing a line he could not cross. She might be attracted to him, but she wasn't a fool. It would be hard enough sharing space and a baby with him, without picking up their love affair where it had left off.

Matt shrugged out of his suit jacket and dropped it on the back of the long, comfortable sofa. Still studying her thoughtfully, he closed the distance between them purposefully. "That was our deal, wasn't it?" he continued bluntly, loosening the knot of his tie. "A marriage in name only?"

Gretchen hazarded a look in the other direction and found herself staring at the king-size bed. She knew at a glance how comfortable it would be. "Yes, that was our deal." Fighting a self-conscious flush, she turned back to Matt.

"However—" he grinned wickedly "—if you want to change your mind—"

Gretchen held up a staying palm, aware he looked more handsome than ever in the late-afternoon sunlight. "We agreed not to complicate things unnecessarily," she reminded him.

For a second he was very still, disappointment flashing across his face. "So we did."

Disconcerted by his nearness, the kisses they'd already exchanged, Gretchen hitched in a breath. "That being the case, we don't really have to stay here tonight. Do we?" Surely they'd courted temptation enough as it was.

Matt shrugged his broad shoulders carelessly as he removed his tie altogether and tossed it on top of his suit jacket. "Depends on whether you want to raise suspicions."

"Meaning?" Gretchen tilted her head back to better see his face.

"Ten to one, Luke has the lobby staked out and will be waiting like any good private detective-to-be for anything out of the ordinary to develop."

"Like one or both of us making a fast getaway from the bridal suite just moments after checking in." Gretchen sighed.

Silence fell between them. "Look, why don't we both try to relax?" Matt suggested. "It's only one night. I'm sure Luke will be back bright-and-early tomorrow morning to get us. Then we can see about moving you into my home."

Gretchen thought about the last time they'd been cooped up together for a mere twenty-four hours. That was how they'd made a baby and gotten into this mess. But there was no reason to think that would happen again, she reassured herself sternly.

She eyed the bucket of champagne, but knew because of the baby that she couldn't indulge. Matt read her thoughts. "We'll save it and use it to celebrate after the baby's born."

"Good plan," Gretchen murmured. It was helpful to think ahead, to focus on the goal rather than the immediate problems yet to be worked out. She took the flowers out of her hair and carefully laid them aside.

"You know, this marriage business doesn't have to be difficult," Matt offered gently.

"Oh, really." Gretchen kicked off her shoes. Wedding clothes or not, she planned to get comfortable. "And how do you figure that?" she asked as she curled up in one corner of the sofa, tucking her legs beneath her.

"Well, think about it." Matt sat down beside her. He folded his hands behind his head and stretched his legs out in front of him. "The first time we were married our emotions were involved. We were both young, idealistic..."

"And we expected our marriages to last forever."

"Whereas this time we're much more realistic. We said our I Dos knowing exactly where we stood."

Gretchen began to relax. She smoothed the handkerchief hem of her dress. "I guess I can study here as well as at your home."

"And I can watch the TV in the bedroom," Matt said, as if it were no big deal. "We'll be like two friends sharing a suite. And to that end—" He vaulted off the sofa, stalked across the room and peered into the well-stocked refrigerator behind the bar. "We've got plenty of milk, juice in here. Care for something?"

"Milk on the rocks, please. And you're right. It's ridiculous for me to be on edge about this. We can live together as roommates, right?"

"Absolutely." His hand brushed hers as he handed her the glass of milk. "I promised not to exercise my conjugal rights and I won't."

"Unless—" Gretchen stood uneasily, guessing there was more.

"You want me to exercise them," Matt added, giving her a meaningful look.

Without warning, Gretchen was trembling. She stepped back a pace. "You think I'm going to change my mind?"

Matt shrugged and replied reasonably, "I think it's entirely possible we both might. And to that end, I think we ought to keep our options open, take it one moment, one evening, at a time."

Gretchen wanted that, too, but she feared that reintroducing lovemaking into their lives was not as simple a proposition as either of them would like to think. It was bad enough that her heart sped up and her breathing became more shallow every time he came within three feet of her. Bad enough that he was beginning to behave and think as if they were very much a couple.

Deciding she needed time to consider, she headed for her backpack and pulled out a textbook and highlighter pen. "Would you mind if I monopolized the living room for a while?" she asked in a brisk, matter-of-fact tone, telling him that for now anyway all the walls surrounding her heart and soul were still firmly in place. "I've got some educational psychology chapters I need to read."

"GET MUCH studying done?" Matt asked Gretchen several hours later when she finally closed her textbooks and got up to stretch.

I tried, but I couldn't comprehend a word, Gretchen thought as she stepped into the bedroom and crossed to Matt's side. He was stretched out in the center of the king-size bed, a pillow propped behind his head. He had a half-finished bottle of beer in his hand and an open pack of peanuts that he'd pretty much demolished beside him. Unlike her, he looked completely at ease.

"I still have a lot of studying to do," she confided, though at this rate she doubted she'd get any work done while they were in the hotel, schoolbooks or no. It was just too hard to focus, with Matt so close by. She knew he didn't mean to wreck her concentration, but he did nonetheless.

He tore his eyes from the NCAA action on the screen and studied her face. "You look tired," he said gently, offering her a shelled peanut.

Ravenous for him was more like it. He looked very sexy stretched out that way. "These days, I want to sleep all the time," she confessed around a yawn.

He patted the mattress beside him. "Want to hit the sack?"

Go to bed? Now? Gretchen shrugged. "It's a little early yet."

"Hungry?" He reached out to catch hold of her hand and tugged her down to sit beside him. "We could call room service."

Gretchen shook her head as his strong fingers closed around hers. She was aware he could see that she didn't know how to be tonight. Aloof? Friendly? Distant but cordial? There was no protocol for situations like theirs—not to her knowledge anyway. And she wasn't sure she was all that good about feeling her way through things. She swallowed hard. "I'm still full from the wedding dinner. But if you're hungry..."

"No." He paused.

An awkward silence settled between them. Not wanting him to see the desire building inside her, she lowered her eyes to the strong column of his throat and the downy black chest hair in the open V of his shirt, before returning her gaze to his face.

He gave her a glance she couldn't read, then reluctantly released her hand. "If there's something you want to watch on TV—" he offered.

"Actually, a hot shower sounds good." If she really took her time, she might be able to stretch the shower out until bedtime. She stood and spun away from him restlessly. "Would you mind if I monopolized the bathroom for a while?"

"Not at all."

Aware he was still studying her thoughtfully, Gretchen picked up her suitcase. She had packed for a night at Matt's home spent in separate bedrooms, not a night in a bridal suite. Hence she had flannel pjs, a terry-cloth robe and slippers, not a negligee. She wondered if he knew that, as she disrobed and stepped into the invigoratingly warm spray of the shower. Or if he was expecting her to try to seduce him and make this a real marriage.

She sighed and tried to relax. But the only thing she could think about was Christmas Eve in Colorado. All the ensuing complications aside, what she wouldn't give for another night of ecstasy like that. But that was a completely unrealistic wish. Her body was going to be changing soon. In a few months she'd be so fat and unwieldy that Matt probably wouldn't even desire her anymore. Then their baby would be born, and they'd go their separate ways, as previously agreed. And then who knew how long it would be before she...

Gretchen groaned and rested her face against the smooth tiled wall. This was nuts. She was here with him, alone with him, married to him, carrying his child and desiring him as she'd never desired anyone, and yet they were planning to abstain from making love. To keep things from getting complicated? They were already complicated, and that wasn't going to change whether anything happened tonight or not.

Okay, she admitted wryly as she began to soap herself from head to toe, so they weren't in love. So this relationship of theirs was not going to last. Did that mean she couldn't enjoy the present—particularly when her future might not hold any lovemaking with anyone at all? Never mind someone who could make her as wild with longing, or make her feel anywhere near as feminine, womanly, sexually satisfied and sensually appreciated, as Matt.

Acting strictly on impulse, Gretchen rinsed off, shut off the shower and stepped out of the tub. Quickly she toweled herself dry and pulled on her thick terry-cloth robe before she could lose her nerve. Not bothering to take down her hair, she marched back out into the bedroom and over to the bed. Matt was still stretched out, his focus on something other than the televised game.

His eyes lit up appreciatively as she neared, but he made no move to take her in his arms.

She shoved her hands in her pockets and looked down at him. She knew she was playing with fire, but she couldn't seem to help herself. "Were you serious earlier when we talked about having a real wedding night? That I can say yes or no?" She regarded him patiently. "The choice is entirely mine?"

Matt's eyes shone with anticipation. His gaze traveled from her bare legs to the curve of her hips and the gentle swell of her breasts. His eyes on hers, he took her hand and brought it to his lips. "I mean it," he promised solemnly. "The choice is entirely yours."

"And you'd feel that way even if it were a temporary situation?"

Matt caressed the inside of her wrist with soothing, gentle strokes. A tantalizing smile tugged at the corners of his lips. "Define 'temporary.'"

Gretchen drew an unsteady breath as she swayed toward him uncertainly. "Today. Tomorrow. Until the doctor says no more or you stop finding me desirable."

"That I can't imagine, because you are one woman who is and always will be desirable to me," he said softly.

"What if...I said yes for tonight?" Gretchen didn't know why, but she felt obliged to test the waters thoroughly before diving in. She sat down next to Matt, the edge of her robe overlapping his slacks. "Does it have to be yes tomorrow?" Gretchen asked.

Matt's brows knitted. "It can be whatever you want in that regard, too," he said cautiously. "Yes today, no tomorrow, yes the day after that...."

Gretchen knew what her body wanted. What her soul needed. And that was to feel loved and cherished... now...tonight. "What do you want?" she asked, her heart suddenly pounding.

Matt's eyes darkened as he hooked a hand in the belt of her robe and pulled her down to him. "This," he murmured, as he delivered a searing kiss. "And this," he said, as he opened the front of her robe.

And as he made love to her, their wedding night was everything a wedding night should be—tender, sweet, wonderful. So much so that Gretchen could almost believe she loved him. So much so that she could almost believe he loved her.

Chapter Six

Rap-rap-rap. Rap-rap-rap-rap-rap.

A feminine groan sounded in Matt's ear as someone warm and cuddly nestled against his side.

Rap-rap-rap. Rap-rap-rap-rap-rap.

"Make them go away," she murmured drowsily in his ear. "So...tired...."

So was he, Matt thought.

"Need...sleep..."

So did he, Matt thought, but whoever was knocking was sure not going to stop. What time was it anyway? He opened one eye and looked at the clock. Ten a.m.! He awoke the rest of the way with a start. He never slept this late.

"Dad?" *Rap-rap-rap.* "Are you in there? It's Luke. I was supposed to pick you and Gretchen up this morning, remember?"

Matt sure did. In fact, it was all coming back to him with a rush. The tension-filled wedding, the surprise of his children's gift to him and the surprise later of Gretchen coming to him, telling him she wanted to make love again. And make love they had—all through the night—in many sexy, wonderful ways.

"Dad?" *Rap-rap-rap.*

"I'll, uh, be right there," Matt called back to his son as Gretchen roused a sleepy head. "Luke's here," Matt said, hating to disturb her.

Gretchen's brows knitted as she struggled to wake up. She grabbed the sheet with one hand, drawing it over her breasts, and pushed the hair from her eyes with the other. "He's here? To pick us up? Already?"

"Afraid so," Matt replied. Reluctantly extricating himself from Gretchen's warm, drowsy form, he scrambled from the bed and reached for his pants. He pulled them on, slipped from the room and went to the door. Luke was standing there with his arms crossed defiantly in front of him when Matt opened it.

"What's going on, Dad?" he demanded. "I've never known you to be late in your life."

Matt raked a hand through his hair. "I overslept."

"Uh-huh." Luke looked him up and down. "Where's Gretchen?"

"Right here, Luke." Gretchen stepped out of the bedroom.

Matt didn't know how she had managed it, but she'd pulled on a white hotel robe and belted it tightly around her waist. Brush in hand, she was restoring order to her glorious mane of glossy mahogany hair. Her cheeks were pink, her deep blue eyes lively.

"It's my fault we overslept. Have you had breakfast?"

Luke shrugged. "Uh, well, actually—"

"Matt why don't we order something up for Luke, for all of us?" Gretchen continued, effortlessly taking charge.

"Good idea," Matt agreed.

"In the meantime, I think I'll shower and get dressed. Luke, I'm sorry we kept you waiting." With a smile, she slipped back inside the bedroom.

As the door shut behind her, Luke turned back to Matt. "I don't believe it," he said in awe. "The two of you...you really...you had a honeymoon, Dad!"

They sure had, Matt thought. And now he was wishing fervently it had lasted more than one night. "What did you think was going to happen?" he drawled.

"I don't know exactly." Luke shoved his hands in the pockets of his jeans. "It's just...I had the feeling...this sixth sense... that this marriage of yours was more like a business arrangement. Like maybe she was going to be your housekeeper or something. But now... I can't believe it, but you look like a man in love, Dad," Luke said in absolute astonishment.

"EVERYTHING OKAY?" Gretchen asked half an hour later as Matt slipped into the bedroom to join her. She had already showered and dressed in the jeans and sweater she'd planned to wear when they moved her belongings into his house, and was in the process of pulling her hair off her face.

"Yes." Matt watched in fascination as she positioned and closed the barrette at her nape. Edging closer as she fastened two sterling-silver Texas-shaped earrings in her earlobes, he continued, "Room service is here. I didn't know what you wanted, so I ordered a bit of everything, including plenty of milk, juice and coffee."

"Thanks. But I meant with Luke." Gretchen stood with a smile and zipped her suitcase closed. Straightening, she propped her hands on her hips. "How's that going? He doesn't suspect, does he?"

Not anymore, Matt thought. "On the contrary." Trying not to let himself get sidetracked by how pretty Gretchen looked in the morning sunlight streaming into the elegant hotel suite, or the way the powder blue of her sweater brought out the soft misty blue of her eyes, Matt unbuttoned his shirt, grabbed his shaving kit and headed for the adjacent bathroom sink. "He thinks we're in love." *And I have to admit it feels that way to me, too,* he thought, surprised.

Gretchen did a double take. "You're kidding, right?"

"Nope." Matt stripped off his shirt and slacks. "Somehow seeing us together this morning has erased all his doubts on that score."

Gretchen followed him, her mood decidedly upbeat. She leaned toward the mirror and applied lipstick. "Well, lucky we slept together last night then, I guess."

"Can't say that I mind." Matt grinned as he shot shaving cream onto his palm and then spread it on his face.

She added a hint of blush to her cheeks, then paused. "What did you tell Luke when he said that?" she asked with curiosity, edging closer.

"I didn't say anything," Matt said quietly as he began to shave. He rinsed his blade, then turned to Gretchen, drinking in the morning fresh scent of her. "I don't care if he is my son. I don't think the intimate details of our marriage are any of his business."

Gretchen nodded her agreement and Matt went back to shaving with short, precise strokes. "I can't stop him from speculating, of course."

"Of course not," Gretchen murmured.

Finished, Matt dropped his razor. "He's free to make whatever assumptions he chooses in that regard as long as he doesn't do or say anything detrimental to either you or me on the subject." He splashed water on his jaw, dried it with a towel. His arm hooked around her waist, he pulled her close. "Or in other words, don't take any gaff from him, Gretchen, and if he tries to give you a hard time—if any of my kids do—you let me know," Matt said, promising firmly, "and I'll handle it."

He'd meant to reassure her. His words had the opposite result. Her face falling, she turned away.

Alarmed by the sudden tenseness of her shoulders and swift change of mood, Matt caught her arm and stepped back to prevent her from leaving. "You're not upset, are you?"

"Why should I be?" She lifted her chin. "I mean, it's not as if..." Her voice dwindled and she shook her head, her eyes glimmering moistly. She backed away, looking even more uncomfortable.

"As if what?" Matt prodded softly.

Gretchen swallowed. "As if we were in love. We know where things stand between us, Matt," she said in a low, depressed tone. "We know why you married me, even if no one else—save Marissa and Cal—does."

Matt knew pregnant women were moody. Sensitive almost to a fault. "Does this bother you?" he asked gently.

"It makes me feel a little dishonest, yes."

"It shouldn't," Matt countered softly, searching for a way—any way—to make her feel better about what was going on. Maybe they had entered their marriage for all the wrong reasons. But that didn't mean the relationship had to stay one-dimensional or practical in the extreme. They'd already started expanding the relationship to more normal boundaries. But he could see that alarmed her, too, now that she'd had a chance to consider things. Maybe he should just take it slow. Not push. Let her get used to their being together, little by little. Then who knew what would happen? Nine months was a long time. Long enough to fall in love, not just temporarily, but in a forever-and-ever way.

He slid his hand down to hers. "There are many reasons for marrying, Gretchen," he said as they linked fingers. "Love is only one of them."

"I know." Gretchen had recovered her composure enough to smile back at him, although in a distant way. "I'm grateful we get along as well as we do under the circumstances."

Matt could hear the truth in her soft, conciliatory words. He still had the feeling he'd put a foot in it, somehow destroying all the joy they'd had the night before in a single instant. It didn't matter that his intentions had been to the contrary, only that a little of the light had gone out of her eyes. "Gretchen..."

Delicately she extricated her hand from his. "I better go out and keep Luke company, Matt."

Damn. "Gretchen..."

She forced a smile, even as she backed away. "Don't be too long. We both have a lot to do today."

"YOU'RE KEEPING your apartment?" Luke asked in surprise as Gretchen indicated the three meager boxes of belongings slated to be moved to Matt's home in Westlake Hills.

"As a place to study during the days," Gretchen explained cheerfully, bracing herself for the first of many questions from Matt's only son. "This way I can come here between classes and at lunch."

"There wouldn't be time for her to drive all the way out to the house and back," Matt said.

And it's a safety net, Gretchen thought, *in case things don't go as smoothly as we hope.*

"Then it's okay with you?" Luke asked Matt, abruptly highly skeptical and suspicious again.

"Sure," Matt said. "With the apartment being so close to campus, the rent so low, Gretchen would be foolish to get rid of it."

"Not to mention it's still under lease for another six months," Gretchen said.

"Oh," Luke said with a shrug, mollified by her answer. "Well, let's get this stuff down to my Jeep. If we all carry one box, that should about do it."

"We'll do the carrying," Matt instructed Luke. "And we'll put the boxes in Gretchen's car. Then she can drive me back to my place." He cut off Luke's protest with a glance. "You need to get back to A & M, Luke. You've got class tomorrow, too. Meanwhile, Gretchen, you look around and see if there's anything you're forgetting."

"That it?" Luke said several minutes later.

Gretchen nodded. She wanted to take her CDs, but until she knew what kind of music Matt liked, or even if they'd be able to live under the same roof peaceably for any length of time, it seemed wiser not to do so.

"Well, then I guess I'll be going," Luke said.

He shook Matt's hand and looked at Gretchen awkwardly.

"Bye, Luke," Gretchen said, not sure what if anything was expected of her now that she was Luke's stepmother.

Luke kept his hands on his hips as he nodded at her from a distance. "Bye, Gretchen." He was out the door like a shot.

Once again, Matt was all business. "Let's get this show on the road," he said.

They were silent as Gretchen drove across town, Matt speaking only to give her directions now and again. Gretchen was glad for the lack of small talk. She needed time to think, she decided as she switched to the far right lane on the Mopac Expressway and took the Bee Cave Road exit. Making love with Matt had been wonderful. She didn't regret that. But as for the rest of their relationship, this morning she just felt confused. Unsure where they were headed, or even how close it was safe for her to get. Matt was her baby's father. She wanted to be close to him; emotional intimacy established now would be a boon later on when they coparented their child. But she didn't want a broken heart or a marriage that was true and real only to her. And the closer she allowed herself to get to Matt, the more she flirted with danger in that regard.

Matt interrupted her thoughts. "You'll need to turn here on Lost Creek Drive," he said.

Several more turns followed, as he directed her around the elegant subdivision in far west Austin. Finally they were there.

"So what do you think?" Matt asked as the two of them got out of her car and she had her first glimpse of his home.

Gretchen caught her breath. "It's lovely," she said. And far more beautiful than she had imagined. The slate gray Cape Cod with white trim was nestled among a dozen live oaks and surrounded by evergreen shrubbery. The large two-story home was exactly the kind of place she had once dreamed of settling into with Robert. But that had never happened. And now, here she was with Matt. It was funny how life turned out sometimes.

"How big is it?" She paused beside the trunk of her car.

"Four thousand square feet. And don't try to lift those boxes. I've got them."

Gretchen shook her head, knowing that one box in particular weighed no more than a basket of clean laundry. "Matt, I'm not an invalid." She didn't want to be treated like one.

Matt's look was autocratic. "You're pregnant. You shouldn't be lifting."

"Heavy objects, no. But things like groceries are fine."

Gretchen could tell he was about to argue. She wondered if he was going to be this protective about everything she did. If so, it would be a long eight months until the baby arrived. Gretchen folded her arms in front of her obstinately. "If you don't believe me, ask Marissa. She's my obstetrician."

Matt grinned ruefully and rubbed his jaw. "I know the drill. I've been through this three times already, remember? As far as any lifting goes, if I'm around I'll do it. Period." He sent her a look of mock sternness. "Got it?"

Gretchen could see a precedent was being set. "Matt—"

He cut her off with a deliberate shake of his head. "No arguing, Gretchen, not about this." He laced a protective arm about her shoulders. "Now c'mon. I want to show you the inside of the house."

Gretchen pretended to pout at the ultimatum he had just handed down, but secretly, it felt nice to be fussed over. No one had done that for her in a very long time.

Matt punched in the security code and let her in. Gretchen was stunned to realize the interior of the home was even more pristinely beautiful and well kept than the exterior. In the kitchen, state-of-the-art appliances gleamed. A side-by-side refrigerator dispensed ice, water and juice. A Jenn-Air grill, microwave, double oven and chef's stove made cooking for a crowd and entertaining easy.

"The laundry room and guest bath are that way." Matt pointed to the right.

"And my den is in here."

Matt led her into a beautifully appointed room with a fieldstone fireplace, oak paneling and saddle-brown leather furniture.

"I do a lot of work here, too," he said, gesturing at the computer, fax, two-line phone, copier and built-in wooden file cabinets.

"It's very nice," Gretchen said, impressed. Definitely a man's domain. She could see Matt working in here in the evenings, maybe on weekends. She could see herself peeking in, maybe joining him occasionally if he asked.

"In here is the dining room—"

With a beautiful chandelier, a hutch full of china and a polished mahogany table that sat eight, it looked cozy and just right for family gatherings, Gretchen thought.

"The family room..." Matt continued.

Furnished with two denim-and-white-plaid sofas, a VCR, television and stereo, the room appeared quite comfortable.

"Which as you can see overlooks the fenced-in backyard. And the formal living room."

Done all in white, it was very elegant, but not exactly baby-proof, Gretchen worried. Was Matt really as ready to change his life as he thought?

"And now for the second story." A hand to her spine, Matt led the way upstairs. "To the left is the master bedroom and bath. My room."

Gretchen peeked in. The room was done in a dark pine green. A fireplace was at one end of the room; opposite it stood a huge four-poster with a luxurious green-and-burgundy plaid comforter. An armoire held a television, VCR and stereo. The dormer windows had dark brown plantation shutters in lieu of blinds or drapes. The adjacent green-and-black ceramic-tiled bath featured a separate black marble shower and whirlpool tub, a dressing area with his and her sinks and two walk-in closets. Like the rest of the house, it was clean and neat. It didn't look like Matt Hale wanted for anything. That being the case, she wondered what he really thought of her small efficiency unit.

Taking her hand, he led her back down the hall, past the three other bedrooms. "Angela's room is here..."

It was pink and utterly chaotic in decor and arrangement. "Luke's is here..."

Gretchen caught a glimpse of rock posters, lacrosse sticks and an unmade bed.

"Sassy's in here..."

The room was mint green and filled with books, with no remnants of the childhood Sassy had recently left behind.

"And last but not least is the guest room." Matt guided Gretchen inside. The pale yellow room was half the size of her apartment, with barely room for a double bed and desk. Opposite the closet was a dormer window with a cozy padded window seat in the same yellow-and-white dotted swiss as the bedspread and curtains.

Gretchen swung around to face him. "The kids are all at school, aren't they?"

Matt folded his arms in front of him and rocked back on his heels. "Right."

Deciding she had looked into his warm silver eyes long enough, Gretchen turned away. "So it'll be just the two of us living here?" she asked, aware her senses were suddenly in overdrive once again.

Matt followed her around the room. "Except for holidays and maybe summer vacation."

As Gretchen drifted toward the window, she slid her hands in her pockets and tried not to remember the magical night they'd shared together in the honeymoon suite. It would be assuming a lot to think that they could share that kind of passion every night. With familiarity, and the progression of her pregnancy, the wild desire they felt for each other was bound to fade. The trick to handling that would be in not letting the normal course of events get to her. Therefore, she needed to brace herself for the inevitable now.

Gretchen looked out at the backyard, then at the room around her, before turning back to Matt, her expression much more stoic. "Is this where I'll be sleeping?"

It was as far away as you could get from the master bedroom. Would they be cordoning off the rest of the house, too, into his and her areas?

He paused thoughtfully a moment, his eyes darkening, before he offered genially, "Unless you'd like the master bedroom, which is bigger."

Gretchen didn't want to kick him out of his room. He had made enough sacrifices for her and their baby as it was.

"In which case," Matt continued, "I'd be glad to trade or whatever—"

"No. This is fine," Gretchen said quickly. "I like small spaces." *And I think I need my own space. I need to figure out what's happening here, what I want to happen.*

"Sure?" Matt persisted, grinning seductively. "You could bunk in with me, you know."

He was taking this all so casually. Gretchen hauled in a shaky breath, knowing, even if Matt didn't, that they were headed for the danger zone.

"Thanks, but don't you think things are getting complicated enough as it is?" she asked lightly, ignoring the sudden rapid beating of her heart.

He regarded her, his face expressionless. Then he shrugged as if it were no big deal to him either way. "Tell you what. Why don't we play it by ear?" he suggested amiably. "For now, you're here and I'm there, and that's that. Okay?"

Gretchen backed up to the window seat, and because her legs suddenly felt a little wobbly, she sat down. "Okay." This was the sensible way to go, after all. So why did she suddenly feel so disappointed?

He flexed his shoulders restlessly. "You probably want to unpack...."

"Yes."

"I'll go down and get your stuff and bring it up."

"Thanks," Gretchen said softly, then watched him go. Once again, she had no clue what he was really thinking or feeling. She wondered if she ever would.

SO MUCH FOR being gallant, Matt thought as he hauled the last of Gretchen's things from the car and carted them, one on top of the other, up the front walk and into the house. He should have just told Gretchen what he wanted here, which was her, in his bed, cuddled up beside him every night. But he hadn't and he wouldn't. He had promised her he wouldn't push her, that this would be a marriage in name only, for their child's sake. He had promised her she didn't have to stay married to him if things weren't working out by the time the baby was born, and it was a promise he would keep, although he was already regretting that, too.

If he'd been smart, he would have said theirs should be a real marriage from the first. But if he had, would she have said yes to his proposal? Somehow, Matt thought with a sigh as he headed upstairs with her belongings, he doubted it.

He would just have to make the best of things, Matt decided as he strode back to the guest room.

THE FIRST WAVE of nausea hit Gretchen by surprise. When the second came, she knew she was going to be sick. It was just a matter of when. Heaven help her, it would not be in front of Matt, on her first afternoon in his home, on their first full day of married life.

Heavy footsteps thudded down the hall. Gretchen ignored the sweat trickling down the back of her neck and the shifting of the breakfast in her stomach, and plastered a smile on her face just as Matt walked in, carrying two of the boxes, stacked one on top of each other. "Where do you want these?" he asked cheerfully.

Gretchen pointed to the bed. "There would be fine." She had to get rid of him. Somehow.

"I'll get the last one," he said, just as the phone rang. Turning on his heel, he added, "I hope that's not Luke with a flat. I told him to check the air in his tires before he left to go back to Texas A & M but I don't think he did."

He strode back to his bedroom. While he was talking at the other end of the hall, Gretchen went to her purse and pulled out a small packet of saltine crackers. She munched on one, determinedly willing the nausea away.

She felt a little better by the time Matt returned. He was carrying the third box. His expression was grim. "What was it?" she asked. Not one of his kids, she hoped.

"That was my foreman on the Lubbock drilling site," Matt related with a scowl as he set the box down beside the others.

Gretchen swallowed as another wave of nausea rolled through her. "Problem?" she asked, aware her knees were beginning to tremble again.

Oblivious to how close she was to getting sick, Matt nodded. "The property owner wants them to stop drilling as of this evening if they don't strike oil this afternoon."

She edged back to the window seat and eased onto it. Maybe if she sat down and held very, very still it would help. "Do you think they will?" she asked.

"Yes, but not necessarily by this evening." He swore and jammed his hands on his waist. Looking past her, he stared grimly out the window. "We've spent a lot of time and money on that site. I'd hate to see it all be for naught."

Again Gretchen tried to will the nausea away. "What are you going to do?"

"Go out and talk to the owner, I guess."

"Tomorrow?"

"Tonight." He paused, his eyes softening as they connected with hers once again. "I'm sorry, Gretchen," he said contritely, before his mouth firmed up decisively again. "But this is my business and I've got to handle this."

Gretchen resisted the urge to blot at the clammy sweat breaking out on her chest. Just a few more minutes . . . then she could throw up in peace, if need be. She swallowed carefully and continued to hold very still. "No problem."

"You're sure?" Matt peered at her, beginning to realize something was wrong. "I mean, you just got here."

"I understand, Matt." Determined to get through this without embarrassing herself in front of him, Gretchen drew a deep breath and stood. "If you want me to pack a bag for you or call the airlines..." *Anything* to get him out of there faster.

But Matt was already shaking his head, letting her know it wasn't necessary. "I'm already packed. I always keep a bag ready so I can leave on a moment's notice. I'm booked on the next Southwest Airlines flight to Lubbock. It leaves in forty minutes, so I'm really going to have to run." He scribbled a number on a piece of paper and handed it to her. "This is where I'll be. You can reach me there day or night."

"Great." Gretchen's stomach heaved as she placed the number on the table beside her bed. The cracker she had just eaten began to come back up.

"Here's your key to the house." He placed it in her palm.

"You better go, Matt." Still holding the key, Gretchen practically pushed him toward the door.

"All right." Matt strode down the hall and grabbed the carryon from his room. "I'll call."

"Do that," Gretchen said brightly, following him down the stairs to the front door, as her stomach roiled again. *Get a grip on yourself, Gretchen. You can handle this—it's only morning sickness.*

Matt paused on the front step and gently touched her hair. He gazed down at her affectionately. "You're sure you're going to be okay?"

Gretchen nodded. "Just go, Matt," she said tightly, knowing she couldn't hang on much longer.

"Right."

Obviously realizing how badly she wanted to get rid of him, looking a little hurt by her attitude, Matt walked over to his truck.

"I'll call," he promised as he climbed behind the wheel.

Not trusting herself to speak, Gretchen merely nodded slightly and lifted her hand in a wave. Five more seconds, four, three... The moment he was out the driveway, she shut the door and ran for the guest bath.

What a disaster her first full day of married life was turning out to be.

Chapter Seven

February

"So how long has Matt been gone?" Marissa Stewart asked, as she palpated Gretchen's abdomen, checking the size and position of the baby.

"Two weeks now." *Though it seems like forever,* Gretchen thought, as she stared at the ceiling above the examining table in Marissa's office. Maybe it was the flood of hormones associated with pregnancy, but she couldn't ever recall feeling more sad and depressed.

"And he hasn't been back since?" Finished with her exam, Marissa helped Gretchen to a sitting position.

Gretchen sighed as she rearranged her clothing. Her first obstetrical visit had required a full physical and gynecological exam. Her second was much easier. She didn't even have to get all the way undressed.

"First there were problems with the owner, then the well, then the oil came in in a much bigger gusher than anyone had expected, and suddenly other landowners in the area were all clamoring to get Matt to drill on their property. Evidently he's been very busy, doing geological surveys and writing drilling contracts." Busy and happy.

"And what about you?" Marissa asked.

Gretchen shrugged as she struggled to keep her emotions under wraps. "I've been busy, too."

"I mean, how do you feel about Matt being gone so much?" Marissa persisted, more best friend now than physician.

"I should be relieved," Gretchen said cautiously.

"But you're not," Marissa guessed as Gretchen hopped off the examining table. She led the way into her private office so the two could talk more comfortably.

"I've already had one marriage where my husband was always running out the door away from me." Gretchen sank down in a chair and stretched her blue-jeaned legs out in front of her in tomboy fashion. "This has made me realize I really don't want another."

Marissa made another note on the chart. "Matt isn't Robert, Gretchen. He won't walk out on you or play around with another woman."

But he doesn't love me, either, Gretchen thought. *Not the way a husband should. Not the way I want him to.*

"It's also unusual for him to be out of town for such a long stretch of time," Marissa continued.

Perhaps he finds it more comfortable being away from me, Gretchen thought. "So he said," she replied lightly. She nodded at the chart Marissa held in front of her. "So, how am I doing? Everything okay with the baby?"

Marissa smiled and folded her hands in front of her. "Everything's great. Your blood count is good, urine fine, weight unchanged, which isn't surprising, since you're only seven weeks along. Have you been having any problems with morning sickness?"

Gretchen nodded. "It comes and goes."

"Do crackers help?"

"Sometimes. Other times nothing does. I just have to lie down and close my eyes and feel like I've died, until the nausea passes."

"Well, take heart," Marissa soothed. "It usually goes away after the first trimester."

Gretchen rolled her eyes. "I'll try to remember that the next time I've got my head in the toilet."

Marissa chuckled. "Bought any maternity clothes yet?"

"No. And I don't need them yet, either."

Gretchen wanted this baby, but she wasn't anxious to have her body bloated and out of shape, to be in a condition where Matt would no longer desire her. Not that that even mattered if he was going to continue being out of town so much.

Marissa grinned. "Well, let me know when you're ready to switch to maternity wear. We'll coordinate our schedules and I'll go shopping with you."

GRETCHEN'S HEART skipped a beat when she saw Matt's truck parked in front of the house. He was home again, after an absence of two and a half weeks. He looked good, too. As though he were in an exuberant mood and very glad to be home.

He was also out the door and striding toward her before she was even out of the car.

"I was wondering when you'd get back," he drawled. That way he had of speaking set her pulse to racing, as she stood, hauling the backpack full of books and notes out of the car.

His eyes roved her with leisurely abandon, taking in everything about her. "Have you had dinner yet?" He leaned forward and brushed his lips casually across her cheek.

Gretchen did not return his distinctly southern greeting. She had promised herself she would remain irritated with him so as to remind herself not to start depending on him. But it was hard when he looked so damn glad to see her, so at ease. Struggling to contain the joy bubbling up within her, she hefted her backpack onto one shoulder. "Sure haven't," she replied breezily. Good grief. She certainly hoped he wasn't expecting her to cook for him tonight. That would be too much.

He removed the backpack from her shoulder, frowning when he discovered how heavy it was. "Want to go out to eat?"

Gretchen favored anything that would help her avoid being alone with him in a truly intimate setting. She'd started to feel like a wife in the twenty hours or so they'd spent together as a married couple. That feeling had faded while he'd been away. She didn't want it coming back again. Not if it meant she had to get used to living without him all over again. And yet they had to spend some time together, work out some plans for the future, for their baby's sake. Maybe a crowded restaurant was the way to go.

"Sure." Gretchen tried hard not to notice how devastatingly handsome he looked in the tan corduroy slacks and dark brown cashmere sweater designed like a long-sleeved polo shirt. She preceded him inside the house and watched him set her book bag gently on the parson's bench in the hall. "When and where?"

Matt turned toward her, unable to tear his gaze from her upturned face. "How about now, and any place you choose?" he asked softly.

Gretchen had been having a lot of cravings lately, for the strangest things. She hadn't indulged any of them. Maybe it was time she did. "How about County Line barbecue?" She didn't know why, but she had been yearning for their hot homemade bread, spread with creamy butter.

"Sounds good to me," Matt said genially.

"Just let me freshen up a bit first," Gretchen said, swiftly stepping past him.

While he continued catching up on his mail—quite a lot had accumulated during his absence—she went upstairs. A quick look in her closet confirmed what she already knew. She had nothing to wear. Nothing that was dressy enough for an evening out with Matt and still comfortable. She might not have gained much weight so far, but her waist had definitely expanded. She could feel the waistband of her jeans cutting into her. Another few days and she wouldn't be able to zip them up at all. She would have to do as Marissa had suggested and switch to maternity clothes.

But she wouldn't think about that tonight.

Tonight she would concentrate on the fact that Matt was back, and he'd looked glad to see her. Maybe they would never be married in the usual sense; maybe they would never even share a bedroom for anything more than an occasional night of lovemaking; but maybe they could still be friends, Gretchen thought confidently. Tonight was the perfect time for them to get to know each other even better.

"STOP EYEING my pickle," Matt teased.

Gretchen finished the last of her potato salad and put her fork down next to her plate. "Not to worry, Matt," she replied dryly, having also demolished generous portions of tender mesquite-smoked beef brisket, tangy cole slaw and ranch-style beans in short order. Maybe it was her pregnancy, but she couldn't recall ever being so hungry, or the food at the famed Austin restaurant tasting so good. "Your dill pickle is safe," she said, patting her midriff contentedly. "I couldn't eat another bite."

He grinned and continued to work on his own man-size combination platter of chicken and brisket with equal gusto.

"Besides," Gretchen said, "pickles are not what I've been craving."

He quirked a brow as he sipped his iced tea. "What have you been craving?"

Truthfully? You, Gretchen thought wistfully, then immediately banished the thought.

It was presumptuous of her to be thinking about sleeping wrapped in his arms again, never mind making wild, hot passionate love with him. But she was thinking it, Gretchen admitted honestly to herself, and had been for days now. Every night he had been away, she had dreamed about him. Every day he had been away, she had thought of him constantly and missed seeing him more than she could ever have imagined possible.

What Matt was thinking and feeling, however, was less clear. She knew he was glad to see her. He hadn't stopped smiling or talking since they'd driven to the restaurant. But beyond that, who knew? To read him better, she would have to get to know him better, Gretchen thought. And there was no time like the present to get started on that.

"So, how are your kids doing?" she asked, turning their attention from current affairs to a more personal subject. "Did you talk to any of them while you were in West Texas?"

Matt grinned, his affection for his college-age children evident. "All of them, as a matter of fact."

"And?" Gretchen sipped her milk and waited with bated breath.

"They mentioned something about wanting to have dinner at the house with us soon."

That sounded ominous. Gretchen watched as Matt took another bite of mesquite-grilled chicken smothered in barbecue sauce. "They're still suspicious, aren't they?" she asked unhappily.

Matt shrugged his broad shoulders acceptingly. "They al
know it's not like me to do something on a whim."

Then why did you? Gretchen wondered. Was it the baby
or something more that had prompted Matt to come to her
rescue? Did she even dare to hope they could ever have more
than they had agreed upon when they'd entered this marriage? All she knew for sure was that going out with him like
this was a very intimate and therefore unsettling experience. Just as living in his home, with or without him, was a
very intimate and unsettling experience, because it made her
feel as if they were married, in more than name only.

Pulling herself together, Gretchen forced herself to smile
and look at Matt. "So what did you tell them?" she inquired cheerfully.

Matt flexed his shoulders restlessly and sat back in his
chair. As he moved, his long legs nudged hers under the table sending a ribbon of warmth shooting through her.

"I set a date for the first weekend in March," he said. His
lips tightened matter-of-factly. "It was as long as I could
stall them."

Finally she was picking up some emotion she could decipher. "So you don't want to do it, either?" she guessed
softly. Trying to form a new family unit, with Gretchen
playing the part of the kindhearted yet undeniably reluctant stepmother, would not be easy. Adding to the trouble
was the fact that Matt's kids were not exactly welcoming her
with open arms.

"It's not that I don't want to see them—I do," Matt said,
leaning forward his feet planted on either side of the chair,
his knees warmly—unconsciously, perhaps—on the outside
of hers. "The problem is I don't want to have to deal with
their suspicions that this marriage of ours is not on the up-and-up."

Gretchen drew a breath, not sure whether it was the topic of conversation or the warmth and closeness of him making her pulse skitter. She lifted her eyes to his, feeling she could drown in the gray depths. "Do you think we made a mistake not leveling with the kids in the first place?"

Again Matt shrugged. "You know what they say, hindsight is always better. If we'd had more time, we might have pulled the marriage together more smoothly, I guess. Considering the pressures we were dealing with, however, we had all we could handle coping with our own ambivalence. Add to that a wealth of other complications..."

"Such as?"

His mouth crooked up ruefully. "That I am their father and they are at a vulnerable age and I'm trying to set an example. As long as Luke, Sassy and Angela can remember, I've been impressing upon them the need to be responsible, to look before they leap, to do not just what I say but what I do, to live an honorable, decent life. Yet here I am, having gotten you in the worst kind of trouble...." His voice trailed off. He shook his head in silent self-reproach, as if, even after all this time, he couldn't believe their predicament.

"So you're embarrassed about the situation, too," Gretchen said gently.

He rolled his eyes and groaned. "Aren't you?"

Gretchen was quiet a long moment. Then, relaxing enough to admit she felt the same, she grinned and, wary of the other diners around them, leaned forward to whisper, "Hell, yes. I never ever thought that I, Gretchen O'Malley, would ever be in a predicament like this."

Matt clasped her hand and lifted it to his lips, kissing her knuckles reassuringly. "But we are," he reminded her, lowering her hand to the tabletop again.

"And you'd like to keep the predicament private."

His hand tightened protectively over hers. She could feel the tension flowing abruptly through him.

"Wouldn't you?" he countered bluntly.

Gretchen nodded, relieved to have some of their most troubling thoughts out in the open. "Yes. Like it or not, I have to be practical here." She looked at him, willing him to understand. "I'm going to be applying for teaching jobs when I graduate. School boards can be very narrow-minded. Most teaching contracts carry morals clauses. I would not want to find myself or my child at the center of any public controversy, either before or after I got hired. I would never want our child to be the object of hurtful gossip or innuendo."

"And the less talk there is about us now, the less chance there will be gossip dredged up later."

"There's also no reason to upset your children unnecessarily, Matt. You're right. They do look to you to set an example. We don't want them following in our footsteps," Gretchen said ruefully, turning her glance toward the large windows that overlooked Austin's picturesque Bull Creek.

"No, we certainly don't. Having a child is a huge responsibility. None of them is old enough or mature enough to handle it at this point."

"Nevertheless, they will have to know eventually," Gretchen said. She wasn't looking forward to making the revelation, either. She could just see them all counting on their fingers, wondering—correctly, as it happened—if that was the one and only reason Matt had married her. And in that respect, she felt guilty. Oh, she knew intellectually that it took two to tango, and they certainly had tangoed the night before Christmas. And she knew that the responsibility for this baby was certainly mutual. But she still couldn't help feeling as though she'd held a shotgun to Matt's head because she had conceived. Even though he didn't seem to blame her; rather, took equal parts of guilt and contrition upon himself. She wondered if that feeling of having been forced together would ever dissipate for either of them, or if they would be stuck with it for life.

"So, when do you want to tell your kids about the baby?" she asked, sipping her milk.

Matt shrugged. "When the time is right," he replied.

"And that will be?" Gretchen prodded.

"When you start to show, I guess." His glance slid appreciatively over her slender form. "Judging from the looks of things, that'll be a while yet."

Maybe not as long as you think, Gretchen thought, aware the waistband of the skirt she had changed into now felt as tight as her jeans had earlier and was cutting into her uncomfortably.

Mistaking her physical discomfort for restlessness, Matt frowned and abruptly signaled their waiter for the check. "I forgot. It's a school night. I'm sure you want to get home. You've probably got studying to do."

MATT WASN'T SURE what had caused the change in Gretchen's mood. He knew only that she grew more moody and restless with every second that passed as they drove over the winding, rolling hills that led to his home in Westlake. He was still wondering what he had said or done to alienate her, when she broke the silence. "How much farther?" she asked tersely, running a hand through her hair.

"Before we get home?"

Gretchen shook her head and continued looking away from him, staring in mute fascination out the passenger window. "Before we exit Loop 360," she stated in the same clipped, highly irritated voice.

Matt knew that she was impatient, that she had a lot to do, but he wished she would quit acting as if she wanted to leap from the Jeep at any second. "It's not much farther. Another mile or so."

"Want to stop and look at the scenery?"

"Now?" Matt knew pregnant women were cantankerous and prone to mood swings that defied understanding, but this was ridiculous.

"Why not?"

He grimaced at the determinedly cavalier edge in her voice. "For starters, we're in the middle of nowhere, on a divided four-lane highway, going approximately sixty miles an hour. Add to that, it's dark, cold and raining." What other deterrents did they need?

"We could look at the city lights."

"I've got an even more spectacular view from my—our—house." He wasn't opposed to enjoying the raw beauty of the February evening, but he wanted to do it in comfort.

"But we're not there yet," she persisted anxiously.

"We will be soon," Matt shot back. She sure was in a weird mood. Why? Was she worried about what was going to happen when they got back to the house? Worried he'd expect something in the bedroom? Surely she knew him better than that, he thought, incensed.

"I was hoping otherwise, but that'll never do," Gretchen muttered.

She sat forward abruptly and grabbed blindly at his leg, her slender fingers curling with surprising fierceness around his upper thigh.

"Stop the car," she demanded harshly.

"What?" Matt quickly slanted her a stunned glance. He knew she could be stubborn, inclined to want her own way regardless, but—

"*Now,* Matt. Oh, no...no..."

She put her hand to her mouth and suddenly Matt knew.

He hit the brakes with as much care as the wet roads demanded. No sooner had he brought the car to a safe stop on the wide, paved berm than she was unsnapping her seat belt, shoving open the door and vaulting from the truck onto the side of the road. By the time Matt had cut the motor and vaulted around to join her, she was already sick.

He went back to the interior of the truck and got a box of tissue from the back seat.

"So much for supper," she said shakily, leaning against the front fender.

"Does this happen often?" Matt asked, wrapping an arm around her shoulders as one car after another whizzed by, splattering them with spray.

She leaned against him weakly and suddenly she was crying. "You don't want to know."

"I'm serious, Gretchen."

"So am I," she quipped miserably as she dabbed at her mouth with a folded square of tissue.

He brushed away her tears with another square of tissue. "Does it always hit you in the evening?"

"No."

She rested her head against his shoulder with a weary acceptance that tore at Matt's heart.

"My morning sickness likes to surprise me," she confided. "Whenever I least need or want it—like tonight—it hits, and it hits with a vengeance."

Matt stroked her hair and continued to hold her close. "What did Marissa tell you to do for it?"

"Eat saltines."

He was desperate to make her feel better. "Do you have any with you?" he asked gently.

She wiped the remaining moisture from her eyes. "If I eat anything right now, I'll throw it right back up."

"Well, let's at least get you back in the Jeep," Matt stepped away from her.

She stayed put. "I'm not sure I'm finished getting sick."

"That's all right."

Her lips curved ruefully. She blew her nose, crumpled up the tissue and stuck it in the pocket of her coat. "You won't say that if I decorate your truck the way I just decorated the side of the road over there."

Matt tucked a finger beneath her chin. "Trust me. I've taken care of sick kids and a sick wife, even sick workers. It's nothing I haven't seen before."

"Even so—"

"In the truck." He guided her back inside, circled carefully around to join her.

She leaned her head against the back of the seat. Her voice was watery again. "I'm so sorry, Matt."

"There's nothing to apologize for."

She closed her eyes, all the more embarrassed. "Right. The perfect end to a perfect evening."

"The evening isn't over yet." Matt could tell she was already starting to feel somewhat okay. He waited a few more minutes. "Feeling better?" he asked after a while, wishing they were already home so he could take care of her properly and tuck her into bed, maybe make her a cup of hot tea or bring her a glass of ginger ale....

Gretchen drew a deep breath. "Yes."

"Well enough to risk some motion?"

"Yes." Keeping her eyes closed, Gretchen settled deeper into her seat. "Just...drive...slowly."

"I THOUGHT you were going to go to bed," Matt said an hour later, when he found her in the kitchen.

Gretchen looked up from the textbook and a folder of notes spread out in front of her, shrugged and put down her pen. "I took a shower and put my pajamas on, instead."

He surveyed her tenderly. "Stomach feeling all right?"

Gretchen nodded and took a sip of ginger ale. "Like it never happened." She shrugged, admitting happily, "That's the up side of morning sickness. Once you're sick, you're usually okay."

He hunkered down beside her, not touching her. "You know, if you'd just told me you were going to be sick, I would have stopped long before I did."

Instead, Gretchen thought, chagrined, she'd tried her best to hide it. She hadn't wanted him to see her that way, for fear it would be the ultimate, perhaps final, turnoff. "I was hoping I could brazen my way through the drive home, then throw up sans audience," she confessed wryly. "Unfortunately, it didn't quite turn out that way." Although Matt had been great about helping her, gentle and patient, nurturing in the extreme.

"No, it didn't," he agreed with amusement. "So next time..." he began with mock sternness.

Gretchen crossed her heart, promising, "Next time I give you my word pride will not stand in my way."

"Glad to hear that." He paused and they exchanged grins.

Matt straightened and headed for the fridge. "So how much longer are you going to be up?" he asked as he extracted a pitcher of orange juice.

Gretchen rubbed the tenseness from the back of her neck. "Awhile. I've got my first exam tomorrow in my ed-psych class and I want to do well on it." She watched as he poured himself a tall glass of juice. "But if you want to talk for a bit, I'm ready for a break." Eager for it, in fact.

"As it happens," Matt drawled, sauntering to the fridge to replace the pitcher and then to her side, "there are a few things I'd like to know."

"Such as?" Gretchen prodded, wondering if he had any idea how much she had missed him while he was away.

Matt pulled out a chair, turned it around and straddled it. He sipped his juice, looking as though he had missed her, too.

"Such as what inspired you to become a teacher."

That was easy. "My love of kids," she said simply. Realizing he was listening intently, she continued, a little shyly, "For years, I put off a family because Robert wanted us to wait. Then, when the time was finally right, he left me."

"You must have been ticked off."

"Royally. But when I got over my hurt, I realized this change in my life was also an opportunity to start over. So I figured if I couldn't have a family of my own, maybe I could love and nurture other people's kids. So here I am."

"Why secondary school, instead of elementary education?"

"My mother died when I was in the seventh grade. I was at a pretty vulnerable age and my dad didn't handle things all that well. Oh, he cooked for us and cleaned and took me to my piano lessons and all that, but he never talked to me about his own grief or what he was feeling." Gretchen cupped both hands around her ginger ale. "To make things worse, he had no clue what to say to a girl going through adolescence." Aware Matt was listening intently, his eyes alight with compassion, she shrugged and continued ruefully, "I mean he just did not consider matters like how I should wear my hair or what I should say to a boy of tremendous importance. Nor did he want to get bogged down in emotional discussions about anything. Luckily I had a teacher who stepped in and helped me handle some of the growing pains in junior high. And another two or three who mothered me on and off during my high school years." She shook her head. "I don't know what I would have done without them." Gretchen paused and drew a deep breath as she lifted her eyes to his. "I know this sounds corny, but I hope I can return the favor someday by doing the same for other girls that age."

"It doesn't sound corny. It sounds sweet and selfless, just like you."

Gretchen warmed to the approval in his low tone. "What about you?" she asked, curious. "What got you into wildcatting?"

"I grew up in West Texas, where there are hundreds upon hundreds of wells. Started working on the rigs summers, during college, and found I had a knack for knowing instinctively where and when and just how deep to drill. As soon as I could, I started my own business, a real shoestring operation, and have never looked back."

Gretchen took a moment to absorb that. "It's funny. Here we are married, and we don't know these basic things about each other."

Matt grinned as if they had just passed a major milestone. "We're learning. And speaking of learning..." He stood reluctantly and replaced the chair. "I guess I better let you get back to hitting the books. I wouldn't want you to flunk an exam on my account." He slid his empty glass into the dishwasher, then ambled past her toward the door.

"Matt—" Gretchen stopped him before he could leave the room.

He turned, his expression expectant.

"Thanks for tonight," she said softly. It felt good knowing she had Matt there to take care of her. It had made her feel safe. "You were great tonight—really." He'd taken one of the most humiliating and embarrassing experiences of her life and made it bearable.

He grinned again. "No problem."

TO BUY or not to buy, that was the question, Matt thought, standing before a Valentine's Day display in the front of the grocery store. Discovering they were out of milk, he had volunteered to go, only to be reminded by the throngs of men waiting in the express lane, their arms full of last-minute gifts of flowers, balloons and heart-shaped satin candy boxes, that it was February 14.

Which put him in a quandary the likes of which he'd never experienced. If he forgot the holiday, Gretchen might be hurt by his insensitivity. Then she would be ticked off at him.

If he honored it by giving her a gift, she might think he was taking a lot—like the bedroom privileges he had not enjoyed since their wedding night—for granted. Or worse, that he thought he could buy her attentions.

The truth was, of course, that he wanted bedroom privileges back. But since his business trip Gretchen had not looked as if she wanted lovemaking reinstated in their lives. If she wasn't studying, she was sleeping. One or the other activity took up almost all the time she spent at home. Neither was something he could interrupt.

Of course, he had only been back a couple of days now. Their one and only dinner out had been a start toward normalizing their relationship to that of a typical married couple expecting a child. And she might have a gift for him, too. So, there was only one thing left to do.

Unfortunately, what had seemed like a brilliant idea at the store did not seem nearly so bright when Matt saw the look on Gretchen's face. He had expected her to like the gift he'd had specially made up for her. Instead, she appeared ready to burst into tears at any second.

"You needn't read too much into this," he said casually. "It's just something I felt I ought to do, under the circumstances, you being the mother of my child and all."

Gretchen froze. The tears sparkling in her misty blue eyes were fast replaced by a flash of fiery anger as she lifted her chin to confront him.

"Ought to do?" she echoed coolly.

Wincing inwardly, Matt amended cautiously, "Well, yes. We are husband and wife. At least for now. That being the case, Valentine's Day gifts are...expected."

"I see."

Gretchen sauntered closer, in an intoxicating drift of perfume.

"Kind of like sex is expected between married couples on their wedding night, right?"

Matt recognized a dig when he heard one. Worse, he had no defense for his behavior. He'd said all along theirs was to be a marriage of convenience; yet at the first opportunity to hold her in his arms again, to make wild passionate tender love to her, he hadn't been able to resist. Nor had she, and that, he felt, irritated her more than anything. He sensed she wasn't used to being driven by her passion any more than he was.

Noting she was still furious with him, knowing hormones were at least partially responsible for her highly emotional state this evening, he attempted to calm her. "Look, I'm just trying to make the best of a difficult situation." Maybe he should have gone with the candy instead of the fruit. Or bypassed food altogether, since it could be a tricky issue during pregnancy, and gotten flowers and perfume. Hell, maybe he should have sprung for lingerie, or even a book of baby names. But it was too late now. Judging from her expression, it was going to be a while before she forgave him for this . . . misstep . . . in their courtship.

Pretty lips set in a stubborn line, she shoved the heart-shaped basket back at him.

"I don't want gifts that are insincerely given."

Irritated that she was deliberately taking this the wrong way, Matt jammed his hands on his waist. "There's nothing insincere about that fruit!" he countered flatly.

"Oh, really." She spun away, temper flaring.

Matt followed fast on her heels. "It's just what I thought you should have. Under the circumstances," he added specifically, as she reached the counter and whirled around in mute aggravation.

Tears sparkled in her eyes, right along with the grief. "I suppose now you're trying to tell me I'm fat?"

"Of course not. Not that gaining weight in your condition is anything to be sensitive about anyway," Matt continued quickly.

She arched a dissenting brow, and Matt flung up his hands in frustration. "I mean, it's supposed to happen," he said. Dammit, judging by her increasingly wounded, increasingly furious expression, that hadn't come out right, either.

"Of course."

She glared at him, then sidestepped him altogether, like some odious piece of trash.

He caught her arm. She flung off his staying grip. "Gretchen . . ." Matt said wearily.

"Can it, Matt." Chin held high, she marched out of the kitchen, pausing only long enough to say, "And keep your basket. I don't want that, either."

Matt sighed as all hope of having a romantic evening with Gretchen faded. He pressed his lips together grimly. Some Valentine's Day this was turning out to be.

Chapter Eight

March

"I've never known Dad to be out of town so much in one month's time," Angela said, as she and Gretchen roamed the grocery aisles together, carefully selecting the ingredients for their first family dinner that evening. "Doesn't it bother you?"

Gretchen put fresh broccoli in the basket. "I've been busy, too, Angela." But not too busy to miss Matt, or feel lonely and miserable as hell, living more or less alone in that big house.

"But the two of you just got married six weeks ago!" Angela protested emotionally.

"Your dad has a lot of work to do." And besides, Gretchen thought, it was all her fault Matt had made himself so scarce. She had overreacted to his Valentine's Day gift, first thinking it meant something much more than it did and practically bursting into tears of sheer, unadulterated joy, then flying off the handle when she realized it had been a "duty" gift because he'd felt she expected it from him.

He'd been wrong about that, Gretchen thought sadly. She hadn't "expected" it. Being the hopelessly sentimental fool that she was, she had hoped he would remember the holiday in some small but heartfelt fashion, and in fact still had a gift for him tucked away upstairs. But thinking that way, Gretchen reminded herself sternly, was hopelessly naive. Now, more than ever, she had to be practical, for her sake and the baby's.

Angela crossed out the last item on their shopping list. "I think that about does it."

"Then let's hit the checkout and go home," Gretchen said. "Sassy and Luke will be coming in, in a few hours, and I want everything to be ready for them."

"What about Dad?"

"He said he'll be home by the time they arrive."

Half an hour later, they were home and had all the groceries put away. As Gretchen raced into the laundry room to start a load of clothes, she felt something peculiar. Heart pounding, she detoured into the bathroom. Then came out, knowing she looked white as a sheet.

"Gretchen? What is it?" Angela demanded in alarm.

Trembling, Gretchen eased herself into a chair. "I think," she began slowly, "we'd better call the doctor."

MATT CHARGED into Marissa's office. Angela shot off the waiting room sofa and hurled herself into his arms.

"Dad, I'm so glad you got here."

His heart thudding heavily in his chest, Matt hugged his daughter reassuringly. "Where's Gretchen?" he asked.

"In one of the examining rooms with Marissa." Angela drew back and stared up at him in confusion. "Dad, what's going on?"

Matt didn't know how to answer that, particularly since he and Gretchen had agreed they would not tell his children the news just yet. Fortunately, Marissa came out to get him before he had a chance to reply.

He whirled to confront her. "How is Gretchen?" he asked immediately.

"Not to worry, Matt. Everything's going to be okay." Marissa shot a cautious glance at Angela, then turned back to Matt. "Look, why don't you come back to the examining room with me and I'll explain what's going on to both you and Gretchen simultaneously."

"I don't suppose that invitation includes me," Angela said.

Marissa shook her head.

Angela gave Matt a plaintive look. "I'll explain everything later," he promised.

"All right."

Angela sat back down reluctantly. She continued to appear worried and upset, despite Marissa's calm reassurance. Matt knew how his daughter felt; he was having the same reaction.

His heart still pounding, Matt followed Marissa. Gretchen was dressed again and putting on her shoes when he and Marissa entered the room. "So what's happening?" Matt asked.

Marissa led them both into her office and indicated that Matt and Gretchen should sit in the side chairs in front of her desk. "Gretchen's had a little bleeding this morning."

That sounded ominous. Matt reached over and took Gretchen's hand in his. "Do you know what caused it?"

"Yes. Gretchen has a small polyp on her cervix. That's what caused the staining."

"So I'm not in danger of losing the baby?" Gretchen asked, anxiously gripping Matt's hand.

"No. Not at all," Marissa reassured her calmly.

Matt breathed a sigh of relief and held on to Gretchen all the tighter. "So what do we do?" he asked.

"Nothing, at the moment. Often these polyps will grow to a certain point, then atrophy and go away by themselves—kind of a case of Mother Nature spotting a problem and taking over, and the body healing itself. In fact, it looks like this has already started to happen—hence the staining."

"What happens if it doesn't go away on its own?" Matt asked, leaning forward.

Marissa finished making notations on Gretchen's chart, put her pen down casually and sat back in her chair. She made eye contact with both Matt and Gretchen. "If it is still there at delivery, we'll remove it. But at the moment, I promise you both, that polyp poses absolutely no threat to either Gretchen or the baby. Nor is it ever likely to do so."

"That's good to hear," Gretchen murmured, still gripping his hand.

Marissa nodded agreeably. "In the meantime, we'll keep an eye on it," she promised. "You can let me know if there's any more staining, Gretchen. But frankly, from the looks of things, I'm not expecting you to have any."

"Thank goodness." Gretchen sagged in her chair, her entire body going limp with relief. "That really frightened me this morning."

Me, too, Matt thought. He looked to Marissa for advice as he squeezed Gretchen's hand. "Are there any other precautions Gretchen should take?" he asked. "Bed rest or anything?"

Marissa grinned. "Well, I could prescribe it," she drawled, "but it'd be like going to bed for a mosquito bite."

Lively color came back into Gretchen's face. "Not exactly my usual practice," Gretchen murmured, tongue-in-cheek.

"I didn't think so," Marissa quipped. She turned back to Matt and continued seriously, "No, there are no precauions necessary. Nor is there any reason for you two not to make love at this point. The baby's fine. And so is Gretchen."

Matt didn't have to look at Gretchen to know she was blushing. He was feeling a mite uncomfortable himself.

Marissa stood. "I'm going out to chat with Angela for a moment, since I didn't have time to talk to her earlier. What you two tell her about this is up to you. I'll give you a moment to discuss it."

"Thanks, Marissa," Gretchen said.

Marissa waved off the thanks. "It's my job as your OB-GYN." She slipped from the room.

Matt faced Gretchen. He was happy to see she was looking better with every second that passed. "What does Angela know?" he asked pointedly.

"So far, only that I had some unexpected bleeding that threw me into a panic." Gretchen paused and slowly raked her teeth across her lower lip. She surged to her feet. Folding her arms in front of her, she regarded him nervously. "We're going to have to tell her, Matt. We're going to have to tell all your kids."

Although he detested the timing, Matt agreed reluctantly that because of the "emergency," they had no choice. "Then it might as well be tonight," he said, "when we have them all together."

"AND THAT'S what happened today," Matt finished quietly as his children sat in shell-shocked silence around Gretchen and him.

"Thank heaven everything's okay with the baby," Angela murmured, shooting Gretchen a compassionate glance as she pressed a hand to her chest. "You were so white when it was all happening. You really had me scared there."

"I was scared," Gretchen said softly. "But you were great. Driving me to the doctor, getting ahold of your dad." She shrugged helplessly. "I don't know what I would have done without you."

"Well," Luke said after a moment, looking only slightly less stunned than his two sisters by the news Matt had just tactfully relayed. "As long as I'm going to have another sibling, I hope the baby's a boy." His expression turned wistful as he smiled at Gretchen. "I'd like a brother. I've always wanted one."

Sassy stared at Luke as if he'd lost his mind. "Are you nuts?" she demanded, jumping to her feet as suddenly as if the sofa had burned her. "How can you be happy about this, even for one second?" she demanded, her hands balled into fists at her sides.

"Because having a baby is a blessing," Matt said firmly.

"Maybe under normal circumstances," Sassy muttered.

Gretchen stood. Sassy appeared ready to explode, and if she did, Gretchen did not want to be there to witness it. "I think I'll go out in the kitchen and get started on the dishes," she said.

"Good idea," Sassy glared at Gretchen as if she were the worst kind of interloper.

Matt caught Gretchen's hand before she could bolt and drew her back down beside him on the sofa. "There's no reason for you to run off, Gretchen," he told her firmly, as he directed a censuring glance at his youngest child. "Anything Sassy has to say on this subject can be said to both of us," he remarked sternly. "Although I would advise Sassy to think carefully before she says anything else."

"Yeah, Sassy," Luke interjected, beginning to look a little nervous. "There's no reason to start anything tonight. Especially since Gretchen cooked us such a great dinner and everything."

Sassy glared at Luke. It was clear she felt him the worst kind of traitor for taking their dad's side in the brewing argument. "I'm not starting anything," she cried in an anguished tone. "This all started when Dad married Gretchen. And even that makes sense now," Sassy blurted out angrily as she stormed about the living room. She whirled toward Matt. "I knew you never would have married Gretchen under normal circumstances—"

Unfortunately, Gretchen thought, Sassy was right. If not for the baby, she and Matt would not have married. Guilt filled her anew.

"Sassy, that's enough," Matt reprimanded, looking as if he, too, were about to explode. "Gretchen is my wife and your stepmother, and you will treat her with respect."

"Well, I guess I know who and what matters to you, don't I?" Sassy shot back furiously, tears glimmering in her eyes. Shoulders shaking with silent sobs, she raced from the room.

With an apologetic glance at Gretchen and an exasperated glare at her dad, Angela ran after her. "Sassy, wait!"

"No! I'm getting out of here."

The front door slammed once, twice.

Luke lurched to his feet and glared at Matt. "Nice going, Dad."

In the driveway a car started.

Matt scowled at Luke. "Got a hankering to join your sister in the doghouse?" he drawled. "'Cause that's where she is right now, and where she'll stay until she comes back here and apologizes to Gretchen and to me."

Luke rolled his eyes. "She won't do it," he predicted direly.

"Then she'd better get used to her fall from grace," Matt retorted.

Near tears herself—it seemed she had brought nothing but turmoil to Matt's life—Gretchen pushed to her feet once again. "Where do you think the girls went?" she asked Luke.

"To Angela's apartment, down by UT."

Gretchen turned to Matt beseechingly. There was still time to prevent an all-out family feud, if only he would act. "Why don't you go after them?" she suggested gently.

Matt shook his head, stood and began collecting coffee cups and dessert plates. "They know how to find me when they're ready to talk," he replied stubbornly.

"Please, Matt—"

"Dad's right," Luke interjected. Gretchen looked at him and he jammed his hands in his pockets of his jeans. "As upset as they both are, I doubt it would do any good right now. But I'll try to talk some sense into them anyway. Thanks for dinner, Gretchen." Luke patted her on the shoulder. He turned to his dad, merely shook his head in remonstration and exited the room.

Once again the front door shut—quietly this time. Gretchen and Matt were alone.

The tension dissipated, but did not fade altogether. "I'm sorry," she said after a moment, as she, too, began to pick up.

Matt's expression was grim, his irritation with the situation evident. "You have nothing to apologize for," he stated flatly.

Gretchen swallowed, the remorse she felt going soul-deep. Knowing the last thing Matt needed right now was another emotional scene, she stood in front of him and kept her voice as even as she could. "I never meant to come between you and your kids," she apologized softly.

"You haven't," Matt replied shortly, his expression bleak.

Recalling what had happened, Gretchen was not so sure.

THE PHONE RANG at midnight. Gretchen heard Matt answer it. He talked briefly, then hung up.

Unable to stand the suspense—calls that late at night almost always brought bad news, she got up, pulled on a robe and went down the hall to his bedroom. The door was open, the bedroom shrouded in darkness. He was lying on his back, both powerful arms folded behind his head, a brooding look on his face. His sinewy chest and shoulders were bare, the covers drawn only to his waist.

She paused in the portal, memories of their previous nights together flooding her senses, making her aware how very much she longed to make love to him again. But that was probably not going to happen until Matt restored some equilibrium to his life. And since she had helped destroy it, perhaps she could help put it back to rights. Clutching the lapels of her robe, she asked softly, "Was that the kids?"

His look turned even more brooding as he leaned over and switched on the bedside light, then turned back to her. "Yes."

Shivering in the nighttime coolness of the house, she edged closer. "And they're all okay?"

"And spending the night at Angela's place," Matt reported wearily, rubbing his hand across his brow.

Gretchen sat on the opposite edge of his king-size bed, facing him, and pleated the spread with her fingers. "Are they planning to come by tomorrow?"

He turned so he was lying on his side. "Luke and Sassy are both leaving first thing in the morning to go back to school. Angela plans to spend the day researching a paper at the library."

Knowing how much he had looked forward to having all three of his kids with him that weekend, she knew how that had to hurt. "Maybe you should have breakfast with them," Gretchen suggested.

"No. They made it pretty clear they don't want to see me."

"Oh, Matt—"

"It's all right, Gretchen," he said gently, his expression becoming more aggrieved. "They've all been mad at me before. They'll get over it in time."

"What if they don't?" Gretchen asked. When he was silent, she rushed on emotionally. "Matt, I couldn't bear it if I were responsible for alienating you from your family." Whether he admitted it, he would not be able to bear it, either.

"Don't worry about it," he advised brusquely. "Any alienation my children and I are feeling tonight is strictly of our own making."

Was it? Gretchen wondered. "That may be," she allowed slowly, "but you can't deny that the blowup tonight wouldn't have happened if you hadn't married me." And for that she felt an incredibly heavy burden of guilt.

Irritation sharpening his features, Matt got up, stalked to the closet and pulled on a robe. "That was my choice, Gretchen," he reminded her.

Gretchen swallowed the growing knot of emotion in her throat. "Choice or obligation?" she countered.

He gave her a sharp look as he strode to her side. "No one forced me into anything," he informed her. "I married you because I wanted to marry you, Gretchen."

As much as she would've liked to think so, Gretchen knew that was not the case, not really. "You married me because of the baby," she corrected icily. "And as much as I want to forget it, I can't, Matt." And neither can you or your kids.

Tears trembled on her lashes. Determinedly she blinked them back. Damn it all, she had known their hasty marriage was a mistake. Tonight had proved it. But it wasn't too late to rectify the situation. "Which is why I'm moving out,'' she continued quietly, her mind made up as soon as the impulsive words were out.

''What?'' Matt did a double take. ''When?''

Before I lose my nerve, Gretchen thought. *Before I think about all I'm giving up and will wish forever that I still had.* ''First thing tomorrow morning.''

MATT STOOD in the doorway to the guest room. It was barely six-thirty in the morning, and Gretchen was already up, dressed in oversize navy sweats and a white T-shirt and folding clothes back into boxes.

He had hoped she would calm down if he gave her some time to get a night's sleep and think about what she was doing. Apparently that was not the case. He leaned a shoulder against the portal, glad he'd gotten up when he'd first heard her moving around, and hit the shower, too. ''Don't I get any say in this?''

Her glance moved cursorily from the top of his damp hair to his moccasin-clad feet, the determination in her eyes appealing to him every bit as much as the passion.

''Nope.''

Matt blew out a weary breath. ''I see.''

Her mouth crooked up in a knowing smile. ''I don't think you do,'' she countered ruefully, ''but you will. Eventually.''

It took every ounce of self-control he possessed for him not to cross the small room and take her in his arms. ''Suppose you explain it to me, then,'' he told her with deceptive tranquillity, his temper beginning to flare.

''That's easy.'' Gretchen tossed her hair. ''I'm giving you your life back.''

''No,'' he amended. Pushing away from the door, he circled around the other side of the bed and slouched on the window seat. ''You are making my life harder.''

Color flooded her cheeks. "I don't see how you can say that," she muttered emotionally.

Matt watched as she stuffed an armload of books in the box. "Has it occurred to you that I want you here, with me, so that I can keep an eye on you?"

Gretchen lifted her chin haughtily. "I assure you I am quite trustworthy," she snapped back.

That had never been under dispute. Matt stood and paced the U-shaped area around the bed. "You are also pregnant, Gretchen."

The color in her cheeks deepened. "I'm fine."

Matt braced his hands on his waist and towered over her. "What if something happens?"

Gretchen slipped by him and stuffed a handful of lacy lingerie in her suitcase. "I can dial 911 as well as anyone," she responded, as if there were no other way to go.

"Uh-huh." Matt didn't even want to think about how long it had been since he had seen her in that lingerie. "What about your desire to give this baby the best possible start?" he demanded, standing close enough to inhale the sexy fragrance clinging to her skin. "Or have you forgotten about that, too?"

Tears of fury glimmered in her eyes as she pivoted away from him. "I was fooling myself thinking that this was the way to do that."

Matt grasped her shoulders and turned her to face him. "No, Gretchen, you weren't." She remained stiff in his arms. "Look, I know our relationship has had a most unconventional start."

Gretchen quirked a brow. "Now, that's putting it mildly," she drawled.

Ignoring her sarcasm, Matt continued, "We got involved too soon. We never had a chance to let our relationship grow. And when we did get married, it was with both feet out the door."

Gretchen folded her arms in front of her but made no move to escape his hold. "So what's your point?"

Matt shrugged and dropped his hands. "Maybe the kids are right. Maybe this marriage of ours is a farce. But it doesn't have to stay that way."

Gretchen grew very still for a long moment. "What are you suggesting?" she asked warily.

"That we make a real go of it. That we sleep together and eat together and act like a real husband and wife. Who knows? The feeling just might take," he said with amiability.

"Oh, Matt."

Gretchen sighed, in that instant looking more vulnerable than he had ever seen her. Tears sparkled in her eyes but did not fall.

"Why are you suggesting this now?" she asked in a low, anguished voice.

"Because I realized something yesterday in Marissa's office," Matt said hoarsely, threading both hands through her hair and tilting her face up to his. "I realized how much I wanted you to have this baby. I also realized how much I'm beginning to care about you. I want those feelings to be mutual, Gretchen. I want us to care about each other as much as we both care about the health and safety of our baby."

"I want that, too," Gretchen whispered back, as the tears she'd been valiantly withholding rolled down her face. "But I'm afraid, Matt."

"Afraid of what?" Matt asked as he swung her up into his arms and carried her down the hall to his bedroom. He shut the door behind them with his foot, then crossed the room and lowered her gently onto the unmade covers of his bed. He lay down beside her and took her in his arms.

"I thought I could handle this as long as I didn't invest too much of myself." Gretchen drew a deep, hitching breath as he aligned his length intimately with hers, cuddling her close as she buried her face in his shoulder. "What you're asking me for is an all-out effort."

Matt cupped a hand beneath her chin, forcing her face up to his, then smoothed the hair from her face with long, gentle strokes. "An all-out effort is what I'm promising to give in return."

Gretchen studied him. "What if it doesn't work?" she asked as she smoothed a trembling hand across his chest.

"Then we'll be able to look back," Matt said softly, kissing first her brow, then her temple, then her cheek, "and know that we both gave it our all. No one can ask for more than that, Gretchen." Giving in to the desire that had been haunting him for days now, he pressed a hand to her spine, urging her closer, until her breasts were against his chest. He ran his hand up and down her spine. As she melted against him, his lips met hers in a searing kiss. Twining her arms about his neck, Gretchen murmured her pleasure and surged up to meet him.

Her mouth was pliant beneath his, warm and sexy, and Matt put everything he had into the kiss. This time, he did not want her running away.

He was kissing her the way he had during their wedding night, Gretchen thought, the way he had the first time they'd made love, with a sure, sweet tenderness that rocked her to her soul and left her feeling as if she were in heaven. Unable to help herself, she began to return his kisses, first shyly, then with growing ardor. The scent of his cologne, so brisk and masculine, filled her senses. She moaned as he pushed aside the layers of her clothes, baring her breasts, his thumb and fingers playing over her nipples until they were tight, aching buds. Still kissing him voraciously, she unbuttoned his shirt, unzipped his jeans. His arousal, so hot and hard, pressed against her palm. He was as eager to please her as she was to please him, and they swiftly shed their clothes, their words coming on ragged breaths.

"I can't believe—"

"I know."

"I want—"

"So do I, sweetheart, so do I." Pulling her back to him, he caressed the gentle slope of her abdomen wonderingly, slid a hand between her thighs. She cried out as he touched her, arching her back as heat spread through her in waves. "Oh, Matt," she murmured, raining kisses across his collarbone and his chest as the need to be part of him grew ever stronger.

"Let me love you," he whispered as he laved her breast with his tongue and blew it dry with his breath.

And all the while his hand stroked, bringing her to a fever pitch. She arched against him again, needing to give, even as she took. Her hands caressing him, she straddled his hips, then knelt, her knees aside his thighs. Slowly she lowered herself, took the hot hard length of him inside.

Matt groaned and caught her hips in his hands, drawing her into an even deeper union. Then his fingers were sliding down their bodies, tracing tantalizing patterns in hidden places, searching for and finding her pleasure. The need within her exploded and her self-control evaporated. She cried out. The next thing she knew she was beneath him again. Thighs pressed against thighs, hips against hips.

She moaned as his mouth came down on hers, and then they were one again. Connecting...everywhere...body and soul. Gretchen hadn't known she could need anyone like this, but she did. Perhaps always would. And then they were cresting together, wave after wave, moving headlong into fire, holding each other in a manner that took all the questions, all the doubts, away. Satisfaction came easily, for both of them, and with it the peace she hadn't felt in weeks.

Matt was right, she thought sleepily, long minutes later as he continued to hold her in his arms, creating a safe loving haven that was invulnerable to the pressures and responsibilities awaiting them in the outside world. They did owe it to each other and their baby to give this relationship of theirs more than half a chance. There was no telling what the future was going to bring them, of course, but right now, they needed each other. So right now, they would take it one day, one moment, at a time....

Chapter Nine

April

"Well? What do you think?" Marissa asked.

Gretchen examined herself in a three-way mirror and started to laugh. "I think I look like a big yellow blimp." The maternity dress had bell-shaped sleeves that poofed off her shoulders like a bad soufflé and a hem that hit at a dowdy middle of the knee. She leaned against the dressing room wall and shook her head, her only comfort the thought that Matt was not there to see her. "I can't go to class at UT dressed like this. If the other students saw me in this they'd think I was two bricks short of a load. And I can't say as I'd blame them."

Marissa grinned. "You're right. It's so bad it's ridiculous. You'd probably be laughed off campus if you wore that."

"And those two jumpsuits I had on a minute ago were just as poorly cut," Gretchen moaned as she shimmied out of the dress. "Honestly, who designs these things?"

"Who knows. Who cares. Let's just try to find you something to wear, and to that end, let's try the maternity jeans and that white turtleneck sweater."

Gretchen slipped off the dress and put on the jeans. The sweater was too bulky and the jeans were a miserable fit. "There's no way these are going to stay up," she lamented as she moved slightly to the left and the denim eased down her hips. Lifting the hem of her sweater, she pinched two inches off the waist of the stretchable front panel. "Maybe I should try a smaller size."

"If you try a smaller size they won't fit when you reach the third trimester," Marissa said practically. "Let's try the khaki slacks. There's no polyester panel on these and the waist is elasticized all the way around."

"Much better." Gretchen noted the trim line of the straight-legs pants and breathed a sigh of relief. Finally a pair of maternity pants that didn't make her backside appear twice its size. "Now, if I could just find a shirt that didn't have polka dots or bows on it, I'd be in business."

"Look, here's one that's designed like a man's shirt, with a shirttail hem. Try it."

Gretchen slipped it on. The white-and-khaki plaid was flattering and she liked the tailored construction and crisp cotton fabric. This was more like it. Maybe Matt wouldn't feel like running the other way when he saw her in it. "Maybe if I could get the same thing in another color?"

Marissa grinned. "No problem. I saw something similar in navy on the rack."

"Good, then let's get it and go."

As they approached the register, Marissa stopped her and said, "That's only two outfits, Gretchen."

Gretchen didn't want to admit it, but that was all her budget would allow this month. Since starting college, she had taken out the minimum in education loans and lived frugally to avoid going any deeper into debt than she absolutely had to.

"Are you sure you don't want to try on the knit separates or the wind suit?" Marissa insisted.

"Positive." Gretchen smiled, knowing she could always come back later, perhaps during the Memorial Day weekend sales. "This is all I need right now." Besides, there was no use investing a great deal of money in clothes she'd wear only for a few months and never need again.

"So how are things with you and Matt?" Marissa asked, when they were back out in the mall again.

"Okay." Gretchen shifted her shopping bag to her other hand.

"That's all? Just okay?" Marissa teased when they stopped to examine some handcrafted sterling silver-and-turquoise earrings in a jeweler's display window.

Gretchen paused, thinking not only about what was right with their life together, but what was wrong with it. "Matt's been very good to me," she said cautiously. He was always looking after her. They took turns cooking dinner, spent time talking every day and made love almost every night.

"And?"

Gretchen shifted her shopping bag to her other hand, trying to find a more comfortable way to carry it. "And nothing."

"Gretchen, I can tell when something's wrong," Marissa persisted, her expression tightening into one of deep concern.

Gretchen glanced away a long moment before turning back to face Marissa. "Things *are* getting better between us. But they're worse between him and his kids," she confided, "and the baby and I are responsible for that."

Marissa took Gretchen's elbow and guided her away from the jewelry center and out of earshot of other shoppers. "Are you saying that Matt blames you for that?" she asked, growing very still when they'd paused again.

"No." Gretchen shook her head emphatically. She sat down on a polished wooden bench and settled her shopping bag between her knees. "He would never do that. But I still feel responsible as hell. I mean, sooner or later this is bound to come between us, too. Sooner or later he is bound to realize that none of this would have happened if I hadn't been around."

Marissa was silent as she sat down beside Gretchen. "Then you have to fix it," she said simply.

"I know," Gretchen said with a heartfelt sigh. The question was how. Thus far all the calls she had made to his children—and she'd made one per child per week—had been either cut short or left unreturned. Thus far, her efforts to mastermind a reconciliation between Matt and his kids were not working at all.

"GOOD HEAVENS, Matt. What happened to you?" Gretchen asked several hours later, aghast. She'd never seen anyone so completely filthy. Matt was covered in grease and dirt from head to toe. Only his wrists and hands were clean.

Matt stepped inside the kitchen door and, still standing on the welcome mat beside the entrance to the garage, carefully removed his boots. He set them down, then came inside. "We were working on drilling equipment all day." He spread his hands wide and looked down at himself with the contentment of a man who'd put in a hard day's labor. "Scary, huh?"

Gretchen pushed away from the table spread with textbooks. "Only in that I wasn't expecting you to look quite so..." she hesitated, not wanting to insult him.

"Grungy?" Matt supplied with a wink.

Gretchen grinned and sashayed closer. "You said it, not me." She looked him up and down mischievously. "Although now that you mention it, you'd be perfect as the before screen in a detergent commercial."

He tilted his head to the side. "Cute."

"I thought so."

Chuckling, Matt headed for the adjacent laundry room. "Washer empty?"

"Yep."

Though they were living together, sleeping and eating and even cooking together, they were still doing their own laundry and errands most of the time. It was as if they were afraid to get too close, or come to depend on each other too much just yet.

Gretchen lounged against the doorway, enjoying the view of Matt in such a masculine, earthy state. She folded her arms in front of her. "Are you really going to try to get those clean?"

"Honey, I've washed out a lot worse," Matt drawled as he shucked his jeans and socks, stripped off his denim work shirt and pulled his T-shirt over his head. He dropped them all in the washer, turned the temperature selector knob to hot, pushed the buttons for heavy-duty cycle and soak, and added hefty amounts of detergent and all-fabric bleach.

"That'll really do it?" Gretchen asked. She would've sworn nothing would get that grime out.

Matt nodded. "Should. If not, I'll run them through a second cycle." He caught her glance and continued, deadpan, "In case you're wondering, I am planning to get a shower before dinner."

"It never would've occurred to me to ask," Gretchen shot back wryly. Unlike his first wife, Gretchen didn't mind a little dirt. In fact, one of the things she liked most about Matt was that he wasn't afraid to get dirty.

Matt took her hand in his, tugged her close and kissed the top of her head. "Come upstairs with me. We can catch up while I shower."

"I gather you had a good day," Gretchen said, as he kicked off his boxers and stepped into the shower.

"The best. It was very productive. What about you?"

As she turned to answer him, Gretchen couldn't resist a look at his silhouette through the glass. Brawny shoulders tapered to a narrow waist and leanly sculpted hips, muscular thighs and calves. And the rest of him was just as beautifully made. Swallowing around the sudden dryness in her throat, she looked away. There was a danger in wanting too much. "I had a good day, too," she reported casually. She picked up her brush and ran it through her hair. Noticing her lipstick could use touching up, she did that, too.

Matt turned toward her as he soaped down his body. "That lecture you were looking forward to today..."

"Was great. My other classes were interesting, too."

"Did you meet with your adviser?"

"Yes." Gretchen spoke loud enough to be heard above the shower. "No luck on substituting the prerequisite speech class. I'm going to have to take it second summer term if I want to enroll in the required class in the fall."

"That's awfully close to your due date, isn't it?"

Gretchen shrugged, bracing herself for the argument sure to come. If she had a complaint about Matt, it was that he tended to worry a little too much, believing that if one should err it should be on the side of caution. "I should be done with my exams a week or so before I deliver."

"That's still cutting it awfully close." Matt frowned as he cut off the water and stepped out of the shower.

Gretchen watched, dry mouthed, as he dried off briskly, then wrapped a towel around his waist. With effort, she forced her mind back to the conversation. "I know." She pushed the hair from her face. "But what's the alternative? Wait another year to take that class? The professor I want only teaches it fall semester."

"Would it be such a crime to take it with another professor?" Matt asked gently, stepping closer.

"In this case, yes," Gretchen explained patiently. "I told you, Matt. My having a baby is not going to interfere with my getting my degree. In fact, my having a baby doesn't have to change my life—or yours—at all."

"Right," Matt replied, deadpan, as he led the way out into the bedroom.

Gretchen sensed a lecture on the perils of parenthood coming on, by one who had experienced it all. She leveled a warning look at him as he rummaged through his bureau. "Matt, don't start."

"Hey!" Matt dropped his towel and pulled on his boxers. "Who said anything?"

Gretchen lifted her brow. "But you're thinking it," she accused.

"That's because it's true." Matt put on a fresh pair of socks, disappeared into the adjacent walk-in closet, then returned, carrying dark brown slacks. "Having a baby does change your life in myriad ways."

Gretchen sat down on the edge of the bed as he finished getting dressed. "Maybe in the old days, before almost all women worked—"

"The old days?" he echoed, chagrined.

"Sorry." Gretchen blushed. "I didn't mean to imply you were behind the times on this subject."

"But you think it," he countered, as he shrugged on an ecru cotton polo shirt.

"Now who's reading minds?" she exclaimed.

Before he could reply, the doorbell rang. Before either of them could do much more than move toward the door, they heard the front door open and close. "That's probably Angela. She said she was going to stop by tonight," Matt explained. "She has something for you."

Gretchen blinked in surprise. "For me?"

Matt lifted his shoulders in a decidedly casual shrug, but there was no hiding the happiness in his eyes. "That's what she said," he replied. "I think she's trying to make amends for the way they all charged out of here last month after we told them the news."

Maybe miracles did happen after all, Gretchen thought. Now, if she could just get Matt to meet all his children, including Sassy, halfway, they'd be able to blend their family into one happy unit. So far, Matt was proving as stubborn as the rest of them. "It was hard on all of us," Gretchen said.

"And it's past time to make amends," Matt said, both happy and relieved. "I'm glad she's here."

"Dad? Gretchen? Are you up there?" Angela called impatiently from the bottom of the stairs.

"I'll go down and talk to her while you finish getting dressed and dry your hair," Gretchen said.

"Thanks."

"Your dad will be down in a minute," Gretchen told Angela as they met at the bottom of the stairs.

Awkwardly, Angela thrust a baby quilt at Gretchen. It was bordered in white, yellow, pink and blue, and decorated with the alphabet and stuffed-animal appliqués. "Oh, Angela, this is beautiful."

Acting as if the family argument had never occurred, Angela beamed. "Do you really think so? I made it myself from scraps of material and stuff I had around."

"It's gorgeous. Really." Gretchen had never seen anything so lovely.

"Thanks." Angela smiled shyly. "I wanted it to be really special. I've been working on it in my spare time for the past month."

Gretchen hugged her. "We'll cherish it. Your dad is going to be so pleased."

"Where is he?"

"He's getting cleaned up. They were working on the drilling equipment all day."

"Oh, yuk," Angela said. "My mom always hated that. He came home looking and smelling really gross."

"Yeah, but he cleans up nice." Gretchen grinned.

Angela brightened. "You're right about that."

Gretchen led the way into the kitchen. "We were about to have dinner. Want to eat with us?"

Angela paused shyly. "If there's enough and I wouldn't be intruding."

"Angela, this is your home," Gretchen said sincerely. "You will always be welcome here. And I mean that from the bottom of my heart."

"I know, Gretchen. And I was never really mad at you. It's just... Dad can be so stubborn sometimes."

"I know."

"And someone had to side with Sassy."

Gretchen wasn't so sure about that, but she didn't see the point of getting into an argument about it, either. "How are she and Luke?" she asked casually.

"Still upset with Dad and, by default, you," Angela said honestly.

"Will they get over it?" Gretchen asked bluntly, not certain how much more of this feuding she could take.

Angela bit her lip. "I'm not sure."

"What usually happens when the family has a disagreement like this?"

"I don't know. It's never happened before."

A chill slid down Gretchen's spine.

An awkward silence fell. Angela glanced at the course descriptions and registration catalog on the table. "So you're registering for summer classes, too," she said brightly, changing the subject adroitly.

Gretchen forced a smile. She went to the stove and stirred the pot of simmering chili. "I'm trying. I keep changing my mind about what I want to take this summer."

"Me, too."

"So how are your classes going?" Gretchen asked, as she brought out the ingredients for corn bread.

"Okay." Without warning, Angela looked glum.

Maybe here was her chance to be if not exactly a stepmother, at least a friend. "Something wrong?" Gretchen asked, as she measured cornmeal and flour into a bowl.

Angela pulled up a stool. "Promise you won't tell Dad?"

They were treading in dangerous territory. Gretchen did not want to be in the middle of any quarrels between Matt and his daughter. On the other hand, Angela looked like she needed someone to talk to. Gretchen knew she couldn't turn away. "If you tell me something in confidence, I promise it will not go any further."

"I want to change my major again. And Dad is going to absolutely freak when he hears."

"What happened to psychology?" Gretchen went to the refrigerator for eggs and milk.

Angela waved airily. "I'm not cut out for that."

"Then what?" Gretchen asked, perplexed as she broke eggs into a bowl.

"That's just it. I don't know. The more I try to settle down and pick something out the more scared I get. I'm terrified of making a mistake. I don't want to end up like my mom and my dad."

A chill went down Gretchen's spine, as she switched the oven knob to 350 degrees. Was there more to the failure of Matt's marriage than she knew? "I'm not sure I understand," she said slowly.

Angela's expression became even more troubled. "They were my age when they got married. They both thought they knew what they wanted out of life—each other—only to find out they didn't belong together at all. They were miserable in the years before the divorce, Gretchen." Lip quivering, she glanced up and continued in a whisper, "They tried not to let on to us, you know, but we all saw it. I can't go back to living that way again. Feeling like...nothing in my life is right." Her eyes gleamed moistly as she pushed away from the stool and began to clear the kitchen table. "And yet I'm so tired of being in school, of putting my whole life on hold. I need to know what to do."

Gretchen drew a deep breath, feeling as if every ounce of maternal instinct she had was being put to the test. "Have you checked with the career counselors?" she asked gently as she walked over to help.

Angela nodded. "I've taken all the aptitude tests countless times."

"And?" Gretchen carried her stack of papers and books over to the far kitchen counter, out of harm's way.

Angela sighed and looked even more miserable. "I get a different result every time. One time, I'm suited for a career in sales, the next medicine, the next law, the next accounting."

"Well, maybe you're going about it the wrong way," Gretchen said at last, as she returned to her corn bread.

Angela brightened. "How so?"

"Maybe you need to stop thinking about what you ought to be and concentrate instead on what you like to do."

Gretchen added the eggs and milk to the dry ingredients already assembled. "In your spare time, what do you do?"

Angela shrugged. "Sew, read. Make things."

Next Gretchen added salt and baking powder. "So maybe fashion design is where you should be. Have you taken any human ecology or home economics courses?"

"Well, actually, yes, when I first got to UT, but I just couldn't see myself as a department-store buyer or a home-ec teacher, and that's where most of the kids were headed...."

"Then maybe you should set your sights a little higher. Think about opening your own clothing shop. Or sewing clothes on commission, for individual customers to suit their individual needs."

"But what if I go ahead and get a degree in design and then find out I can't make a living?" Angela asked anxiously.

Gretchen mixed the batter with a wooden spoon. "Angela, if this quilt you've sewn is any indication of your talent, that will never be a problem. You have style and creativity in abundance. And if it's something you like to do... At least think about it," Gretchen urged softly.

"What's going on?" Matt stood in the doorway of the kitchen.

"Angela made us a quilt for the baby," Gretchen said, changing the subject adroitly, as she moved to spoon batter into a pan. "Isn't it beautiful?"

"Very." Matt admired it quietly, then hugged his daughter. "I'm glad you came by," he said softly, feeling more content than he had in weeks. "I've missed you."

"THAT WAS FUN," Gretchen said after Angela had left.

Matt waved goodbye to his daughter, all the love he felt for his eldest child reflected on his face. "Yeah, it was." He smiled with a deep, paternal satisfaction as her car disappeared from view, then slowly shut the door.

Gretchen knew that Matt did not like to discuss the current difficulties he was having with his kids with her, but maybe it was time to take the bull by the horns whether he liked it or not. It was pretty clear this situation was not going to get resolved by itself, at least not anytime soon. And Gretchen, for one, thought it had dragged on long enough.

"Have you heard from Luke and Sassy?" Gretchen asked as she and Matt gravitated back to the living room, where a fire was still burning in the grate.

"Not since the blowup, no," Matt confirmed as he sank down on the sofa beside her.

Gretchen turned toward him, her cheek resting against the hardness of his shoulder. "Have you tried?"

He nodded and absently stroked her hair. "I've left messages on their machines at school."

So had Gretchen. "And?"

He dropped his hand. "They haven't called back."

Her, either. Gretchen exhaled wearily. Once again, they were headed into tumultuous territory. "So what are you going to do?"

Matt shrugged and pushed away from the sofa restlessly. "The only thing I can. Wait."

"Matt..."

"As much as I would like to do so, Gretchen," he countered quietly, almost apologetically, "I can't force them to feel good about the new baby."

Nor could she. Gretchen watched him remove the fire screen and kneel before the grate. The disappointment he felt showing on his ruggedly handsome face, he picked up the poker and arranged the burning logs more efficiently. Finished, he put the poker back in the firestand and replaced the screen. Dusting off his hands, he turned back to her, his expression grim but accepting as he leaned against the mantel.

Gretchen shook her head sadly. She lifted her eyes to his. "This is all my fault," she whispered.

"No, it's not." He closed the distance between them and, pulling up the ottoman, sat down opposite her. He covered her hand with his and continued softly, "What's happening between us began years ago, when my marriage to Vivian first began going bad."

Needing to hear about this, Gretchen leaned forward raptly. "And that was when exactly?"

"When the kids were in junior high. She was really restless, tired of the status quo." He tightened his hand over hers. Recalling, he shook his head grimly. "I'd had some lucrative offers for Hale Drilling and she wanted me to sell my business so that we could concentrate on living the good life." His lips set unhappily. "When I refused, she became increasingly restless. She began taking off for days at a time, just to get away, to think. The kids began to get a little nervous. Maybe I should have let her go then," Matt said, the hurt he'd felt reflected in his eyes.

"But all I could think about was the happy, solid upbringing I'd had as a kid and how much I wanted that for my children." Matt grimaced. "So I pressured her into staying in the marriage until all our kids were finished with high school. I promised her that if she did, I'd be much more generous in the divorce settlement."

"So you knew all along it was going to end," Gretchen stated cautiously. *Just as we know our marriage is going to end.*

Matt shook his head. "I kept thinking this was just a phase she was going through, a midlife crisis. I thought all I had to do was try hard enough and everything would work out, that we'd be able to sort through our problems and keep our family together."

"But it didn't work," Gretchen guessed. Realizing how much Matt had been hurt, her heart went out to him.

"Not only that, our staying together was ultimately harder on the kids." Again he shook his head in silent regret. "The turmoil bubbling just below the surface left them feeling more insecure, unhappy, than they would have otherwise." Matt clamped his lips together in weary self-remonstration. "I should have let Vivian go when she first wanted out of the marriage. But then, hindsight is always better."

Gretchen nodded, understanding. She had made her own share of mistakes. She knew how hard it was to give up on a marriage, even one that wasn't working. She linked hands with him. "If only we knew then, what we know now."

Their eyes met.

Another, longer, silence fell between them, and the peace that came with understanding each other a little more.

"About ready to go up to bed?" he asked finally.

Gretchen nodded as he got to his feet. She was as eager to leave their tumultuous romantic pasts behind, and move into the future as he was. She rose gracefully. "I just need to get a glass of milk and take my prenatal vitamins."

"I'll bring the milk up to you," he offered, before she could even start in the direction of the kitchen.

"All right. I'll meet you in the bedroom."

Gretchen had just slipped off her sweater and tugged a thigh-length flannel nightshirt over her head, when Matt came in and set the tray on the bed. He'd brought a glass of milk for himself, and a small plate of oatmeal-raisin cookies. When she grinned at the sweet treat, he shrugged offhandedly and said, "What's life without a little indulgence now and then?"

Gretchen sat down and kicked off her tennis shoes. One thing they'd found out about each other quickly was that they both liked cookies and milk before bed each night. "Somehow I knew you'd say that," she murmured.

Matt caught a glimpse of the garments hanging in the front of her walk-in closet, price tags still attached. "New clothes?"

Gretchen nodded as she slipped off her slacks.

"I didn't know you'd been shopping."

She sat down on the edge of the bed and began her twice daily ritual of smoothing lotion on her legs and arms. "Marissa and I went the other day."

He pointed to the price tags. "You haven't worn them yet," he noted.

Gretchen defended herself staunchly. "I'm working up to it." She didn't know why, but she felt a little shy about him seeing her in maternity clothes.

He looked through, finding only two pairs of slacks and two shirts, then turned back to her, watching intently as she rubbed lotion over one calf. "That's all you got?"

Gretchen put a final dollop of scented lotion on her palm and recapped the bottle. "There wasn't much selection." *At least in my price range.*

His expression gentled as she transferred the lotion to both palms and smoothed it over her forearms. "Maybe I should go with you," he suggested. "Help out, drive you around. At least help pay for them—"

Blushing, Gretchen held up both hands in stop sign fashion. "No...no...." This was her expense. She'd taken enough from Matt as it was. He was also going to be footing the hospital costs for both her and the baby. Besides, it was bad enough Marissa had seen her in one fashion disaster after another.

"Gretchen, you need more clothes than this," Matt insisted.

"Not to worry." Gretchen bounded off the bed and, clad only in socks and nightshirt, raced into the adjacent bath. She picked up her hairbrush and began running it through her hair. "Angela promised to help me find some material, when we were doing the dishes tonight. I think we're going to sew most of my other maternity clothes. That way I can have exactly what I want."

Matt, who'd followed her to the door of the master bath, quirked a brow. "Particular, hmm?"

Gretchen made a face. "As if you're not," she retorted.

"So, what about your new clothes?" He folded his arms in front of him and braced a shoulder against the frame. "Going to model them for me?"

"One of these days." When I work up the nerve.

He sauntered closer. "You're blushing."

"No." Gretchen spun away.

Hand on her shoulder, he spun her back. "You're self-conscious about being seen in maternity clothes."

"No. Well, yes." Gretchen held her hairbrush in front of her in a two-handed grip. "All right, I am."

He studied her upturned face and asked softly, lovingly, "How come?"

Gretchen's heart pounded at his nearness. She wished he didn't see so much. "I don't know." She wet her suddenly dry lips. *I just don't want things to change between us.*

"It won't make a difference," Matt said, reading her mind. He stroked a hand down her hair, teasing gently, "I'm going to desire you to my dying day."

Keeping her eyes locked on his, Gretchen put her hairbrush aside. "We'll see," she replied cautiously, but inside her heart was already soaring.

His eyes sparked with an ardor that promised many more nights of passionate lovemaking. "Probably," he drawled.

Gretchen tossed him a sassy look. "Help me turn down the bed," she ordered playfully, already anticipating what was going to happen next.

He saluted her, his mood just as playful. "Yes, ma'am."

They had just positioned themselves on opposite sides of the king-size bed and begun to turn down the bedspread, when Gretchen felt it. A tiny flutter, like a quickening. "Oh!" Startled, she put her hand to her tummy.

"What?" Matt looked instantly alarmed.

"My God." Gretchen froze. There it went again.

He leapt across the bed to her side. "What is it?" he demanded, his face ashen.

Gretchen took his hand and put it on her tummy. No sooner had his palm flattened over her skin than she felt it again. A slight flutter. Kind of like a... a kick?

"The baby moved," Matt whispered, as awestruck as she was. "Gretchen... our baby moved."

Without warning, happy tears were flowing down Gretchen's face. "I can't believe it," she murmured, feeling completely overcome with maternal pride.

"This is the first time then?" Matt asked hoarsely, his eyes shimmering as their baby kicked again and yet again.

Gretchen nodded excitedly, joyful tears still sliding down her cheeks, and let out a shaky laugh. She looked down at the curve of her belly. Suddenly, losing her shape did not seem the tragedy that it had in the dressing room. Suddenly, she thought it was a very good thing. She patted the curve of her belly affectionately. "I think he's a rodeo star."

Matt grinned. "She might be a girl, you know."

Without warning, the fluttering faded, then disappeared altogether. Her heart still racing with a mixture of joy and excitement, Gretchen waited and waited. Nothing happened. "Oh," she said, disappointed as the moments drew out, one after another, with no further baby activity. The corners of her mouth turned down sadly. "She's stopped."

Matt's elation hadn't faded in the least. Every inch the proud papa, he said, "Trust me, it won't be too long before she's doing gymnastics in there at all hours of every day and night."

Gretchen couldn't wait. "Oh, Matt," she murmured, so glad he was there to share this miracle with her. "I've never felt anything so great."

Face full of wonder, Matt agreed. "That's because it's not a pregnancy anymore, or a cause for morning sickness and leg cramps and all sorts of other indignities. It's a baby."

"A real, live, kicking, playing baby," Gretchen finished through her tears. *Their baby.*

Wrapping an arm about her shoulders, Matt bent and kissed her tenderly. "You are beautiful, you know that? Beautiful and incredibly radiant."

So are you, Gretchen thought, the sentimental tears flowing down her face all the harder. She launched herself all the way into his arms and hugged him hard. "Oh, Matt. Thank you," she whispered against his shirtfront, holding him close. "Thank you so much." Standing on tiptoe, she kissed him joyously, fully, on the mouth.

Matt threaded his fingers through her hair, trailed a hand down her face. "For what?" he asked softly.

Gretchen splayed her hands across his chest. Beneath her fingers, she could feel the strong, steady beat of his heart. She could feel for herself what a solid, wonderful man Matt was. "For being here. For the baby." *For everything.*

"Oh, that." He grinned at the memory. "That was my pleasure."

Their look lengthened longingly.

"Mine, too," Gretchen replied.

Matt glanced at her tummy, then her face, before his expression became completely unreadable once again. Gretchen would've given anything to know what he was really thinking and feeling at that moment, but once more he had reined in his emotions, worries and concerns and put up a firewall she couldn't cross. It was as though he would allow them to become so close, and then he would stop.

"Don't forget to take your vitamins," he reminded her gently.

She nodded, knowing as did he, how important it was that she take care of herself and the baby. "Right."

Realizing they'd never been so emotional, so vulnerable around each other, thinking that perhaps this was what was bothering him, that their temporary coparenting/shared-space arrangement was beginning to seem a little too permanent, Gretchen pulled herself together and turned away. She drank her milk and swallowed her pill.

Still unusually quiet, Matt went to brush his teeth. He returned clad only in his boxers and helped her finish turning down the bed. They climbed in on their respective sides. He set the alarm and switched off the light.

They lay on their backs in the darkness. Hand on her tummy, Gretchen waited for another kick, another flutter. But none came. She waited for Matt to go to sleep. That didn't happen, either. They just lay there, the moonlight streaming over them in ribbons of iridescent light.

"Matt?" Gretchen murmured after a while.

"Hmm?"

She stared at the ceiling, knowing she had to ask, even if she wouldn't like the answer. "Do you think it's possible to have a good marriage—a real marriage—without traditional romantic love?" Or were they fooling themselves into thinking this could actually work...on any level?

Matt rolled onto his side and smoothed a hand down her hip. "So far it seems to be an effective and successful arrangement for us," he replied cautiously, feeling an overall contentment.

But right now was a very magical time, Gretchen thought wistfully. She turned toward him, laying a hand on his chest, as the doubts and fears that had been with her since she had first agreed to marry him for the baby's sake began to crowd her thoughts. She bit her lip uncertainly. "But when the baby's born..."

"That's a long way away," Matt reminded her as he shifted toward her impatiently and drew her into his arms. He aligned her against him, surrounding her with his warmth. "A lot can happen between now and then."

Gretchen splayed her hand across the downy mat of hair on his chest. "But—"

His kiss was his reply. Saved from further discussion, Gretchen lost herself in the wonder of the passion they shared. This was enough, she thought, for now. It had to be enough. For their baby's sake, for her own, she couldn't, wouldn't, allow herself to think any other way.

MATT LAY in the darkness, a sleeping Gretchen cuddled in his arms, his body sated from their lovemaking. He knew he had taken the coward's way out by cutting short their conversation, instead making love to her with every ounce of passion and tenderness he possessed.

She'd given him no choice.

He didn't want to think about her leaving him once the baby was born and she no longer needed him to see her through her pregnancy.

Maybe their splitting up was inevitable, given the circumstances of their involvement, but he wouldn't think about it now or let that spoil things. Right now, he wanted to stay in the present, enjoy the moment, savor having Gretchen in his life, carrying his child. As for everything else . . . they had already discovered they had more than just a baby in common, that they lived together well and got on great.

Who really knew what the future would bring? They had five more months in which to work things out. Five more months in which miracles could happen. . . .

Chapter Ten

May

"Gretchen, are you comfortable?" Marissa asked, as she turned on the ultrasound equipment.

Gretchen took Matt's hand, glad he had come to this doctor's appointment with her. "My position on the table is fine," Gretchen replied, working to curtail the edge of nervous anticipation in her voice. "I don't know about the rest of me," she confided wryly as Matt squeezed her hand reassuringly. "All that water I drank twenty minutes ago is beginning to weigh on me." She felt as though she'd been driving on a freeway for hours with no rest stop in sight.

"Ah, yes, I remember *that* feeling well from my own pregnancies," Marissa quipped back as she spread a film of gel over Gretchen's abdomen. "But hang on. The pictures we're going to see in a few minutes will make you forget all about the discomfort."

"What's the gel for?" Matt asked as he settled more comfortably on the stool they'd brought in for him.

"It improves the conduction of sound." Marissa turned on the TV monitor and the nurse moved around to adjust the screen so Matt and Gretchen and Marissa could all see it easily.

Marissa held up a medical instrument with a long cord. "This is a transducer," Marissa explained. "I'm going to move it over your tummy and it's going to record echoes of sound waves as they bounce off parts of the baby. From that, we'll see a picture on the television screen."

"Will it hurt?" Gretchen asked.

"Nope. Not a bit," Marissa said.

All eyes turned to the screen. "Oh, my gosh," Gretchen said as a blurry picture of a gently moving baby began to appear. "Is that...is that the baby?" she asked, incredulous.

"Yes. If you look here," Marissa said softly, pointing out a small, throbbing area in the center of the baby's chest, "you can even see your little one's heart beating. And here's the curve of the spine...the head...the arms...and the legs."

"Wow," Matt breathed. Like Gretchen, he was unable to take his eyes off the screen. "The technology is so much better these days than when I had my other kids."

Marissa grinned, every bit as happy about the advances in technology. "Isn't it, though," she said softly.

"This is so incredible," Gretchen said, totally blown away by the enormity of actually seeing, not just feeling, her baby in her womb. "I can see the baby. I can see everything!"

"Mmm-hmm. Even the sex," Marissa said, smiling, moving her pointer lower still. "It's a—"

"Boy," Matt and Gretchen said in unison.

"Oh, my gosh, Matt, we have a son." Tears sparkled in her eyes as she turned to look up at him.

"Incredible," Matt murmured in a choked voice, looking down at Gretchen. Again he squeezed her hand. Gretchen knew she had never seen him happier than he appeared at that moment. She knew exactly how he felt. This had to be one of the very best moments of her life, too.

"You all decided on any names?" Marissa asked as the nurse stepped forward to help take some measurements of the image on the screen.

"No, not really," Matt said as Marissa took a picture of the screen and the nurse handed them the developing Polaroid.

"Now that we know, though, I guess we could go ahead and decide," Gretchen said as she admired the black-and-white photograph of the baby in utero.

Matt grinned. "I guess we could at that."

"Well, you'll both be glad to hear everything is okay. Your son is progressing right on schedule, and it appears the due date is what we initially thought, around the twenty-third of September, give or take a few days either way."

"Yeah, well..." Matt began, grinning.

"We never had any doubt about that," Gretchen finished.

"SO WHAT do you think—about names, I mean?" Gretchen asked Matt as he drove them home in his Jeep. Tearing her eyes from the beautiful Texas wildflowers growing on either side of the highway, she turned to face him. "Do you want to get a baby book and figure out one from that or go the more sentimental route?"

Matt decided he might as well be honest. "I wanted to name the baby after our parents."

Gretchen smiled at him radiantly. She was wearing that tan-and-white striped maternity outfit. Her mahogany hair curled softly around her shoulders and gleamed in the sunshine. Excited color filled her cheeks. She had never looked prettier or more content, Matt thought. He felt good knowing he'd had a hand in giving her the child she had always wanted.

"I want that, too," she admitted softly.

"My dad's name was Zach," Matt said, as they passed numerous families photographing their children—and occasionally even their pets—in the thick fields of Texas bluebonnets and Indian paintbrush that bordered the hillsides in and around Austin.

"My dad's name was Devin."

"Devin Zach?" Matt suggested, as he passed yet another mom and dad snapping photos of their toddler romping in the wildflowers.

"Actually, I like Zach Devin a lot better," Gretchen said.

Matt contemplated the sound of that a moment, even as he wondered if he and Gretchen would one day be taking their son to the wildflowers for photos jointly, or if they would do those activities solo, as most parents without partners did. He admitted he was hoping for the former. He slanted Gretchen a smile. "Zach Devin is good. Zach Devin Hale is very good," he said.

"Gosh, that was easy," Gretchen said with relief, as Matt turned in the driveway and parked his Jeep.

Matt cut the engine and unclasped his seat belt. "I know. Boggles the mind, doesn't it? How well we get along sometimes?" he said lightly as he bent toward her impulsively. He took her in his arms and was about to kiss her, when the sound of a car motor interrupted. They turned in the direction of the sound and saw Luke park behind them.

Matt felt a rush of ambivalent feelings. He had missed his son, but he was also highly irritated with him. Semester exams had been over for nearly a week. Yet Luke hadn't even bothered to call to let Matt know of his plans for the break. In fact, it had been almost two months since the two had even talked. "I was wondering if he was going to come home," Matt murmured.

Gretchen withdrew from his arms, her expression stern and maternal. "Now, Matt. He's got to be here because he wants to make peace," she chided.

"Let's hope that's the case," Matt said dryly. Inwardly, he wasn't counting on it.

They assembled in the driveway. To Matt's relief, his son was cordial as the three of them greeted one another and entered the house. As always, upon arrival, Matt and Luke gravitated toward the living room.

This time Gretchen did not follow. "You know, I think I'll go in the kitchen and start dinner," she said.

"You don't have to do that, Gretchen," Luke interjected, his manner both adult and direct. "You're Dad's wife. You can hear what I have to say to him."

Gretchen looked to Matt.

"Stay," Matt urged. He didn't know what Luke had on his mind. He did know he wanted Gretchen by his side, just as she had wanted him to be with her during the ultrasound she'd had earlier.

As uncertain about what was going to happen next as Matt, Gretchen sat down on the sofa. Matt sat next to her, with Luke in a wing chair opposite them.

Luke leaned forward in his chair, clasping his hands between his knees. "About this summer..." he began earnestly. "I've decided to stay with my original decision and not go to summer school at A & M."

Matt nodded his approval, his mind already racing ahead. "I can use you right now, either out in Lubbock on one of the drilling sites or here in town at the office and warehouse."

"Yeah, well, I don't think you should count on that."

Matt looked at Luke, sure he hadn't heard right.

"I've accepted another job this summer, Dad," Luke continued bluntly. "I'm going to be working for a private investigation agency here in town, instead."

This, Matt thought, was not good news. Gretchen felt the same, if the new tenseness in her demeanor was any indication.

"And if you give me any grief about it," Luke went on defiantly, "I may not go back to school next fall."

Matt did not abide being threatened. But he saw no reason to lose his temper, either. "Don't you think you're acting a little hastily?" he asked Luke calmly.

"No, I think I'm taking charge of my life and doing what I want to be doing, just like you are, Dad," Luke shot back.

Matt saw no reason to hide his feelings. "You know I totally disapprove of this?" he asked his son grimly.

"You know I have to follow my heart," Luke countered, just as grimly.

At the thought of a whole summer wasted, when it could easily be put to better use, Matt felt his patience waning. "Are you moving back in?" he asked curtly.

"No," Luke snapped back. "Angela said I could stay in her apartment, so that's what I'm going to do." He paused to look over at Gretchen. "You two being newlyweds and all, I figured you could use the privacy."

"You don't have to do that," Gretchen interjected, raising both hands in silent entreaty. "This is your home, too, Luke," she added softly, as her compassionate glance lasered in on his willful one. "I don't want to be responsible for pushing you out."

"You're not," Luke said frankly. He pushed to his feet and began to move about the living room restlessly, his attention still focused on Gretchen. "Dad is. If I were here all summer, he'd be haranguing me constantly to go to work for him. Frankly, I don't want to listen to it."

"That's because you know I'm right," Matt retorted hotly.

Luke blew out a weary breath and ran both hands through his tousled, unshorn hair. "Look, Dad, I love you, and I admire what you've built for yourself, but for the last time, your business does not interest me. Not in the least. P.I. work does."

Matt had known Luke long enough to realize this was just a whim. "You've never given the family business a chance," Matt countered equably.

"You're right. I haven't." Luke shoved both hands in the back pockets of his jeans. "And that should tell you something, too."

Matt frowned.

"I'm taking this job this summer. So like it or not, you're going to have to live with it," Luke decreed.

"Fine," Matt said. It'd be one less problem for him to deal with.

"Fine," Luke snapped back. "I've got to go." Without another word, he walked hurriedly toward the door. Seconds later, the front door slammed behind him.

Matt looked at Gretchen in frustration. Half an hour earlier, she had been radiant and happy. Now she was pale and upset. Worse, Matt thought, he should have seen this coming and handled it better, somehow spared Gretchen the stress of sitting in on his quarrel with his son. But he hadn't, and now he would just have to find a way to lessen the tension between them. "So much for my superior parenting ability," he said drolly.

Struggling to understand the inherent difficulties in parenting an almost grown but not quite yet independent offspring, Gretchen stood. "What does it matter what kind of summer job Luke gets as long as he's working?"

Matt did not want to argue the subject with Gretchen, too. Working to contain his aggravation, he stifled a sigh and explained, "Because I want him to learn the family business from the ground up. This is the perfect time for him to be out on the drilling sites."

"Hasn't he already done that, other summers?" Gretchen persisted as she headed toward the back of the house.

Matt nodded tersely, as she glanced over her shoulder, and followed her into the laundry room.

"Then this'll give him something to compare that with. Maybe when he spends the whole summer hunting people down and staking people out, he won't think it is so glamorous," Gretchen suggested, as she bent to take laundry out of the clothes dryer.

"I don't know about that." Matt watched as she spread the clean clothes out on the folding table. "Luke is and always has been awfully nosy."

"Well, then, maybe he is suited for—"

"Don't say it," Matt interrupted with a warning glance. "Don't even think it." He stepped forward to lend a hand with the towels.

Gretchen spun toward him. They were so close they were standing toe to toe. "What is this? So now I'm admonished to be silent, too?" Gretchen demanded.

Looking into her upturned face, Matt frowned. "It's not that," he said.

"Then what?" Gretchen cried, her eyes brimming with exasperation.

"I don't know what it is about this past year or so but none of them listens to me. I'm beginning to think I have no influence over any of my children," he lamented as he speedily folded first one towel, then another and another.

Determined not to relent, Gretchen pitched in with the sorting and folding. "Listen to me, Matt. Your kids are finding their way in the world. It's not an easy process, no matter how old or young you are."

Matt tackled the washcloths, while she mated the socks. "I know you mean well, but there is nothing you can say about this that is going to make me feel any better."

Gretchen's chin lifted. For a moment she looked as defiant and argumentative as Luke had.

"Right, and I suppose you were the perfect son when you were your kids' age?" she demanded, planting her hands on her hips.

Matt grabbed a laundry basket. "Damn straight I was."

"And you never did the slightest thing to annoy your folks?"

Matt paused as he layered stacks of clothes, to take upstairs for distribution. "That was different," he allowed reluctantly.

She tilted her head to the side, surveyed his scowl and grinned. "Hmm."

Matt waited for the teasing sure to come. He wasn't disappointed. "I'm beginning to see a whole new side of you, Matt Hale," she declared, as he picked up the basket of folded laundry and carted it up the stairs. She followed him to the linen closet in the master bathroom and perched on the marble countertop. Her hands braced on either side of her, she swung her legs back and forth. "So," she began still regarding him with a sparkling look, "what did you do to irritate your parents?"

Matt stacked the towels and washcloths on the shelf. "Nothing major."

"Mmm-hmm."

Matt turned around to face her. "Okay, so I broke curfew a few times," he admitted reluctantly, "and left the house without telling them where I was going or when I was going to be back."

"Bet that went over well," Gretchen drawled.

Chagrined, Matt rubbed the back of his neck. "Yeah, there were a few times when my mother would've liked to wring my damn fool neck." Looking back, he was surprised his folks hadn't lost their temper with him more than they had.

"And were there other instances where you disappointed them—perhaps in a more serious way?" she asked gently.

He nodded. Sobering, he took her hand in his and intertwined their fingers. "I didn't finish college." She waited, listening, really wanting to know what had happened and why. Succumbing to the compassion in her eyes, he found himself continuing intimately, "I didn't return my senior year when I was offered a cut of the profits to stay on and bring a well in. It was a gusher and I used the proceeds to start my own company. My mom and dad were disappointed." Matt shook his head unhappily. "They'd never had the opportunity to go to college at all. To see me throw it all away when they'd scraped and saved to send me to Texas A & M... well, I think it really hurt."

Gretchen took his other hand in hers. "But they must've been proud of your success in starting your own company."

His eyes on the way their fingers were entwined, Matt acknowledged that with a nod. "They were, although my company wasn't as hugely successful when they passed away as it is now. But yeah." He smiled, the satisfaction he felt for what he had built welling in him. "I think they felt I had made something of myself in the end."

Gretchen lifted his left hand to her lips and kissed the back of it gently. "Maybe Luke will do the same thing."

Even as shivers of desire went through him, Matt couldn't help but worry. "The PI business is a tough one."

"So is wildcatting," Gretchen said, moving to the edge of the countertop and all the way into his arms, "but he's got your genes, and your love." She smiled up at him. "I'm betting on him."

"Anyone ever tell you you're a born peacemaker?"

"Yep." She splayed her hands lovingly across his chest, in much the same way she did when they made love. "But I don't mind hearing it again and again and again." She lifted her lips to his. He kissed her lingeringly. "So what are your plans for today?" he asked. He knew what he wanted to do—take her to bed and spend the rest of the day and all night making mad, passionate love to her.

But as he had half suspected, Gretchen had other plans.

She leaned her head on his shoulder. "I've got to go over to my apartment building and talk to the manager about signing a new lease."

Matt frowned. "I didn't know your current lease was up."

"At the end of June," she confided matter-of-factly.

Matt tried not to think about why she wanted to re-sign a lease on a place she was no longer using. His manner casual, he asked, "Mind if I go with you?"

"Actually—" Gretchen smiled "—I'd be glad for the company."

"SO BACK TO OUR earlier conversation about what I did in my adolescence to consciously or unconsciously irk my folks," Matt said as he drove to the university. He slanted Gretchen a teasing glance. "You never got around to discussing what you did on that score."

Gretchen groaned. Matt persisted. Finally, he got her to fess up, her hands pressed against her very pink cheeks.

"Okay, okay, I confess. I refused to make my bed—and, when forced, did a very sloppy job of it."

Matt quirked a brow. The image of a much younger Gretchen, in the midst of a teenage rebellion was a compelling one. "But you make your bed these days," he said.

Embarrassed, Gretchen rolled her eyes. "That," she remarked sagely, "is because I've grown up and discovered the pleasure of climbing into a neat and tidy bed every night."

Thinking how seldom their sheets stayed neat and tidy once the two of them were between them, Matt grinned. No one, he had decided, could tangle a set of sheets and use an entire king-size bed the way they did. But back to her true confessions... "Okay. That's on the small score," he said, as they stopped at a street sign. Because there was no traffic coming in any direction, he paused to look at her. "What about on the larger score?"

"I married Robert, which, as we all know now, was a big mistake. And I mean a big mistake."

Wishing he could hold her in his arms, but knowing they'd be at her apartment in another minute and she might talk more if not distracted, Matt drove on.

"My dad told me I was too young, of course," Gretchen continued with a heartfelt sigh. She turned her gaze to the narrow tree-lined street. "He suspected that Robert was rushing me into marriage for his own convenience and needs—that he was more eager for a paid way through med school and a wife to take care of him during the long, arduous process—and not because of any real desire to be with me."

Listening to her talk, Matt hoped he never ran into "Robert," 'cause if he did he would be seriously tempted to punch the guy's lights out for hurting Gretchen the way he had.

Oblivious to his thoughts, she shook her head in regret. "I should have listened to my dad, but I didn't because I was just too young and stubborn."

Matt parked his Jeep in a shady space in front of her apartment building. He turned to her, not sure why this was important, only knowing that it was. "What would your parents think about us if they were here?"

"They'd be happy for me," Gretchen said softly, self-assuredly, as she absently brushed a speck of lint from the knee of his jeans. "They'd be happy for us."

"Even with the circumstances of our marriage being what they are?" Matt asked gently, wondering if the sheer unexpectedness of her pregnancy was still driving a wedge between them.

"Yes."

Gretchen leaned forward to kiss him on the cheek, the way Matt imagined that she might kiss an old and dear friend. Her blue eyes shining, she looked up at him.

"Because they know, as do we, that a child is a wonderful and precious gift."

"UH-OH. You have that look on your face again," Gretchen said as she entered her apartment a few minutes later.

"What look?"

"The look that says you have an opinion about something."

He didn't deny it. "Anything wrong with that?" he asked as he shut the door behind them.

"Plenty, when it doesn't concur with mine." Gretchen opened the drapes. The golden glow of the sun on a summer evening poured in the room.

"In this case, I've got a valid point," he countered amiably.

"Which is...?"

Matt braced a hip against the back of the sofa and watched as she went through the mail that had accumulated the past two days. "I'm not sure you should renew your lease."

Gretchen paused in the act of opening her electric bill. "Matt, I was on a waiting list for two years to get this apartment. It's within easy walking distance of all my classes."

His mouth curved briefly. "And you're hardly ever here anymore."

Gretchen looked around with a sigh, knowing he was right. She hadn't been there much. The apartment was dusty, the air stale, the plants in need of watering. "Well, that was certainly true in May. I mean, I had a two-and-a-half-week break between spring and summer terms."

"And since the first summer term started two weeks ago?" Matt prodded, a gleam in his eyes.

Gretchen shrugged, the electric-bill envelope still in her hands. "I lucked out. All my classes arc back to back. I can come here, go to class and go home."

"Exactly. Home isn't here anymore, Gretchen. Home is with me, in Westlake Hills."

Gretchen eyed Matt cautiously. "For now, yes..." she agreed reluctantly.

He levered himself away from the sofa and closed the distance between them lazily. "For as long as we both can see in the foreseeable future."

As he neared her, Gretchen had to tilt her head back to see his face. "We agreed I'd stay with you until the baby was born," she began in a low voice choked with emotion.

Matt flattened his hands on her shoulders, then swept them down her arms to her wrists. "No, we agreed we'd stay together as long as you and our baby needed me. That could be six weeks or six months or six years...."

Gretchen swallowed nervously. Matt was upsetting the delicate balance of their relationship again; she didn't like it. "Aren't you jumping the gun a bit here? Babies cry a lot. They're up all night. They have smelly diapers and mysterious rashes and they teethe and do all sorts of things."

"Exactly. And you're going to need help seeing our little one through all those things. I want to be there for you, Gretchen. I want to be there for Zach Devin. Let me be there for both of you."

"Oh, Matt..." Gretchen teared up as she let go of the half-opened envelope in her hand and watched it flutter to the small table-for-two next to her stove. She knew what her parents would think about this if they were here. *They'd think I'd found a great man and could have all the happiness they'd ever wanted for me if only he'd fall in love with me. But that was a very big if only...*

Matt hooked a foot beneath the rung of one chair and pulled it out. In one economical motion, he sank onto the chair, circled his arm about her waist and drew her down into his lap. "I know I'm pushing you and I said I wouldn't do that."

Gretchen laced one arm about his neck and flattened the other across his chest. Beneath the soft cotton of his shirt, his chest was warm and solid. She felt very safe in his arms, very much cared for and about. "Then why are you?" She fastened her eyes on his.

Matt contemplated her for a long moment. "I guess it has to do with the way I grew up, the way I know you grew up, in a warm, loving home with two parents who adored you and lots of laughter and familial support. I don't want Zach Devin growing up without all that, do you?"

No, she didn't. "This is because of your fight with Luke, isn't it? Because you're more or less on the outs with all your kids."

His lips thinned. "I readily admit that I feel I failed them in some ways. I won't fail Zach Devin if I can help it."

Duty again. Gretchen worked to suppress a sigh of supreme disappointment as she launched herself off his lap and began to pace the room restlessly. "Aren't you forgetting one little thing?" Gretchen asked, deliberately keeping her voice light, noncommittal. No use adding embarrassment to injury. It wasn't as if they were actually in love with each other...was it? "Marriage isn't ever easy, under even the best of circumstances. And to know that we only have to look back and remember," she reminded him sadly. "We both went into out first marriages with all sorts of romantic expectations. We were both deeply in love with our mates, right?"

"Right."

"And yet we still both had spouses who fell out of love with us in the course of the marriage."

"You can't compare our previous situations with our situation now," Matt said slowly, beginning to feel very unhappy again.

Gretchen released a troubled sigh. "I don't want to be hurt, Matt." The hurt and humiliation she'd felt when her marriage to Robert ended had been staggering, and she hadn't felt half as passionately about Robert then as she did about Matt now.

Matt began to relax. "You don't have to worry about that, Gretchen." He stood and replaced the chair.

Silence fell between them, more complicated and intense than before. Matt drew her gently into his arms. "I know this is a confusing situation."

"And then some."

Cupping a hand beneath her chin, he tilted her face up to his. "I also know there are no guarantees here. Only risks," he soothed. "But I think they are risks worth taking. Not just for the baby, but for us. No one's going to love Zach Devin the way we will, Gretchen, not from the very first, not he way we already do." He paused, then continued per-uasively, "Don't we owe it to ourselves to see if we can't ransfer some of that magic to our relationship? Don't we we it to ourselves to see if we can't make this marriage vork on an even higher level, even if we do so gradually?"

Still wrapped in the warmth of Matt's embrace, Gretchen nulled over what he'd said. There was no doubt about it; he first five and a half months of her pregnancy had been ough on both of them, full of turmoil and change, but also ull of wonder and love. Especially lately. "You mean let ur love for the baby expand to include ourselves in a sort f familial way?" Gretchen asked.

Matt's eyes were dark and fathomless, then ever so slowly hey began to light. "That's how families are made." He raced the curve of her cheek with the pad of his thumb. Still tudying her, he murmured thoughtfully, "It's worth a shot, lon't you think?"

"If it provides a loving home for Zach Devin, yes. But if t doesn't work out..."

Matt leaned forward to kiss her brow in a swift, reassur-ing manner, before he promised, "Then as I said before, we'll look back and know we tried. And that things have enfolded the way they're meant to be. But in the meantime, Zach Devin will have a great start with two parents who love him more than life."

Gretchen had to admit the rent she was paying on the apartment was taking a great dent out of her savings. And these days she was hardly ever there. "I guess I could al-ways get another apartment if and when the time comes," she offered slowly, amazed as always at how easily Matt could talk her in or out of things.

Matt grinned. He hugged her close. "You won't regret it," he promised happily.

Gretchen hoped he was right about that, because she was now walking the high wire of an unexpected pregnancy and forced marriage, without a net.

GRETCHEN LEANED over Matt and shook her head. "Matt, I don't think you should put that there," she warned solemnly.

"Sweetheart," Matt replied, not bothering to hide his growing exasperation with her. "I've done this before—numerous times."

"I know, but everything's different these days," Gretchen said anxiously, glancing over to study the paper-clipped pages of the instruction manual.

"Not that different," Matt drawled with a sexy please-let's-cooperate-here wink.

"Want to bet?" Gretchen quipped, as a film of perspiration broke out on first Matt's forehead, then hers. She didn't know how Matt felt, but this was so much harder than she had anticipated!

"Just...hold it in place," Matt instructed firmly, albeit a little breathlessly. "Let me...yes...all right." He slid around on his back, moving his upper torso slightly to the left of Gretchen. "That's perfect." He leaned back to view his handiwork.

Gretchen looked at the same thing and knew they still had much to test out. She thought of the homework she had left to do that evening and bit her lip uncertainly. Maybe she shouldn't have insisted they get started on this right away, or that she and Matt do everything together from now on, including this. "How much longer do you think this is going to take?" she asked worriedly.

Matt shook his head, glancing back at the manual. "I'm not sure. A while."

"Maybe we should've started with something easier," she said. She didn't want their first truly mutual, planned effort to be a disaster.

He put a reassuring hand on her arm. "Rome wasn't built in an hour, Gretchen. And neither will this crib be...."

"OH, MATT, it's gorgeous," Gretchen breathed, two more weeks of part-time labor and endless planning later. "I've never seen a more beautiful nursery."

Matt surveyed what had once been the guest room with a deeply felt satisfaction he knew Gretchen shared. "We did a great job, didn't we?"

"We certainly did." Gretchen tucked an arm around his waist.

Liking the easy way she touched him—she initiated physical contact as much as he did these days—Matt wrapped his arm around her shoulder as they surveyed the new kid-proof medium blue carpet, white waist-high wainscoting and lighter blue walls. The bleached-oak baby furniture they'd painstakingly assembled was arranged practically, the closet transformed with additional shelves for toys and baby linens and appropriately spaced hanging rods for baby-size clothing. An alphabet border and a Sesame Street mural on one wall further brightened up the nursery.

Beaming, Gretchen turned to face him. The softness of her breasts pressed against his chest.

"I worried that shade of blue we picked out for the new curtains was going to be too light, but you're right," she announced delightedly. "It's perfect."

Matt grinned as he surveyed the excited color in her cheeks. When she looked at him like that he wondered how he had ever gotten along without her. "I've got one more surprise for you," he promised, kissing the top of her head. "Wait here."

Short minutes later, he came back with a Bentwood rocker in the same bleached wood as the nursery furniture.

"Oh, Matt, a rocking chair." Gretchen's eyes shone with happiness.

Matt had no trouble picturing Gretchen in it, their baby in her arms. The vision brought a lump to his throat. "Every new mother needs one. Sit down and try it out."

She launched herself into the chair and rocked back and forth gently, her eyes shutting briefly in silent accolade. "It's wonderful. Thank you." Her eyes misting, she braced a hand on the arm and gracefully levered herself to a standing position. Leaning forward, so her expanding tummy was between them, she stood on tiptoe, wreathed her arms about his neck and kissed him soundly on the mouth. "It's like all my dreams are coming true," she said softly.

Matt wrapped his arms around her. "Mine, too," he admitted huskily. How could he ever have thought he didn't want to do this all again? Gretchen...the baby...had brought new vivacity to his life. The thought of losing her brought an unexpected desperation to his life.

Gretchen hugged him harder. "Oh, Matt," she murmured in a contented voice. "We're really doing this, aren't we? We're building a family and a home and a marriage for our child, and we're doing it against impossible odds."

Matt knew in his case the odds weren't that impossible. He wasn't sure when it happened...if it had been the night he had pulled her out of the wrecked car, or the night he had first made love to her, or the night she had moved into his bedroom for the duration of her pregnancy, but somewhere along the way, he had fallen in love with her. Deeply, irrevocably in love with her. Somewhere along the way, he had stopped being able to imagine ever being happy without her.

The trick was going to be in finding a way to make her love him back, to make her want to share their life, not just for Zach Devin's sake, but for their own. He had promised he wouldn't pressure her. And he wouldn't. But that didn't mean he wouldn't work on it gradually. And the nursery was only part of his strategy to make Gretchen fall in love with him.

"Yes," Matt said, folding Gretchen even closer. "We are."

Chapter Eleven

June

"What do you think, Gretchen?"

Gretchen twirled in front of the full-length mirror in the master bedroom. She was six and a half months pregnant, she had gained almost fifteen pounds and she couldn't believe how slim she looked in the silky navy blue maternity dress Angela had designed and sewn for her. "You're a genius, Angela," she said gratefully, unable to resist checking out the view from all sides once more. "The fabric, color and style are perfect for me."

Angela grinned. "I'm glad you like it."

Gretchen returned to Angela's side so her stepdaughter could finish pinning the hem. "Your fashion design classes must really be helping you."

Angela nodded. "I'm really enjoying them, especially the sewing part. But as good as my professors are, I don't think they're responsible for my flair for this." She waved vaguely at Gretchen's tea-length dress. "I get that from Dad's mother. She's the one who taught me how to sew. She was a seamstress, you know. Worked at the best department store in Lubbock, altering men's suits, and sewing formals and wedding dresses for her private clientele."

"Matt never mentioned that."

Angela put in the last pin, then stepped back to admire her handiwork. "He doesn't talk about sewing much," she said distractedly. "It's not his thing."

"When are you going to tell him that you're switching your major again, this time for good?"

Angela made a face as she began gathering up her things. "I think that news can wait."

"Maybe you're right," Gretchen conceded, as Angela stuffed a pincushion and scissors in her sewing kit. "Although sooner or later he's going to figure it out."

"Normally, I'd agree with you there," Angela murmured as she rerolled her measuring tape, "but lately he's been so preoccupied with the coming baby that he hasn't even asked me what classes I signed up to take this summer."

Gretchen felt a flash of guilt. She knew she had taken up quite a bit of Matt's time the past few months and added even more strain to what he promised was a temporarily difficult and complex period of time for his nearly grown children.

"Well, I know one thing. He's been very impressed by the clothes you've sewn for me the past two months." Angela had added three pairs of slacks, three pairs of shorts and four tailored menswear-style shirts to Gretchen's wardrobe, all in mix-and-match colors that allowed her to make the most of what she had.

"I'm hoping that if he sees what I can do, this will soften him up, too." Angela grimaced, feeling suddenly older than her twenty-four years. "So he doesn't hit the roof again, when I do tell him, you know?"

Gretchen touched her stepdaughter's arm gently. "He doesn't mean to lose patience, Angela."

"I know. On the other hand—" Angela blew out a weary breath "—he does have a right to be a little frustrated with me. I have been working toward an undergraduate degree for six years now." She shook her head. "Most parents would've cut me off long ago. But not Dad. He just keeps hanging in there."

Yes, Gretchen thought, Matt did. She slipped out of the dress and handed it to Angela. "Have you heard from Sassy lately?"

Angela reached for a hanger. "Yes. I talk to her about every week. You know this is the first summer she hasn't come home to work in that law firm, don't you?"

Gretchen nodded. As Angela hung up the dress, she slipped on her maternity jeans and an old white oxford-cloth dress shirt of Matt's that he had lent her.

"Matt told me that she had elected to go to summer school at SMU, instead." Gretchen paused as she buttoned the shirt, then admitted wistfully, "I wish she and Matt would patch things up." It was obvious to Gretchen that the continuing cold war between them was bothering Matt a lot, even though he refused to talk about it in depth.

"Not much chance of that at the moment," Angela declared as she perched, Indian-style, on the edge of the bed. "She's pretty angry with Dad for not leveling with her about the baby and everything."

Gretchen sat opposite Angela. "Do you think it would help if I talked to her?" Gretchen asked. "Told her how confused everything was for us at that point?"

"I don't know, Gretchen. With Sassy, it could go either way. And if you made things worse... Let's just say Dad would not be a happy camper."

"True."

"But back to my studies. Would you—Dad!" Angela broke off as Matt appeared in the doorway of the master bedroom. She turned slightly pink. "I didn't know you were home."

"Just got in." He smiled at the sewing basket. "Sewing for Gretchen again?"

Angela nodded proudly. Bounding off the bed, she held up the navy blue maternity dress. "What do you think?"

"It's very nice." Matt sauntered farther into the room. He looked from one to the other with curiosity, then drawled casually, "So what were you two talking about just now?"

Gretchen and Angela exchanged a glance. It was clear from the pleading look in Angela's eyes that Angela wasn't ready to confide in her father yet. "Nothing much," Gretchen said, and immediately felt all the more guilty for keeping something from Matt.

"You look a little flustered," Matt observed.

"We're just surprised to see you." Gretchen took a deep breath. With effort, she forced herself to meet his perceptive gaze with a welcoming smile. "Why are you home so early in the day?" she asked. "I wasn't expecting you for several hours."

Without warning, Matt frowned unhappily. "I've got to go out of town. Tonight," he specified, looking even more reluctant to leave.

Gretchen understood Matt's ambivalence. He wanted to protect her and the baby as much as possible. Even when it wasn't necessary. "Need any help packing?" she asked gently, already knowing she would miss him terribly, too.

"If you wouldn't mind." Matt looked very stressed. "I don't have much time to catch my flight. And I'm going to need a suit, so I've got to iron a dress shirt, too."

"I'll do that for you." Gretchen set up the ironing board as he brought out a bag. She plugged in the iron and switched it on as Angela tactfully excused herself to go downstairs and work on the hem.

"You two are getting along well," Matt said, once he and Gretchen were alone in the master bedroom.

Gretchen nodded, her joy over that apparent. "Angela's very sweet. She's really welcomed me to the family with open arms."

Matt quirked a brow. "Unlike her siblings?"

"Luke's warming up a little every time I see him," Gretchen said, wishing her and the new baby's assimilation into his ready-made family had gone a little easier.

"But not Sassy," Matt said grimly.

"She'll come around, you'll see. But back to your trip." Gretchen followed Matt into the bathroom and watched him run a cordless shaver over his face. "How long will you be gone?"

"I'm not sure. Maybe a couple of nights." Finished, Matt snapped the cover on his razor and slapped on some after-shave. He turned to her, his eyes brooding. "I wish I didn't have to go. But there's no help for it," he confided sadly, laying his hands on her shoulders briefly before sliding them over her spine. "We've got a major contract on the line in Amarillo and the landowner won't sign unless he meets with me personally."

Gretchen fought for composure as she let him draw her close. She placed her head on his shoulder, savoring his warmth and his strength. She was not going to break down in sobs just because they had to sleep apart for the first time in months, although she would miss him terribly, and maybe more than she had a right to. "I understand," she said in a muffled voice. Her fingers curled more tightly into the fabric of his shirt.

Matt drew back, but kept his arms locked around her waist. "I don't think you do," he said huskily as he searched her eyes. "I don't want to be away from you at all."

The implications of that statement had her reeling. Could it be a miracle was happening? Could it be their marriage was turning into a real one? Warning herself not to jump to any conclusions, Gretchen asked warily, "This isn't going to be another two-and-a-half-week trip, is it?"

"No. I won't let it. In fact," he continued determinedly, "I plan to be back here forty-eight hours from now. So you can count on seeing me in time for dinner that evening. Meanwhile, I'll call every night." Matt hugged her tenderly. "And I'll miss you," he whispered against her hair, holding her close.

Happy tears glittered in Gretchen's eyes. He might not love her yet, but they were getting so close. It was only a matter of time. She hugged him back and replied thickly, "I'll miss you, too."

"LET ME GET this straight. You're not telling Dad you're flying up to Dallas while he's gone," Angela said the following afternoon as she drove Gretchen to the Austin airport after class.

Gretchen nodded confidently as Angela maneuvered the three lanes of through traffic leading up to the terminal. "There's no reason he needs to know at this point, particularly since my dinner with Sassy might not go all that well. If it works out, of course I'll tell him what I've done."

Angela pulled into a spot against the curb in the loading zone and shifted into park. "Is it okay for you to fly?"

Gretchen smiled. In this regard, Angela was every bit as fiercely overprotective as her father. "Marissa says it's fine."

Angela nodded. "So when are you coming back?"

"On the first inexpensive commuter flight out tomorrow morning. I'll be back in time for my first class." Trying not to feel too much like a double agent on a secret mission, that of reuniting Matt and his estranged youngest child, Gretchen thrust a folded piece of paper at Angela. "Here's the name of the hotel where I'm staying, in case anything comes up on this end and you need to reach me."

Angela glanced at the paper, then slipped it into her purse as a shuttle bus rolled by in the outer lane. "Is Dad supposed to call you tonight to check in?"

"No, I'm calling him. I told him I wouldn't be in earlier because I was having dinner with his daughter."

"And he assumed by 'daughter' you meant me," Angela said.

"Right. So if he should get to you before I get ahold of him..."

Angela smiled, promising, "I'll cover for you."

Gretchen pushed open the passenger door with one hand and grabbed her slim carryon and her purse with the other. "I feel really guilty about this."

Angela soothed her with a glance. "Your heart's in the right place. Maybe Sassy will finally notice that, too."

Gretchen sighed, knowing how much of her future happiness was staked to achieving a good result on her peacemaking mission. "I hope so," she said earnestly.

Angela's eyes, so like her father's, shone encouragingly. "Have a good trip," she said softly.

Gretchen leaned over and gave Angela a maternal hug goodbye, aware that in marrying Matt she had gained at least one friend. "See you tomorrow."

MATT KNEW it was ridiculous for him to be worrying so much, but he couldn't help it. He hadn't been gone overnight since that first month they were married. If he had to be out of town, he left and came back in the same day so they wouldn't have to spend any time apart. He had hoped Luke would be around this summer to act as his eyes and ears and to help pick up the slack, but that wasn't happening.

In the meantime, something was going on with Angela and Gretchen. They had looked as guilty as hell and had cut off whatever it was they'd been discussing when he'd walked in unexpectedly yesterday afternoon. It was as if they had a secret... a mutual secret.

And that took him back to the waning days of his marriage to Vivian. Vivian had enlisted the kids in keeping things from him just prior to the divorce.

He knew it was wrong for him to compare the two women. They were as different as night and day. Forever restless and dissatisfied with life and with him, Vivian had wanted to get out of the house, to get away. By then, she had been cheating on him with her present husband, but the kids hadn't known that. All the kids had known was that she needed for them to help her achieve some personal space and time away from the house and from Matt because she felt trapped by their life together.

The way Gretchen felt trapped by the baby?

No. He was being ridiculous. So what if Gretchen and Angela were spending a lot of time together. So what if every time they thought he wasn't within earshot or eyesight lately, they bent their heads together and had whispered conferences about something they were loath to disclose to him. It meant nothing. Women did that all the time, right? They talked about feminine stuff... periods, cramps... who knows what. It meant nothing. It was just stuff they didn't want men to hear about.

He was being ridiculous.

All he had to do to achieve some renewed peace of mind was to get home as soon as possible, make sure everything was all right, breathe a sigh of relief and move on, away from the heartbreak and disillusionment of the past. What had happened before was not going to happen again, he told himself firmly.

"I DON'T KNOW what you hope to gain coming here," Sassy began cantankerously, as they met for dinner in the Galleria Mall.

"How about peace in the family?"

Gretchen's remark was met by silence. She tried again, saying gently, "Sassy, your dad misses you so much."

Hurt shimmered in Sassy's eyes. "I doubt that," she mumbled impatiently.

Gretchen winced at the accusation in her stepdaughter's words. "Sassy—" she began as amiably as possible.

"Look, Gretchen," Sassy interrupted, taking a sip of her iced tea. "He doesn't need me around anymore. And why should he? He's got a new family now. A new wife, a baby on the way."

"Yes, he does," Gretchen countered gently. "But that doesn't erase everything he feels for you, Sassy. He still needs you and loves you, and he always will."

Sassy stabbed at her salad with her fork. "Then why did he side with you against me?"

It was Gretchen's turn to be silent. She didn't know what to say without making matters worse. Pointing out Matt had merely been instructing Sassy on familial manners and courtesy when he'd reprimanded her about her behavior toward her new stepmother was not bound to help the situation any.

So Gretchen bypassed that and went on to the real issue. "In retrospect, I know we should have leveled with you about the baby earlier."

"Then why didn't you?"

Because we could barely cope with the information ourselves, Gretchen thought as she forced herself to finish her salad. "Your dad and I were very surprised. We felt it was enough for you to get used to the idea of our being married, before tackling anything else."

Sassy sat back, a smug look on her face. "As it turns out, we were right to regard the nuptials so suspiciously," she said in a low voice laced with tension and anger.

"Yes, you were. There was more going on than Matt or I let on at the time."

Sassy studied the people coming and leaving the busy restaurant. "He'd never hidden anything from us before then, were you aware of that?" she informed Gretchen resentfully.

Knowing Matt, Gretchen could have guessed that. She also felt that Matt, as a consenting adult whose grown children were almost completely out of the nest, had a right to some privacy. "I care about your dad," she said simply. *I care about him so much.*

"Then why didn't you leave him alone in the first place?" Sassy demanded, her jealousy and insecurity evident. "Why did you ever have to pick him to be the father of your child?" Sassy threw down her napkin. Her eyes were brimming with tears. "You have no idea how much he's already been hurt. The divorce from Mom almost destroyed him. And now...now this." She pushed away from the table.

Gretchen stood and caught her arm before she could flee. Sensing other diners were staring, she asked gently, "What do you want me to do?" Silence. "Sassy, please," Gretchen pleaded, wanting more than anything to reunite Matt's family, for all their sakes. "How can I make this better?"

"That's just it. You can't," Sassy replied stonily. Ignoring Gretchen's plea for peace, she spun on her heel and stomped away.

WHAT A WASTED TRIP, Gretchen thought as the cab let her out in front of the house shortly after midnight. She paid the driver the last of the cash she had withdrawn from her savings to finance the venture, then started wearily up the drive. She was going to have to call Angela first thing tomorrow morning and tell her she had decided not to stay in Dallas overnight after all. Then she was going to have to telephone Matt in Amarillo and see how his trip was going thus far and if he still expected to be home in time for dinner tomorrow night. She hoped so. Though they had only been apart thirty-six hours, she missed him terribly.

She headed up the stairs, turned the corner and walked into the master bedroom. To her surprise, Matt's suitcase was just inside the door, to the right. Matt was lying on what she had come to think of as their bed, his hands folded behind his head. He hadn't bothered to undress or turn down the bedcovers. The only light in the room came from the master bath.

Resisting the urge to gasp in surprise, Gretchen reached for the switch and turned on the lights. She didn't know what it was exactly, but there was something dangerous about him tonight, something faintly predatory and overtly watchful in his manner.

Was it possible? Had he found out where she'd been and what a mess she'd made of things? Deciding to give nothing away until she absolutely had to, she carried her own bag into the room. Giving him an innocent smile that belied the sudden wobbliness of her knees and the racing of her pulse, she remarked pleasantly, "You're home a day early."

He took her in from head to toe, noting the undeniable dressiness of her silky new navy blue maternity dress. "I worked overtime so I could get back tonight. I didn't tell you because I wanted to surprise you. It would appear I did," he

awled as if there was suddenly too much at stake between
em.

Gretchen unzipped her carryon and removed the bag that
ntained her cosmetics, and then her clothes. "How was
ur trip?"

Annoyance sparkled in his gaze as he fastened on the satin
ghtshirt and handful of clean undies in her hand. "Not as
citing as yours, I bet." He swung off the bed in one lithe
otion and strode toward her, not stopping until he stood
ose. "Where've you been?"

Gretchen crushed the satin-and-lace undies in her palm.
I went to Dallas this afternoon."

He lifted a brow and said softly, "And conveniently for-
ot to mention it to me?"

Gretchen wet her lips and instinctively stepped back, only
find herself up against the armoire containing his clothes.
It was a spur-of-the-moment decision." One she'd since
ad occasion to lament a hundred times over.

"I see." Matt closed in until she was pinned between him
nd the armoire. "What did you do there?"

Gretchen paused, torn between her desire to make him
uffer for thinking her capable of who only knows what in
allas and her even stronger desire to protect him from the
ings and arrows of those closest to him. Should she tell him
he'd gone to see Sassy, against his wishes and advice, and
n the process likely made his estrangement with his daugh-
er worse? Or just let him think she'd gone all that way to
hop...while she continued to try to work things out with
assy. Because she was unsure, it seemed wise to be cau-
ious. "I went to the Galleria Mall," she replied calmly, re-
ealing as little as possible as she sucked in her tummy and
idled past him.

"And took a suitcase?" he asked incredulously, follow-
ng her into the master bath.

Gretchen shrugged, aware of his eyes upon her as she took off her pearl necklace and earrings, then headed back out into the bedroom in search of her jewelry case. "I thought I might stay overnight." If things with Sassy had gone well which they hadn't.

"What did you need in Dallas that you couldn't get at one of the malls here?" Matt asked, watching as she rifled through her travel bag, finally emerging with her velvet-lined case.

"Nothing, really." Gretchen breezed back to retrieve her jewelry and put it away, then closed the case with a snap. "I just thought I'd see what they had there in Dallas for me that might be more exciting than what was here in Austin." Too late, she realized that hadn't come out exactly right.

He reminded her tersely, "When I called last night, you told me you were having dinner with Angela tonight."

No, what she'd said was that she was having dinner with his daughter. She hadn't mentioned which daughter. It did not seem politic to admit that. "I know I didn't tell you in advance, but I—" *followed my heart and,* she added silently "—acted on the spur of the moment."

"And flew to Dallas with a suitcase, and checked into a hotel—for the afternoon—instead," Matt stated grimly, bracing his hands on his hips and drawing himself up to his full six feet two inches.

Okay, so on the surface that looked bad, Gretchen admitted reluctantly to herself as she caught a glimpse of her pink-cheeked countenance in the mirror. Used to total freedom all her adult life, she found she resented being checked up on now—a lot.

Maybe it was time they established a few ground rules on that score, too, Gretchen thought. She arched a brow, asked suspiciously, "How do you know about that?"

He regarded her grimly and refrained from touching her in any way. "You left a note beside the kitchen phone, with the hotel confirmation number on it. A quick call to the hotel this evening when I got home established that you had indeed checked in at four p.m. and checked out again at eight-thirty this evening. Which quite naturally led me to wonder why anyone would check in and out of a hotel for a period of four and a half hours. Of course, I know the usual reasons for such actions—at least in the afternoon."

Her heart raced at both the ludicrousness of his suggestion and the implication in his tone. "As though I'm in any shape for a hot love affair," she scoffed.

His eyes slid over the inviting curves of her breasts, the swell of her tummy and slim, sexy legs, before returning to her tousled hair, softly glossed lips and wide blue eyes. "I find you very desirable," he said in a husky voice that vibrated with suppressed emotion. "It follows other men would, too."

When he looked at her that way, she felt very sexy. She sucked in a breath and pivoted away from him. "Careful, Matt, you're beginning to sound jealous," she warned.

He followed her back into the bedroom. "Ticked off is more like it. And having just found my wife deliberately deceived me, flew to Dallas and spent the afternoon cavorting in a hotel room doing who knows what, I have every right to be ticked off." He glared at her, desire and a wealth of feeling glimmering in his eyes, as he waited for her to defend herself.

She had the sense they were skirting dangerously close to the edge. She didn't want to fall off the cliff and into an abyss. She didn't want to lose what they had. And she saw only one way to avoid that. "Matt, I don't want to hurt you, so don't ask me any more about my trip."

His temper simmering, Matt demanded, "Dammit Gretchen, what aren't you telling me?"

Aware her feet were aching, Gretchen stepped out of her pumps. A mistake, she swiftly decided. In stocking feet, she was a full eight inches shorter than Matt.

She lifted her hands in silent supplication for peace. "Matt, please—"

"There's someone else, isn't there?" Hurt and disappointment glistened in his eyes.

"No!" She grasped his hands in both of hers. "How could you even think such a thing!"

He tightened his fingers over hers. "Then what are you hiding?"

Gretchen drew a breath. Like it or not, there was no other course to take. She drew her hands away, breaking contact. "I saw Sassy."

"What?" He did a double take.

Reluctantly she admitted, "I went to Dallas specifically to see her, to try to get her to come home, or at least see you, talk with you."

"And?" Matt's face was full of hope.

It broke Gretchen's heart to have to give him bad news. "She's angry. She feels betrayed." She paused sadly, then began to pace the length of the room. "I was hoping to mend the rift, shop, whatever. Get to know each other."

"But she refused," Matt guessed grimly.

Gretchen turned back to face him. She braced her hands on either side of her and her fingers curled around the edges of the bureau behind her. "She thinks there's no room in your life for her, now that you're married to me."

Matt's eyes were bleak as he squared his shoulders, as if for battle. "There's no room in my life for her anger and resentment," Matt corrected.

Gretchen crossed to Matt and caressed the hard muscles of his chest. "Maybe Luke and Angela are right. Maybe you should go to her and apologize, make peace at any cost." Whether Matt wanted to admit it to her, Gretchen could see this continuing rift between him and his children was tearing him up deep inside. Sassy, Luke and Angela, too. They all longed to have their family back, intact, the way it had been before Gretchen got involved with Matt.

"No," Matt disagreed firmly, even as he wrapped a comforting arm about Gretchen's shoulders. "She's a grown-up and she needs to behave like one. She'll come around, given time."

"And if she doesn't?" Gretchen asked anxiously.

"She will." Of that, Matt had no doubt.

"I hope you're right," she said softly.

Matt sighed reflectively. "From the time a baby is born, it seems all we parents want to do is protect it and all the baby wants to do is break free. And yet the letting go is a very necessary and ultimately healthy step in growing up. Don't you see? Whether I'm ready to have Sassy so completely independent from the rest of us is beside the point. On this score, it's what she wants and needs that counts. Yes, it's painful having this distance between us, especially over something that should be so joyful for all of us. Yes, I miss her more than I can bear to think about sometimes. But as for me backing down on one of the basic covenants of this family, that we don't hurt each other deliberately or out of spite, I can't and won't do that. Not for Sassy. Not for anyone. You are my wife," he said sternly. "We are having a child together, and like it or not I expect her to respect that and honor that and treat us accordingly, and until she can do that, then...well—" Matt offered a helpless shrug "—we'll just have to stay apart."

Gretchen toyed with the buttons on Matt's shirt. She loved the solid warmth of him, his innate dependability and old-fashioned gallantry. "I agree with everything you're saying," she began carefully, wanting to examine this problem jointly, from every angle, now that Matt had finally consented to talk about it in-depth.

"But?"

She tilted her head to look up at him. "I don't want to be responsible for you losing your relationship with your daughter, Matt." To her mounting horror, it seemed they were close to making that a reality.

"You aren't," Matt stated with a slow, sad smile. "Sassy is. Besides," he continued with gentle confidence as he trailed his fingers through her hair, "I have faith that she'll come home eventually, when the time is right."

Gretchen released a shaky sigh and tightened her hold on his waist. Matt was so sure of himself. She could almost believe this was a normal part of the growing up process. "Anyone ever tell you you're stubborn as a mule?" she teased with a tremulous grin.

"Runs in the family."

She gazed at him, aware there was yet another matter they needed to discuss. "That it certainly does," she drawled, turning so he could unzip her dress.

He parted her dress obligingly. Watched with undisguised pleasure as she picked up the satin nightshirt. "Sure you want to join this family?"

"That all depends." Gretchen stepped out of her dress and dropped it in the hamper for laundering later.

"On what?" Matt wrapped his hands around her waist, drew her back against him and pressed his lips to the exposed column of her throat.

Shivers of desire swept through her. Gretchen closed her eyes and let her head fall back upon his shoulder. "No more third degree,'' she murmured in the most dictatorial tone she could manage.

Matt made his way languorously down to her collarbone. ''No more laying down the law?''

''That's absolutely right!''

He turned her gently to face him. ''Why not?''

Gretchen looked deep into his eyes and knew she could drown in their silvery depths. ''Because I love you,'' she said softly, meaning it from the very bottom of her heart, ''and— Oh, no...no.'' Gretchen put her hand to her mouth, stunned by what she'd just blurted out.

Matt went stock-still. ''What did you say?'' he commanded hoarsely, completely thrown for a loop by her disclosure.

Gretchen shut her eyes in misery. She had promised herself she wouldn't pressure Matt or reveal the depth of her feelings for him, not until well after the baby had come and Matt had had a chance to see if he really wanted to put in another twenty years of day-in, day-out fatherhood again. Only then, if the answer was in the affirmative would she tell him how she felt.

''Gretchen...'' Matt prodded.

Stunned by the flood of emotion she felt, Gretchen put up a hand in stop-sign fashion. ''Forget it, Matt,'' she advised, shaken to the core by the intensity of her feeling for him and her unconscious willingness to transmit that feeling to him.

''Now, why would I want to do that,'' he drawled, shifting her closer once again. ''When for the record—'' his eyes turned unbearably tender ''—I love you, too.''

Joy bubbled up inside her, along with an overwhelming desire to reach out to him and make love to him, again and again and again. ''Oh, Matt...'' Gretchen whispered, wreathing her arms about his neck. The knowledge that he loved her filled her with a happiness unlike any she had ever known.

"I know, I know," he soothed, then continued their mutual confession of their feelings with a cocky grin. "I don't know how or even when it happened, but the feeling is here—" he placed her hand and his over his heart "—deep inside. And it has been for quite a while."

Gretchen's emotions soared, even as the pragmatic side of her, the side that had been hurt before, warned her to be wary of promises given in the heat of the moment. "Oh, Matt. We promised we'd keep this as uncomplicated as possible. And now look at us."

But Matt couldn't have been happier. "The hell with our promises," he said huskily. "Even the best-laid plans go awry." He turned her palm up and kissed the middle of it. "We have to go with what we feel, what we want."

The touch of his lips against her skin sent shimmers of fiery sensation rushing through her. Gretchen forced a trembling smile. She stood on tiptoe and pressed her lips playfully to the underside of his chin. "Did it occur to you that this is how we got in trouble in the first place, Matt?"

Matt lifted her in his arms and carried her the short distance to the bed. He swung her down, removed her slip, then her bra, panties. "One day at a time, Gretchen. Remember what we promised ourselves? One day at a time. And right now," he continued, as his fingertips moved lightly, lovingly over her breasts, "all I can think about is how very much I missed you."

Gretchen had missed him, too. Desperately. Needing him more than she had ever thought possible, she swiftly divested him of his clothes.

Desire swirling in their veins, they came together in the center of the bed. Kissing sweetly, then desperately, then sweetly again. Touching...everywhere. Commanding everything they had to give. Until Gretchen felt the shudder start deep inside her.

Toes pointed, she arched up off the bed. Steeped in the warmth and scent of him, she ran her hands down his taut, muscular inner thighs. It didn't seem possible, but their lovemaking had become more intense, more satisfying, as her pregnancy progressed. Perhaps because they knew each other better, wanted each other more. Perhaps because of the fragility of the moment, the wonder they felt at having found each other and being together, for however long—though she hoped it was forever.

Her hands trailed up and down his damp back, drawing him closer. With a guttural moan, he shifted her onto her side, cupped her and brought her forward, entering her gently. He kissed her again and again, matching the shallow strokes of his body with enticing sweeps of his tongue. Until she was writhing against him, coming apart in his hands, catapulting over the edge. And then he, too, was following. They were lost in each other. They were freed. They were a happily married couple, in every way, at long last.

Chapter Twelve

September

"I think I would know if I was in labor, Matt," Gretchen said.

"At least call Marissa," Matt urged as he finished loading the dishwasher and shut the door.

"And tell her what?" Gretchen inquired, rubbing her lower back as she paced aimlessly back and forth. "That I can't get comfortable sitting in a chair?"

Matt watched her pass by the kitchen windows for the hundredth time since dinner and wondered if she knew just how beautiful she was in the very last stages of her pregnancy, with her rounded tummy, radiant skin and Madonna-like serenity.

"Or standing or lying down," he added. She hadn't eaten much, either, he noted silently, even though he'd made her favorite meal, fajitas on the grill.

Gretchen shoved a hand through her hair. "So? This is what it's like being nine months pregnant."

Exactly, Matt thought. He closed the distance between them and massaged the tenseness from her shoulders. "I think you may be in labor."

Gretchen rolled her eyes and leaned against him, her back to his front. "I'm not due for another twelve days."

Matt wrapped his arms around her. He buried his face in the soft fragrance of her hair. "Babies have been known to come early," he whispered in her ear.

Gretchen patted her tummy affectionately. "Zach Devin wouldn't dare." She inclined her head toward the textbooks spread out across the kitchen table. "He knows I have a test tomorrow."

"Zach Devin and I have news for you," Matt said dryly, turning Gretchen around to face him. "You will be missing more than one or two classes this semester when Zach Devin is born."

"I've already talked to my professors," Gretchen said, her chin taking on a stubborn tilt. "They assure me I can catch up, as long as I don't miss more than two weeks. Besides, I'm taking just three classes this semester, and only have class on Monday, Wednesday and Friday, from nine to twelve. That's really not so much."

Maybe not for someone who was getting a full night's sleep, Matt thought. But if he knew newborn babies, and he did, that would not be the case, either, once Zach Devin was born. More than likely, he and Gretchen would both be up for part of every night.

"And with Angela agreeing to baby-sit for us while I'm in class and you're at work, it should be a snap," Gretchen finished confidently.

"Don't forget. I can take some time off, too," Matt reminded her gently.

"I know." Gretchen studied him. "Something else is bothering you, isn't it?" she said at length.

She read him too well.

I don't like the fear I see in your eyes, Matt thought, *the suspicion that you're just waiting for all our happiness to be taken away at any second.* Which was also why, he thought, she had elected to stay in school right through labor and delivery rather than sit out a term.

"Maybe we should talk about the future," Matt suggested practically. Maybe if they did, it would ease their minds.

"I thought everything was set," Gretchen said. Moving away from him, she began to rub her back again.

Matt knew they had accepted their love for each other during the past two months—reveled in it, in fact—but they had also avoided talk about anything much beyond Zach Devin's birth. Of course, in many ways that was understandable. They'd been unwilling to upset the delicate balance of their lives together by discussing their future ad nauseam. Considering the losses she'd already sustained in her personal life, the fact that he and his own daughter Sassy were still on the outs, it made sense that she might worry he would not always be there for her and their baby. So he'd done his best to alleviate her fears about the future on every score.

"I was going to wait until Zach Devin's birth to tell you what I'd done," Matt began, his lips curving in a satisfied smile. "But perhaps now is the time."

Gretchen blinked in confusion. "Time for what?"

Matt took her hand in his and led her into his den. "I know you don't like to talk about these kinds of things, but I think it's something that needs to be faced, for our peace of mind and for Zach Devin."

Gretchen put a hand behind her to steady herself and backed onto the sofa. "And that is?"

"I've set up a trust fund for the baby," Matt said. He went to his desk and brought out a set of documents. He took them back to her and handed them over. "As you can see," he began in a low tone, "it's a substantial amount of money. Enough to ensure that you and Zach Devin will be taken care of for the next twenty years—even if I'm not around."

Gretchen continued to stare at the documents in shock. Matt knew how she felt; it was a lot of money. But was it enough to make her finally feel secure in his love for her and their baby?

Finally, she looked up. She was trembling, ashen; a bead of perspiration had broken out on her upper lip. "How do your other children feel about this?" she asked hoarsely.

Matt shrugged matter-of-factly. "I haven't told them. But I don't imagine it would be a surprise to them, since they have similar trusts."

Gretchen swallowed. "I had no idea that you had anywhere near this amount of money."

Matt shrugged and explained, "It's why Sassy wanted the prenup."

"And yet you didn't ask me for one," she said in awe.

That's because I never for one moment felt I needed one, Matt thought to himself as Gretchen abruptly let out a gasp of surprise and cupped both arms across her middle.

"Contraction?" Matt asked, resisting the urge to panic.

"A doozy," she confirmed.

"First one?"

Gretchen nodded.

Adrenaline surging through his veins, Matt sprang into action. "I'll get the stopwatch."

He returned with the watch two minutes later. Gretchen was still doubled over. Working to stay calm, Matt hunkered down beside her. "Another one?" he asked as he struggled to recall everything he'd learned in Lamaze class.

Gretchen's face was beet red. She was perspiring in earnest now. "Same one," she huffed. Matt turned on the stopwatch. Thirty-one seconds later, the contraction ended.

The minute it did, Gretchen collapsed against the back of the sofa, as limp as a piece of lettuce. She put a hand to her brow and dabbed at the perspiration dotting her forehead with her palm. She looked at Matt and shook her head in admonition. "They said it would hurt in Lamaze class, but—oh!" She cried out and shot forward. Began to turn red again.

Matt sat down next to her. He put his hand on her middle. He could feel the strength of her contraction; her abdomen was as hard as a rock. This was not good. It shouldn't be happening so fast.

"How...long...between...?" Gretchen panted, looking both determined and triumphant.

"Thirty seconds," Matt said, knowing Gretchen needed him now as never before. And that could only mean one thing. She had been in labor all along, just as he'd thought. "I think," he said briskly as he gripped her hand in his, resolved not to let her and the baby down, "it's time to call Marissa and get you to the hospital."

"YOU'RE DOING GREAT," Matt announced cheerfully.

Gretchen was sure it was the thousandth time he'd said this. And while she appreciated his enthusiasm, she had not appreciated the various and sundry indignities of being prepped for delivering a baby. "Only someone who wasn't having labor pains would say that," she replied dryly, grimacing and pressing her hands to her middle.

Matt picked up another ice chip and offered it to her. "Marissa said it would help speed things up if you got up and walked around."

Not bloody likely. "Marissa is out of her mind," Gretchen replied irritably as she pushed the perspiration-damp hair from her face and waved away the ice chip Matt kept trying to push at her.

Matt grinned. "C'mon now, Gretchen, cooperate," he coaxed.

"You cooperate," Gretchen grumbled as her body once again demanded her complete and utter attention. "I've had it with this," she vowed emotionally, deciding maybe she didn't want to have the baby now anyway, maybe she would just wait a few more weeks. Even a month. "I want—agh—" Gretchen froze as another contraction racked her middle.

Matt talked her through the contraction, allowing her to squeeze his hand until she damn near broke it, helping her focus and breathe. When the contraction was over, she gasped, "How many centimeters did they say I was dilated?"

"Four."

Hell, no wonder she hurt. "How many to go?" Gretchen panted miserably.

"Six."

Gretchen swore like a sailor and pushed herself up to sit on the side of the bed.

"Now what are you doing?" Matt asked.

"What does it look like I'm doing?" she replied through gritted teeth. "I'm going to speed things up."

She slipped her feet into her slippers and stood. Matt was right beside her, a steadying arm wrapped around her waist. "What are you doing?" she demanded.

Matt walked her back and forth across the soothing light green labor room. "Keeping you company."

"As I recall, that's exactly what got me into this mess," Gretchen chided with comic irritability.

Matt grinned appreciatively, as tireless and gung ho about all this as she was wrung out. "It'll all be over soon," he soothed, kissing her brow. "And when it is, you'll barely remember the pain."

Ha! "Spoken like someone who will never actually give birth." She stopped her aimless trekking and stared at the apparatus plugged into the wall outlet, next to the visitor's chair. "What's that?"

"The battery for my video camera."

She pivoted toward him. "You are not seriously thinking..."

"Don't you want a record of Zach Devin's birth?"

"Yes—and no." Gretchen glowered at him. "Can you do it without videotaping me?"

"Probably," Matt shot right back, regarding her with a lazy sensuality, "but that kind of defeats the purpose, doesn't it?"

"Not from my point of view," Gretchen muttered. If the worst happened, if they did break up, she didn't want Matt remembering her in labor. She'd rather he remember her on her wedding day...or their wedding night.

Determined to get this over with as soon as possible, she forced herself to make another pass across the room, huffing and puffing as she went. "I mean it, Matt. I'm all for seeing Zach the moment he comes into the world, but I am not so sure I want to remember me this way." All sweaty and icky, clad in an ill-fitting hospital gown, her face as red as a fire engine, her hair plastered to her head.

He brushed his mouth across her nape in an incredibly gentle, almost reverent kiss. "I'll be discreet, I promise."

Unable to bear much more, she rested against him weakly.

"Another contraction?"

She nodded, incapable of speech, as she wreathed her arms about his waist. She was so glad he was there. She didn't think she'd be able to make it without him.

"Lean on me." Matt whispered sweet words of encouragement and lavish praise in her ear. "That's it. I've got ou. Breathe now, just like they showed us in Lamaze lass...."

When it was over, she stayed in his arms, incapable of oing much more than recuperating from the immobilizing rength of the contraction.

"Perhaps you should go lie down again," Matt sugested, holding her close, smoothing her hair with long, entle strokes.

Gretchen shook her head. This walking around was orking. She pushed away from Matt, aware she was tremling, and set her chin. "Let's walk again."

Marissa came upon them four contractions later, just as retchen's water broke. She and Matt helped Gretchen back bed. Marissa got a nurse to assist and did another exam.

"How much?" Gretchen asked between pants as Matt eld her hand.

"Seven centimeters."

Then it was eight, nine, and they were wheeling her into he delivery room. Matt was at her side, garbed in sterile lue and a surgical cap, a compact videocamera slung round his neck.

He talked to her softly as they strapped her onto the tale and adjusted the mirror so she could see. The epidural rought a blissful relief to the pain. And then everything egan to happen with amazing swiftness.

"Push when I tell you, Gretchen," Marissa directed. 'Now. That's it. That's it. One more time."

The delivery room resounded with their baby's lusty cry. Tears of relief, of joy, streamed down Gretchen's face. She gazed at their baby in wonder, looked up and saw Matt was rying, too. Then the cord was cut and the baby was placed n her chest. Gretchen wrapped her arms around Zach Devin, soothing him with her voice, stroking his downy ead and perfect little body. Matt touched him, too. Remembering the camera, he picked it up, turned it on with shaking hands and recorded the moment, and their joy, for all posterity.

"I COME bearing gifts," Angela announced as she entered the hospital room, her arms laden with gaily wrapped presents and a basket of flowers. "How are you?" She bent to give Gretchen a hug. "Dad said you came through the birth with flying colors."

"We all did," Gretchen was pleased to report. Matt in particular had been so relieved everything was all right with her and the baby. Maybe it was because he tended to worry but it had been as if a burden had been lifted from his shoulders.

Gretchen focused on her stepdaughter. "How are you?"

"Great. I just stopped by the nursery to see Zach Devin." Angela clapped a hand to her chest. "What a handsome charmer he is!"

Gretchen smiled. She and Matt thought so, too. In fact, she had never seen Matt look happier than when he'd held his son for the first time.

Unfortunately, since then they hadn't had much time alone. Matt had had business and personal phone calls to make while she slept. Then the nurse had come in to help Gretchen get cleaned up while Matt went down to the nursery to check on the baby. After that, there'd been forms for him to fill out in the business office downstairs.

Matt, who'd had even less sleep than she had, had begun to look tired and preoccupied—as though something worrisome were on his mind. Gretchen had urged him to go home and get some rest, too, but Matt had gotten that determined look on his face and absolutely refused. It was his place, he had said, to be with Gretchen and the baby, and that was where he was going to be. It had taken all her and

Cal's persuasion to get him to leave long enough to eat dinner in the cafeteria. And now the family was coming in. Which probably meant they wouldn't have any time alone together this evening. But that was okay, Gretchen thought. Right now it was important they share their joy. And maybe even use it to pull their family together, the way Matt had wanted for months now.

"Do you think they'll bring Zach Devin back to your room, so I can hold him?" Angela asked, dragging over a chair and settling in.

Gretchen smiled. "Marissa said all we have to do is tell the nurse when we're ready. Was Zach Devin asleep when you saw him?"

"At first. Then he started waking up and yawning and looking around. He's so cute, Gretchen," Angela enthused. "I can't wait to hold him."

"I'm glad." Gretchen smiled. She looked toward the door. "Where's Luke? I thought he and Sassy were coming with you." And where was Matt? She missed him, too.

"Luke's here. He went in search of Dad, who, according to the charge nurse, was just seen near the staff lounge with Marissa."

"And Sassy?"

"I'm sorry, Gretchen." Angela's face fell. "Dad called her and offered to fly her down from Dallas to see you and the baby."

"But she refused?" Gretchen guessed sadly.

"I'm sorry." Angela sighed, her frustration with her younger sister evident. "Luke and I called her, too, and told her she was going to be missing out. But she still won't come. I think maybe she's still getting over the divorce. It was hard on all of us, but Sassy took it the hardest. I mean, she knows Mom and Dad will never get back together. I don't think it's that. I think she just wants things the way they were in a general sense. You know, one mom and one dad, and one home during the holidays. Maybe if they'd divorced sooner and we'd grown up always having two homes and split holidays, it would have been easier. But it wasn't that way for us and it's been hard for us to get used to."

Sadness filled Gretchen's heart, for these were days that could never be recaptured once they were missed. "I'm sorry, too," she said softly. "I really wished we could have all been together. Especially now."

"Well, don't give up on her," Angela urged brightly. "Luke and I haven't. And I know Dad hasn't, either. He thinks she's going to come to her senses, realize what she's missing and rejoin the family at any moment."

But what if she didn't? Gretchen wondered. What then? Would Matt always blame her and Zach Devin for the loss of his youngest daughter?

Before Gretchen had a chance to sort out her feelings, Luke poked his head in the door.

"Ready to have your picture taken?" He had a camera case slung over his shoulder.

"Sure," Gretchen said.

"Where's Dad?" Angela asked Luke.

"He'll be here in a minute," Luke said.

Angela frowned impatiently. "What's he doing?" Angela asked.

"Having a midlife crisis or something," Luke said as he took his camera out of the bag.

"What do you mean?" Gretchen and Angela asked in unison.

"Oh, you know. Calculating just how old he's going to be for every moment of Zach Devin's life. Fifty when Zach Devin enters kindergarten, sixty-three when Zach Devin enters college, sixty-six when Zach Devin graduates. Stuff like that.'' Luke laughed as he took in Gretchen's distressed expression. "Don't worry. Dad can get like that. Sometimes he's a real worrier.''

"I agree,'' Marissa said, walking in the door to join the group gathered around Gretchen's hospital bed. "Matt's the kind of guy who braces for the worst and hopes for the best. He'll be okay when he stops trying to prepare for twenty years of devoted fathering and parental crises in one fell swoop and gets some sleep.''

But he was worried, Gretchen thought, as guilt flooded her anew. Maybe even having second thoughts about his ability and desire to do this over the long haul. Wasn't this just what she had feared would happen, once the fantasy and romance of a new baby faded and reality and hardship set in? And if she thought it was going to be hard to divorce Matt when she had lived with him only nine months, what was it going to be like another year or two or three down the road?

"Hey, quite a crowd in here,'' Matt said, striding in to join the group.

He looked tired and haggard beneath the veneer of happiness, and he seemed to be missing Sassy.

There was only one real fix to this situation, Gretchen thought sadly, as guilt flooded her anew, and she knew in an instant what she had to do.

"MARISSA TELLS ME you and Zach Devin are going to be released in the morning,'' Matt began, several hours later, after pictures had been taken and everyone had left. Wrapped in a swaddling blanket, his cherubic features quiet in repose, Zach Devin slept on, cuddled in Gretchen's arms.

"Right,'' Gretchen said, telling herself to be strong. "And to that end,'' she continued cautiously, knowing she would always have a part of Matt in Zach Devin, "I have a favor to ask."

Matt sat on the edge of the bed and smiled over at her and the baby. "You can ask me anything. You know that."

Gretchen braced herself for the test to come. She hoped like hell she was wrong about what Matt really wanted, but only his reaction to her announcement would tell, and right now there was nothing of what he was really thinking or feeling on his face. "I know I've been leaning on you a lot in recent months," she began, albeit a little nervously.

Matt shrugged. "I didn't mind. Under the circumstances, it was the least I could do." He reached over to stroke Zach Devin's baby-soft cheek. "Besides, I got a lot out of the arrangement, too."

"I know, but I think it's time I was independent again." Gretchen took a deep breath and looked away. "I want to move back into my own place."

"What about Zach Devin?"

She looked up to see Matt watching her with shattering intensity. She flushed from head to toe. "He'll go with me, of course." Knowing how selfish that sounded, she rushed to add, "You can see him as much as you want, whenever you want."

There was silence between them for several minutes as he continued to regard her with frustration and uncertainty and, unless she was mistaken, a great deal of guilt.

"I thought—"

"I know," she interrupted gently as he surged off the bed and began to pace. "I wanted to pretend that everything could work out with fairy-tale precision, too, but we were fooling ourselves, Matt." She shook her head as she began to choke up. "I think I knew it all along, but—" She swallowed, terribly afraid she would burst into tears at any second if she didn't keep a tight rein on her emotions.

"But what?" Matt prodded, incensed.

Gretchen lifted her eyes to his. "I was afraid. I'd never had a baby. I had no family to turn to for support. I didn't know how it was going to be or what it would feel like to be a mom."

"And now?" Matt watched her cross to Zach Devin's Plexiglas bassinet and settle him gently on his side. He whimpered once, then was silent.

"With three easy lessons from the nursing staff, I'm a pro." She turned back to him with a confidence she couldn't begin to feel. "I'm letting you off the hook, Matt."

"What you mean is you're kicking me in the teeth." Matt hooked his thumbs through the belt loops on his jeans and stared down at her furiously.

Good, Gretchen thought. *It'll be easier for us both if he detests me.* "We had a deal," she reminded him succinctly. "We'd stay together as long as necessary after the birth to give our child a good start and then we would split, amicably."

Matt was very still. He looked away a long moment, then turned back to her with a knowing expression. "You said you loved me."

"I did and still do." That she wouldn't deny. "But love doesn't solve everything, Matt. Love doesn't guarantee a marriage will work over the long haul of the participants' or even the child's life," she continued earnestly, speaking the words that were in her heart. "But maybe it will mend your family."

Matt's mouth tightened into a thin line. He wanted to smash something with his bare hands. "Let me get this straight. You're leaving me because of Sassy, because you feel I've let her down?" he asked grimly.

Gretchen shook her head. As the color left her face, she willed herself to be strong. "No, Matt," she said softly.

"I'm leaving you because it's the right thing to do, because we're at different places in our lives."

I'm looking forward to an empty nest, he'd said the first night they'd met. *I'm looking forward to having my life back, to being free of parental responsibility on a daily basis for the first time in over two decades.* Gretchen drew a deep breath. "You deserve your life back, Matt. And I deserve mine." I don't want to be a burden or a liability to you. I don't want Zach Devin ever to feel that way, either.

"And suppose I'm not comfortable with that?" he challenged, sauntering closer. "Suppose I think that this idea of yours is just a thinly veiled attempt to give me license to walk out on my responsibility?"

"No one who ever knows you would ever question your gallantry or decency, Matt. But we need to think about the bigger picture. Your divorce was hard on all your kids, Sassy in particular."

"I know that," he said roughly, pushing a hand through his hair impatiently.

"I don't want Zach Devin to have to go through that. I don't want him to grow up thinking we're always going to be together, only to find out one day that you're not around and you're not going to be."

Matt sighed, the depth of his weariness apparent. He closed the distance between them, cupped her chin in his hand. "I feel my responsibility deeply, Gretchen. I won't walk out on you the way your first husband did."

But what if you don't mend your relationship with Sassy, because of me...and Zach Devin? What if one day you wake up and realize you'll never have a chance to be footloose and fancy-free? Will you end up hating me for that? Will the resentment you feel toward me cut so deep it will even end our friendship?

Gretchen knew she couldn't bear that. Agitated, she whirled away from him. "I'm not talking about duty, Matt," she whispered hoarsely. "Or even a sexual fling that turned into a relationship for a brief while. I'm talking lifetime commitment. We can't make that to each other. And considering why and how we got together, we shouldn't even try." They had to be sensible here. They had to protect Zach Devin. They had to do what was best for Matt, and best for his other three children, as well.

He regarded her stoically. "You're saying you want a divorce?" he asked in quiet desperation.

Without warning, Gretchen recalled Angela's words: *Maybe if they'd divorced sooner and we'd grown up always having two homes and split holidays, it would have been easier.*

Gretchen swallowed and wished for strength as their eyes locked. "I'm saying I think it would be best, yes."

"YOU COULD have the house. I could move out," Matt suggested amiably as he parked in front of the efficiency hotel next to Northcross Mall.

"No, Matt. I've inconvenienced you enough as it is," Gretchen said, as if by rote. She wanted nothing more than to say her goodbyes and get this over with. "It's enough that you've insisted upon paying for the hotel. This will be fine, really."

Matt disagreed. "If I'd known you were going to move out right after Zach Devin was born, I never would have encouraged you to give up your efficiency apartment," he said.

"Nor would I have done so," Gretchen said calmly, knowing she was hurting him and hardly able to bear it. "But I didn't know then how I'd feel now." *As though I had given you a son, taken away your freedom and torn apart your family all in one fell swoop.*

Matt nodded stiffly at the hotel. "You're sure this is what you want?" he said.

Gretchen nodded. Hard as it was, she knew she was doing the right thing in moving out now. This way, Matt could bring Sassy back into the fold and have his family once again. He could still love his brand-new son, and spend as much time with him as he wanted, but he'd be free of the sleepless nights and the daily responsibilities he'd worried about before Zach Devin was born. This way, she thought sadly, he would still be able to find a woman who had also already raised her children, someone who was ready to enjoy her newfound freedom. This way he could still be happy.

And, despite the way things had worked out between them, she wanted Matt to be happy, more than anything in the world.

Matt waited in the car with Zach Devin while Gretchen checked in at the front desk, then escorted her to the unit. "Are you sure you're going to be all right here?" Matt asked with a frown, looking around at the clean, contemporary furnishings of the two-room suite.

"Yes. I'll be fine."

Matt reluctantly set down the diapers, formula and canvas bag of baby clothes and blankets. He glanced around in disgruntled fashion. "It doesn't have a full kitchen."

"It has a refrigerator and a microwave," Gretchen replied, hanging on to her temper because she knew he was picking apart her accommodations as a way of not dealing with the painful issues behind their enforced separation. "And a grocery store down the street that delivers." Sensing he needed—wanted—reassurance as much as she did, she turned to him with a smile. "Really, Matt, that's all I'll need for now."

He scowled and peered into the bedroom, saw a king-size bed, television, vanity, dresser and bath. "Where's Zach Devin going to sleep?"

Gretchen set a sleeping Zach Devin down in his combination car seat-carrier and strapped him in securely, trying all the while not to show how truly nervous she was.

She folded her arms in front of her. "The front desk is bringing me a crib."

"How long do you plan to stay here?"

"I don't know." Gretchen shrugged. She felt as if her heart were breaking. "A couple of weeks, just until I find a permanent apartment."

Matt nodded. "If you need help with that..."

Gretchen knew if she spent much more time with Matt she really would burst into tears. She'd grown far too dependent on him as it was. Because she wanted so badly to hold on, she shook her head, refusing his offer. "Thanks," she said stiffly, "but I can handle it." She was out of her depth here, not up to a pretend marriage with very real and heartfelt implications.

"Somehow I knew you were going to say that," Matt replied with a wry sigh.

Realizing they had to find a new way to be around each other, for Zach Devin's sake as well as their own, they exchanged cautious smiles. Matt looked as tranquil and careful about things as Gretchen was pretending to be.

"I guess I better bring in the rest of your things," he said.

"Thanks."

He carried in her two suitcases and a stack of textbooks. "I'm going to be out of town for a few days," he advised her matter-of-factly, more in a hurry now.

"I understand," Gretchen said swiftly, knowing he was running away from the mess they had made of things, just as she was.

"But if you need anything—" He scribbled down the number where he could be reached, cast a last longing look at their baby.

"I'll call," Gretchen promised, watching as he set the paper down next to the phone. But even as she spoke, even as she watched him bend to kiss a sleeping Zach Devin goodbye with exquisite tenderness, she knew she wouldn't. It was going to be a long time, if ever, before she got over Matt. Until that happened, she knew the less time she spent around him, the better.

Chapter Thirteen

"So how long are you going to keep this up?" Luke asked from the door to Matt's office at the drilling company.

Matt glanced up from his computer just in time to see Sassy, Luke and Angela all troop in his office. This was the first time in months he and all three of his children had been in the same room together. His joy over that was lessened by the fact that Gretchen and Zach Devin were not there to join them, as they should have been. "These reports have to go out first thing in the morning," Matt told them grimly.

"You have staff to do that for you," Angela reminded him gently.

His staff had families to go home to, Matt thought irritably. He didn't.

"I suppose you have a purpose in showing up here jointly at 10 p.m.," Matt drawled, and followed that with an expectant look, aimed at all three. He hit the save button on the computer, then started to print the document and letter he'd just drawn up.

The kids exchanged nervous glances, the kind they used to give each other when they were younger and knew they were in trouble and were wondering just how ticked off he was.

"First of all, we've got pictures taken in the hospital to show you," Luke announced cheerfully, stepping forward. He pulled the photos out of a plastic envelope and spread them out over his desk.

Matt looked down and felt immediately overwhelmed as he viewed photos of a newly bathed and dressed-for-the-first-time Zach Devin in an exhausted Gretchen's arms. Zach Devin and Gretchen in the delivery room. Zach Devin in Gretchen's hospital room, surrounded by family and friends. All except Sassy, that is. The poignant feelings the photos conjured were almost more than Matt could bear.

"He's really cute, Dad," Sassy said softly, apologetically, finally understanding what all the fuss had been about. Coming closer, she admitted, "After Luke and Angela showed me the pictures of him and made me realize how much I was missing out on, not sharing in the joy of having a new baby in the family, I went to see him a couple of days ago. Gretchen, too. I even took them both a gift. And I told Gretchen how sorry I was." She shook her head, tears welling in her eyes. Her lower lip trembled. "I've been acting like a total jerk, being threatened by all this. I know that now. If I hadn't been so stubborn, I would've admitted it a lot earlier."

Matt had known Sassy would come around eventually, just as he had known that the growth she'd suffered through this past year was both painful and necessary.

"I'm glad you understand you had nothing to fear," Matt said quietly, opening his arms to her. "Because I've missed you," he said thickly.

He and Sassy hugged. Tears shimmered all around.

"Which brings us to the second reason we're here," Angela said.

"And that is?"

"We're worried about you," Luke said bluntly.

Matt quirked a brow. This was a switch. "All of you?"

Angela nodded vigorously. "It's been ten days now since you took Gretchen and Zach Devin from the hospital to that hotel," she told him gently.

"Yet during that time you've hardly seen our baby brother," Sassy said.

Not because I wanted it that way. "I was in West Texas until the day before yesterday," Matt said gruffly. "And I saw Zach Devin yesterday, practically the moment I got back, while Angela was baby-sitting him and Gretchen was in class. I'm seeing him again tomorrow, when I take him and Gretchen to Cal's office, for his two-week checkup." *And every day after that if I can swing it.*

"Gretchen agreed to that?"

"Of course she agreed." *Via a message left on his answering machine.* "I'm his father. She wants me involved in Zach Devin's life." *She just doesn't want me involved in her life.* And on that score, Matt was still reeling from the hurt.

"Well, in that case, you need to put a new blade in that razor, Dad," Luke said.

Matt clapped a hand to his jaw. Feeling the stubble growing in patches on his face, he belatedly realized his razor was probably a little dull; he just had been so unhappy he hadn't noticed it was no longer doing a good job.

"And a haircut wouldn't hurt," Sassy advised.

"Did you iron that shirt?" Angela asked.

"Yes," Matt said dryly, already knowing he hadn't done a good job with that.

"What with, a rock?" Luke asked.

Figuring he'd endured enough "makeover tips" for one day, Matt glared at him.

"No offense, Dad, but you look like hell," Angela said. "Which, by the way, in case you are at all interested, is the way Gretchen looks, too."

Matt suffered a flash of hope. He quashed it quickly. There was no sense hoping for the impossible. He had already done that, and see where it had gotten him. "Being a new mother is a hard job," Matt replied calmly. Harder than Gretchen had probably realized, he thought.

"So is dealing with all those postpartum hormones," Sassy remarked.

Her tone had Matt thinking maybe he should be a little worried.

"Yeah, Dad," Luke chimed in helpfully. "Has it occurred to you that maybe Gretchen didn't really mean what she said about wanting to be out on her own? That maybe she was just dealing with some giant surge of estrogen or progesterone or whatever it is women get after they give birth?"

Matt only wished that were the case, but he knew better. He had forced Gretchen into this marriage, for their baby's sake. Because she was vulnerable and uncertain, she had agreed. But now that she was no longer pregnant, all bets were off. And as much as he hated to let her go, Matt had to honor his vow. He had promised to let her go without a fight when the time came, and he had. No matter that the gallant move was tearing the hell out of him inside.

"Hormones have nothing to do with what happened between Gretchen and me," Matt said.

His kids regarded him smugly. "How do you know?"

Because we made a deal long before Zach Devin was born, one Gretchen had apparently decided to stick by after all.

Abruptly realizing his printer had stopped, Matt gathered his papers off the printer tray, straightened them and slid them into an envelope. "Is there a point to this?" he asked, as he switched off the machine.

"Yes," Sassy said firmly, taking charge in her usual lawyerly fashion. "The three of us have talked it over. We decided we know what is best."

"And that is?" Matt prodded, curious.

"We want you and Gretchen and Zach Devin back together, pronto," Sassy said.

I want that, too, Matt thought, even as he wondered if the outspoken Sassy had said as much to Gretchen. Aware his heart was suddenly pounding, Matt asked his youngest daughter, "Did you tell her that when you went over to see Zach Devin?"

"We all have," the kids replied.

"And?" Matt held his breath.

Angela sighed. "She just says she doesn't want to talk about it," she admitted reluctantly.

"Sounds like a good policy," Matt said. *One I should adopt.*

"What I don't get is why she left you," Luke continued, as curious as ever. "I thought everything was going great between the two of you."

"It's complicated," Matt said.

"Did you fight for her?" Angela asked.

"I think she knows what she wants," Matt said gruffly. *Her freedom.*

Once again, his kids regarded him, aghast. "Dad, you have to fight for her," Angela insisted passionately.

If I thought it would do any good, I would, Matt mused. But even as he considered the possibility he grimly recalled Gretchen's words to him as she explained why she wanted to leave. *I thought I needed you. I thought I couldn't do this by myself. I was wrong. I can.*

He shook his head, unable to contain the bleak disappointment over the way things had worked out. As much as he was loath to admit it, he knew he had to be honest if he didn't want to hurt Gretchen or himself any more than he already had with his bullheaded, old-fashioned view of what was right or wrong for them. "I'm sorry, kids. As much as I'd like to change things, it's too late."

"Is it really?" Sassy replied. "Aren't you the one who's always telling us that the only thing that ever sat its way to success was a hen?"

"And that we shouldn't be afraid to go out on a limb, because that's where the fruit is," Angela added helpfully.

Luke grinned. "And let's not forget this old saying—To change everything, simply change your attitude."

"It's good advice, Dad," Sassy said.

"You ought to know. You've given it to us often enough," Angela said.

Sassy nodded. She looked at Matt expectantly. "Maybe you ought to take it."

MATT THOUGHT about the unsolicited advice given him, took a good look in the mirror the next morning and reluctantly decided his kids were right. He put a new blade in his razor and shaved with care, ironed his clothes—khaki slacks and an indigo blue dress shirt—then added an eclectic tie he thought Gretchen would like, and some after-shave, too. He hit the barber shop on the way over and had his hair neatly cut. Nevertheless, his heart was pounding as he parked in front of her unit in the efficiency hotel.

He got out and headed for the door. Knocked once. Twice. Three times. He was about to get the manager, when he heard movement on the other side. A chain rattled. The door opened. Gretchen stood there, looking deliciously sexy in a long flannel gown, her hair mussed and her cheeks pink from sleep.

"Matt? What are you doing here?" she asked.

Matt lounged in the portal, enjoying the lush fullness of the curves visible beneath the gown. "Zach Devin has an appointment with Cal, remember? It's time for his two-week checkup."

Gretchen pushed the silky length of her hair off her face. "Oh-my-gosh. It can't be—it's Thursday already?" she asked, panic setting in.

"Looks like," Matt drawled. Now that he was there, he was glad he had come.

"What time is it?" Gretchen asked, still a little disoriented.

"Nine-thirty."

"Nine-thirty!" Gretchen echoed.

"You overslept."

Behind her, Zach Devin stirred, then let out a wail. Obviously, Matt thought, Gretchen wasn't doing quite as well as she'd like him to believe. Maybe she needed him after all. He worked to hide the depth of his elation. "Perhaps I should come in?" Matt suggested affably.

"Uh, right." Gretchen pivoted on her heel and led the way.

"I'll get Zach Devin." Matt scooped his squalling son out of his Port-a-crib. "When did he last have a bottle?"

"Several hours ago."

Gretchen looked drowsy and confused, Matt thought, as if she were having a hard time waking up.

"There's formula in the fridge."

"Great. How long do you think it will take you to get ready?" he asked gently.

"Fifteen, twenty minutes."

"No problem. We'll still make it to our appointment in plenty of time."

Matt had finished feeding Zach Devin when she emerged, fresh and pretty in a loose-fitting madras jumper and long-sleeved white T-shirt. She had drawn her glossy mahogany hair back in a clasp at her nape and applied a touch of makeup. The only signs of her fatigue were the dark circles beneath her eyes.

"I used the last clean diaper in the stack," Matt felt obliged to tell her. "Is there another box of them?"

"Uh, no, unfortunately."

He smiled. "No problem. We'll pick some up. Where do you keep the clean baby clothes?" He still needed to finish dressing Zach Devin, who was clad only in a T-shirt and diaper.

"In the top drawer of the dresser, just inside the bedroom door," she directed.

Matt emerged with a yellow terry-cloth sleep suit in hand. He held it up for approval.

"Those are pajamas, Matt," Gretchen said as she rushed around, gathering rattles and receiving blankets and an extra bottle of both formula and water.

Matt shrugged. "That's the only clean thing left."

"It can't be." She rushed back to the drawer, yanked it open and stared down, reporting glumly, "It is."

"No problem." Matt handed the baby to her. He began stuffing soiled clothing into a drawstring laundry bag. "We can pick up diapers on the way to Cal's office and do laundry after the appointment, back at my place."

Gretchen hedged, but only briefly, before agreeing with a reluctant nod. "Thank you," she said simply. "I would appreciate not having to go to a Laundromat."

Matt planned to do much more than that for her, if she'd let him. "So how're the classes coming?" he asked on the drive over, trying to rein in his own interests and keep things casual. He had made a mistake pushing her too hard once, and had almost lost her. He wouldn't do it again. This time when he courted her, and he was going to court her, he would take it nice and slow.

Slanting her a glance, he continued lightly, "Angela said you're back in class—what, a week now?"

"Yes."

"And Marissa approved that?" he asked gently.

Gretchen nodded and kept her eyes trained on the passing scenery. "She said as long as I didn't overdo the walking or running around campus and got plenty of rest that I'd be okay."

She didn't look to be getting enough rest, but figuring he would trust her to make the right decision on this, Matt didn't push it. "How far do you have to walk from the car to your building?" he asked.

"So far about ten steps." Gretchen's lips curved wryly. "I've been taking cabs. Horrendously expensive, but it's a lot easier than driving down to one of the lots and then catching a bus."

Matt was glad she was trying to take care of herself. Now, if only it wasn't too late for them.

"Nine pounds six ounces. He's gaining right on schedule," Cal announced with satisfaction, after thoroughly examining Zach Devin. "Any questions?"

Gretchen nodded. "Yes. Approximately when can I expect him to sleep through the night?"

Cal grinned. "Hard to say. Could be anywhere from six weeks to six months. Depends largely on the individual—each baby is different in that regard."

"How much is he getting up at night?" Matt asked, easing closer to her, as he walked Gretchen and the baby back out to his Jeep.

"Two, three times. He usually sleeps two, two and a half hours at a stretch, but that's about it for now anyway."

No wonder she looked exhausted, Matt thought, his heart going out to her. As if she were trying valiantly but were wrung out emotionally nonetheless. Matt wanted to demand she move back into his place, even if it meant them sleeping in separate bedrooms—again—so he could give her a lot more help with the baby. But remembering his vow not to push her too hard this time, he reined in his desire to rescue her and continued to talk about other things during the drive.

As they entered Westlake Hills, Matt announced casually, "The kids are coming over for fajitas on the grill this evening."

Gretchen's gaze was reflective. "I imagine they'd like to see the baby."

Matt nodded, still feeling close enough to her to confide. "It's rare during the school term for all three of them to be together under the same roof, with the exception of major holidays, and I admit I'm looking forward to it."

Gretchen smiled, but there was a lingering sadness around her eyes. "So you're reunited with Sassy, too?" she asked gently.

Matt turned onto his street. "Yes." Finally.

Gretchen breathed a sigh of relief. "I'm glad."

"So am I." Matt turned in the driveway and cut the motor. He would have given anything to make the sadness in her eyes disappear. "So what do you say?" he pressed, unable to help himself and pushing it just a little, because he felt she needed him, needed this, even if she was too proud to admit it. "Will you have dinner here tonight, too?" he asked softly. *With the family? With me?*

Gretchen hedged. Her teeth sliced into her lower lip. "I don't know, Matt. I don't want to be in the way."

He shrugged, pretending it wasn't of great importance. "So don't be. It's a big house. We can each do our own thing for a couple of hours. Frankly, I'd like some time to spend with my son, and you could probably use a chance to unwind a little on your own, couldn't you?" Sensing her weakening, just a bit, he continued, "Between school and the baby, who knows when you'll have another chance to pamper yourself a little?"

Recognizing the truth of what he'd said, Gretchen sighed. The wistful look was back in her eyes. "To tell you the truth, I'd kill for a bubble bath, maybe even a nap."

Matt grinned. "Then have at it." He gestured magnanimously. "The master bedroom is all yours."

IT WAS STRANGE coming to the house with Zach Devin and Matt, Gretchen thought as she disrobed and stepped into the hot, steaming bath, and yet in an odd way being there felt like coming home, both physically and emotionally.

Having Zach Devin had changed everything. It had made college seem less important. Oh, she was still determined to be a teacher, and to help children through the rough spots in life the way her own teachers had once helped her. But she was no longer sure that she had to earn her degree that instant. She was no longer sure she wanted to be taking classes that semester, or even if she wanted to go back the next.

What she wanted, more than anything, was to devote her every waking moment to Matt and the baby and his three college-age kids. To go back to the way it had been, to go back to living in the same house with Matt, to sleeping in the same bed with him. She wanted to share every single moment, large and small, of Zach Devin's life with Matt. She wanted to work out the problems with his children with him and form one happy family. And she wanted him there with her, every night in a very traditional, old-fashioned way.

But it was too late now for that, Gretchen acknowledged wearily as she soaped herself leisurely. They'd had their chance to be a family. Only it hadn't worked out. With her and Zach Devin in the picture, his relationship with his other three children had splintered. Knowing she was the cause of such distress, fearing Matt would never be happy unless he regained his freedom and salvaged his relationship with his children, she'd done the valiant thing and walked away.

She'd thought doing that would mend his family—and it apparently had. And bring them less hurt in the bargain. But since she'd left him, she acknowledged wearily, all she'd done was hurt. It was the kind of hurt that had nothing to do with the postpartum blues. And she couldn't see that changing.

MATT FED Zach again, burped and diapered him, rocked him to sleep and put him down for a nap in the bassinet in the family room. Finished, he tossed a load of baby clothes in the wash and then went upstairs to check on Gretchen and see if she wanted any lunch.

He found her curled up on top of the bedcovers, fast asleep. Matt gazed down at her, realized all over again how much he had missed having her in his life on a daily, hourly basis, and knew he didn't have the heart to wake her.

He covered her with an afghan and tiptoed out.

GRETCHEN AWOKE slowly to the sound of rain pelting against the windowpanes. Unsure how long she had been asleep, she sat up groggily and looked at the clock—10:28.

Had she slept all day? Gretchen wondered, pushing the hair from her face. But...wait a minute...it was light outside. It was never light at 10:28 at night. Which meant either the clock was wrong or she'd slept a very long time.

Still struggling to orient herself, Gretchen pushed from the bed, vaulted to her feet and headed toward the master bath to splash some cold water on her face. Two minutes later, she was down the hall to the guest room, aka the nursery.

Zach Devin wasn't there.

The house was totally silent.

Heart pounding, she made her way downstairs. Matt was in his den, looking more deeply content than she could ever recall seeing him, Zach Devin sleeping soundly in the bassinet beside him.

Matt gave her an approving smile, then stood when he saw her.

Gretchen smiled back, then mutely stared down at their baby in consternation. In all the time she had cared for Zach Devin, he had never slept this soundly or looked so utterly content. It was almost as if he, too, knew he was where he wanted to be.

Matt put a finger to his lips, willing her to silence, then took her hand and led her into the kitchen, where a baby monitor sat on the counter. "'Morning," he said softly.

Gretchen tightened the belt of her robe. "Then it's true," she said slowly. "I slept through the night?"

Matt nodded. "As near as I can figure, about twenty hours straight."

She collapsed onto a stool, unable to escape the sensation that Matt was about to say something important to her. "I didn't know that was possible."

"You were exhausted. So apparently was Zach Devin."

Gretchen wet her lips. "He's been sleeping a lot, too?"

"Almost exclusively," Matt confirmed. He took a pitcher of juice out of the fridge and poured them each a glass. Their fingers brushed as he handed it to her.

Gretchen felt the tingle all the way to her toes. Trying not to flush, she sipped her juice. "And the kids?"

Matt smiled down at her compassionately. "Were here last night. They were sorry they missed you, but they understood how tired you must be." His gaze roved her tousled hair, her sleep-pinked cheeks and the robe she had left in his closet and pulled on yesterday after her bath in an innately sexy way. "Can I fix you some breakfast?" he said quietly.

"Oh, no." *I really should have gotten all the way dressed before I came down here.* "I really—I have to be going," Gretchen stammered. *Before I give in to my desire and end up in your arms again.*

He held himself very still. Some of the light left his eyes. "Sure?"

"Yes." Afraid she was about to give herself away, Gretchen turned away swiftly. She wanted nothing more than to launch herself into Matt's arms and take complete advantage of every selfless speck of gallantry and consideration he offered her. She swallowed around the growing knot of emotion in her throat. "Zach Devin and I have already imposed enough."

"Imposed?" Matt echoed. He narrowed his eyes at her. He couldn't possibly have heard right.

"Yes," Gretchen said hurriedly, the guilt she'd felt from the very beginning slamming into her with hurricane force. "I never meant to stay so long."

"You're my wife," Matt said tightly, beginning to feel resentful again.

Not for long, Gretchen thought.

"And Zach Devin is my son," Matt repeated.

Gretchen lifted her chin, using what little pride she had left and all the love she felt for Matt to galvanize her toward a more selfless path than the one she had originally taken in marrying Matt. "A child you never bargained on having to raise," she forced herself to acknowledge honestly.

Matt was so incredulous Gretchen found herself taking a step back from him. Her back bumped up against the kitchen table.

He flattened a hand on either side of her and leaned over, caging her between his arms. "The day my son is an imposition to me is the day the world comes to an end."

He shook his head at her and came closer still, inundating her with the brisk, outdoorsy scent of him.

"Is this what this was all about? Why you left me?" he demanded hoarsely, his eyes shimmering with a mixture of hurt and confusion. "Because you felt you and Zach Devin were a burden to me?"

Gretchen put a hand behind her to steady herself and sat down on the edge of the table. "You made it very clear when you set up that trust fund for Zach Devin that you were making the provisions for when you were no longer around."

Matt threw up his hands in frustration. "I did that in case anything happened to me. Not in case I left."

Gretchen was not letting him off the hook that easily. She folded her arms in front of her. "You told me in Colorado that you were looking forward to an empty nest."

"And I still am." He put his hands back on either side of her. The fleeting contact sent another tremor through her. "In another twenty or thirty years," Matt finished.

Once Zach was raised. Gretchen's hopes rose even as she reminded herself of his reaction in the hospital the day after Zach Devin had been born. Her eyes flashing, she regarded him with exasperation. "Matt, you don't have to be gallant. Luke and Marissa both told me what you said in the hospital."

Confusion darkened the irises of his eyes. "What are you talking about?" he demanded.

Gretchen pushed Matt aside and hopped down from the table. "You were counting the years, figuring how old you would be when Zach Devin started kindergarten and college."

"That," Matt corrected as he caught her wrist and brought her back around to face him, "was nothing new. I felt the same way when Luke and Sassy and Angela were born. I have always worried about being a good enough parent, about doing the right thing. And I always worry more when I haven't had enough sleep. But in the end this all comes down to the fact that Zach Devin is our child and a very, very precious gift. He's a part of our lives now. I can't imagine—I don't want to imagine—the next twenty years or more without him."

His words had the ring of truth. "All right. I accept that," Gretchen allowed stubbornly. After all, who couldn't love Zach Devin, with his baby-soft skin, sweet soul and handsome little face? She could spend—had spent—hours just holding him and loving him and marveling over every tiny inch of him. "It still doesn't mean you have to stay married to me."

"You're right," Matt agreed swiftly, his expression determined. "It doesn't." Matt tugged her against him. "But I want to stay married to you," he said. "And I'd want that even without Zach Devin in our lives. If you had never gotten pregnant, I would still want you to be my wife, now and forever."

Her heart soared. Tears flooded her eyes. "If you felt that way, if you loved me that much—"

"And I do."

The soft way he'd said it had her believing it heart and soul. "Then why didn't you tell me that before I moved out ten days ago?" Gretchen asked hoarsely.

Matt shook his head with regret. "Because I thought that was what you wanted," he said firmly. "And I had promised you that I wouldn't force you to stay once the baby was born."

Relief sent her into his arms. "Oh, Matt, if I had known that, I never would have left," Gretchen whispered, wreathing her arms about his strong shoulders, as all the hopes and dreams she had once had for them surged to new life.

Some of the tension leaving him, Matt caressed her face. "Why did you leave?"

Gretchen swallowed. "Because I thought...when you set up the trust for Zach Devin that you were trying to tell me...in a very nice, sort of roundabout way...that our relationship was going to end...eventually...as soon as you thought your commitment had been met and that I could manage the baby on my own."

Loath to let go of her even for one second, Matt pulled out a stool from beneath the breakfast bar, sank into it and sat her down on his lap. "You should have discussed it with me if it worried you."

"I probably would have if I hadn't gone into labor then. But you're right. It is more complicated than that." Gretchen shook her head in regret. "First, I had promised you that Zach Devin and I wouldn't ever be a burden to you...and here we were, usurping your next twenty-some years and depriving you of your freedom and empty nest. And then I felt so guilty about what our marriage had done to your relationship with Sassy, I decided my leaving was your best chance to bring her back into the fold."

"It worked, but not in quite the way you imagined. It ended up convincing her of the need for us to get back together."

Gretchen blinked in surprise. "She said that to you?"

"Worse. She and the other two confronted me the day before yesterday and literally demanded I do whatever it took to win your heart again and bring you home. Needless to say—" Matt grinned, "—it was comforting to me to know we were all on the same wavelength in that regard, and they were all deliriously happy to find you and Zach Devin were here last night. They're also determined to make things run smoothly this time around. Which means, no more prenuptial agreement." Matt extracted the folded document from his shirt pocket and held it in front of her. "So what do you say? I rip half. You rip half."

Gretchen grinned. "You're on."

They laughed softly as they tore it to shreds, then Matt drew her close again. "And for the record, that empty-nest business is highly overrated."

Gretchen settled more cozily on his lap. "You think so?"

He surged against her, pulling her irresistibly toward him. "After the past ten days, I know so." Where her robe parted, he stroked her knee. "I've missed you, Gretchen," he said softly. "I've missed you and Zach Devin both more than I can say."

"Oh, Matt, I've missed you, too." Gretchen melted against him and kissed him sweetly, aware she had never felt so very loved or so very safe.

"So..." Matt said breathlessly several minutes later, "four weeks left to go?"

Gretchen sighed her disappointment, glad there was no moratorium on sleeping wrapped in each other's arms, for she had missed that, too. "Before we can make love again? Afraid so."

"Hmm. Well, I've heard necking is in again."

Gretchen smiled, her pulse already starting to race. "As in just kissing?"

"Right." Matt grinned and touched his lips to hers. "Think you can handle that?"

Gretchen wrapped her arms around his neck and returned his kiss eagerly, putting all that she felt, all that she needed, all that she had to give, into the caress. "With you by my side, I can handle anything."

SNOW CAME DOWN in sheets as the Hale and Stewart families gathered around the fireplace in the Stewarts' Rocking S ranch house, but this time they had all paid attention to the weather and arrived in advance of the storm. Cal and Marissa and their brood had made the preparations for the Christmas holiday, while Matt's grown children had taken care of the details for the wedding. And as Gretchen descended the stairs in a full-length red velvet dress designed and sewn by Angela, she knew they were doing the right thing in insisting on this second ceremony with their families and friends present. And what better time and place than one year to the day after it had all begun.

Attended by Matt's two daughters, Gretchen, her heart in her throat, joined Matt and his two sons before the fire. Resplendent in a black tuxedo, yuletide cummerbund and red tie, Matt smiled down at her, all the love he felt for her reflected in his eyes, while beside him Luke expertly cradled the three-month-old Zach Devin in his arms.

"Who gives this man and woman in marriage?" the minister asked, as Christmas music played softly in the background.

"We do," Angela, Luke and Sassy said softly in unison. Zach Devin gurgled happily, too, making them all grin.

"'To have and to hold...from this day forward...'" Gretchen repeated her vows in a strong, sure voice.

"'For better, for worse, in sickness and in health. As long as we both shall live....'" Matt promised, brimming with tenderness and wonder.

"I now pronounce you happily married all over again," the minister said. He nodded at them approvingly. "Matt, Gretchen, you may seal those promises you just made to each other with a kiss."

Gretchen went into Matt's arms, putting everything she felt for him in that one kiss. And as he kissed her back, Gretchen felt how much he loved her and always would. Ever so slowly, ever so reluctantly, they drew apart. Cheers erupted all around them.

Luke was the first to offer his congratulations. Sassy, Angela and a gurgling Zach Devin quickly followed suit.

"So, Dad, I see this time you and Gretchen went the traditional-ceremony route," Luke drawled, as hugs and laughter were exchanged.

"You better believe it," Matt said, tucking Gretchen into the curve of his arm. "We wanted to do it right this time—no more halfway measures."

"And that being the case, we figured it was time to give the tried-and-true vows a try," Gretchen said. This time she and Matt were in it for the long haul. This time they were building something real and permanent.

"Just consider us one big happy family," Sassy quipped, as she took her turn at holding her new baby brother.

And as Matt and Gretchen surveyed their brood, they knew it was true. In finding each other, they'd found the kind of love that lasted a lifetime, the kind of love that strong families and everlasting happiness were built on. Matt finally had his family back. Gretchen had both the baby and the large family she'd always wanted. And they'd been blessed with Zach Devin, too. Out of the storm of last

Christmas had come a miracle of new life and the chance to grow and learn together.

Gretchen and Matt smiled contentedly as they came together to share in another joyous kiss. Who said dreams didn't come true?

MILLION DOLLAR SWEEPSTAKES (III)

No purchase necessary. To enter, follow the directions published. Method of entry may vary. For eligibility, entries must be received no later than March 31, 1996. No liability is assumed for printing errors, lost, late or misdirected entries. Odds of winning are determined by the number of eligible entries distributed and received. Prizewinners will be determined no later than June 30, 1996.

Sweepstakes open to residents of the U.S. (except Puerto Rico), Canada, Europe and Taiwan who are 18 years of age or older. All applicable laws and regulations apply. Sweepstakes offer void wherever prohibited by law. Values of all prizes are in U.S. currency. This sweepstakes is presented by Torstar Corp., its subsidiaries and affiliates, in conjunction with book, merchandise and/or product offerings. For a copy of the Official Rules send a self-addressed, stamped envelope (WA residents need not affix return postage) to: MILLION DOLLAR SWEEPSTAKES (III) Rules, P.O. Box 4573, Blair, NE 68009, USA.

EXTRA BONUS PRIZE DRAWING

No purchase necessary. The Extra Bonus Prize will be awarded in a random drawing to be conducted no later than 5/30/96 from among all entries received. To qualify, entries must be received by 3/31/96 and comply with published directions. Drawing open to residents of the U.S. (except Puerto Rico), Canada, Europe and Taiwan who are 18 years of age or older. All applicable laws and regulations apply; offer void wherever prohibited by law. Odds of winning are dependent upon number of eligibile entries received. Prize is valued in U.S. currency. The offer is presented by Torstar Corp., its subsidiaries and affiliates in conjunction with book, merchandise and/or product offering. For a copy of the Official Rules governing this sweepstakes, send a self-addressed, stamped envelope (WA residents need not affix return postage) to: Extra Bonus Prize Drawing Rules, P.O. Box 4590, Blair, NE 68009, USA.

SWP-H1095

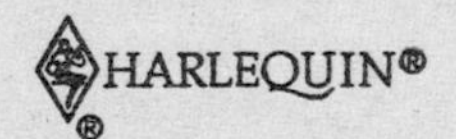
HARLEQUIN®